MOTOR CITY MURDER

MOTOR CITY MURDER

Megan Clare Johnson

To Dean, with much love and admiration.

"Racism is like high blood pressure—the person who has it doesn't know he has it until he drops over with a goddamned stroke. There are no symptoms of racism. The victim of racism is in a much better position to tell you whether or not you're a racist than you are."

- Coleman A. Young (May 24, 1918 – November 29, 1997)
Mayor of Detroit from 1974 to 1993
Young was Detroit's first black mayor.

Table of Contents

CHAPTER 1 – WELCOME TO DETROIT

"This goddamned city," Wanda Doppkowski whispered as she stared straight into the headlights of the jet black Lincoln Continental limousine speeding toward her. The limousine hit Wanda straight on. She let out a grunt as her body collided with the front grille then bounced into the windshield, over the hood, and onto the roof with a thud. Her body tumbled off the trunk and landed hard on a dimly lit city street on the east side of Detroit. Her watch broke as it hit the pavement. It read 12:52 a.m.

Wanda's portly, fifty-five year old body dented the chrome grille badly and shattered the windshield, which had jolted the driver's hands to his face as if her body was going to fly right into the limousine. The passenger in the backseat knew the body wouldn't get through the reinforced glass and he didn't flinch. Where the body ended up was of no worry to the passenger. Just that it was only a body now and not a living person was all the passenger was concerned about at this time.

Wanda's body fluids cooled the hot pavement and sent a puff of white steam up into the air as if her spirit was rising up from the ground in the summer heat wave. Her white skin and blonde hair began to be surrounded in blood. Wanda's body lay in the middle of Mack Avenue, lifeless, with the exception of her left eye—a beautiful green eye, which slowly opened—gazing in the direction of the bushes across the street where a shadow shivered.

Run, Wanda's eye screamed to the quivering shadow. *Run, child. Get out of this city before it kills you, too.*

"Stop," the passenger in the back of the limousine commanded.

1

The driver hit the brakes. The engine idled on the street. The limousine was located fifty feet past Wanda. The driver looked into the rear view mirror to see the results of the order his boss had given him. Sweat ran down his forehead as he looked around the street that was void of pedestrians. He tasted vomit saliva in his mouth.

Joe Dempsey, the limousine driver, had never killed anyone. His mind raced. He could run out of the limousine right now. Go straight to the police station, confess and turn in his boss. But his legs didn't respond to these options. He waited for his next order.

"Back up," the passenger coolly commanded. "You haven't finished the job."

Joe wanted to flip his boss off and tell him to finish it himself but what he feared even more than killing the woman was the man that was sitting in the backseat. He was this man's dog. He owned him and Joe grasped that—now more than ever.

If Joe went to the police he would face jail time and there was no telling if his boss would ever serve one day. Better to just finish the job, as his boss told him. His boss was smart like that. The smartest man in the city, Joe and others believed. Not just book smart, which he was, but street smart. That was the smart that counted in Detroit.

Joe revved the engine.

He slammed the limousine into reverse and within three seconds flat he had made up the fifty feet. The two heavy bumps told him he had finished the job.

"Get us back to the mansion," said the passenger.

Joe shifted the car back into forward drive and swerved around Wanda's body, careful not to run over her a third time. This avoidance wasn't lost on the passenger in the back and he shook his head in disgust at his driver's weakness and sentimentality.

Joe hadn't even known this woman, the passenger reflected. Why should he be sentimental? The passenger had known her, known her deeply. In their younger days they were lovers for four months.

He had known her fears, her favorite movies, her favorite food, favorite sex, cologne, books and booze. He even had fathered a child with her. He turned the back air conditioner knob so that cool air flowed onto his face as the passing street lights flashed in his eyes. A light rain had started and the streets steamed as the limousine ran over them.

"Here we are, sir, the mansion," announced Joe.

The passenger's cell phone rang.

"Hello? That's terrible. Sure, I can help. Call Commander Kavanaugh at the 7th Precinct. Tell him you are a friend of mine and you need two officers down at your bar. Okay…try to sleep Julius. Yes, she was special. Goodbye."

The passenger turned his cell phone off. He pulled his gaze back from the street and saw his own reflection in the window. Grey mixed in with his dark black hair, thin face, long-broken slanted African-American nose and brown, almond eyes. He still had his looks as he matured and was careful to work out five days a week. He straightened his tie in the mirrored reflection. This is my city, love it or hate it, and no one is going to take that away.

Joe slowed and pulled the limousine into the Manoogian Mansion, the residence of the Mayor of Detroit, Hank Jenkins.

"We're home Mayor," whispered Joe.

"Thank you, Joe. For everything," replied Hank.

Back in the dark of Mack Avenue, the shadow stepped out and revealed itself as a thirty-five year old light-skinned African American woman, Ginny Crawford. Her body shook in the soft rain. The sound of music from The Blue Monk, a blues and jazz bar, across the street was muffled in her ears. Ginny stared at Wanda's dead eye that had previously screamed at her.

The screaming was now in Ginny's head and she listened to it this time. She turned and ran. She didn't know where she was running, it didn't matter. The instinct for survival was in control and she let it be.

She wasn't familiar with the Detroit streets she was running down, the street people that rushed past her and threw out obscene commentaries at her, or the burned out houses and buildings she passed in her marathon. Ginny had witnessed the murder of a woman she was about to meet for the first time—her biological mother, Wanda Doppkowski.

Ginny had seen the fear in her mother's eyes, those same green eyes that they shared. Now, while running, she felt a craving to touch Wanda's skin. It was still a shock to see it—the skin. She knew her mother was white but to see Wanda, this blonde bombshell of a woman, walk toward her was still shocking.

Since finding her birth mother, Ginny had only two months to intellectualize that inside her ebony skin lived whiteness. Now the origin of her whiteness was dead.

The urge overcame her. Ginny had to touch her mother's skin. She stopped running, turned around and stared down the street panting hard. She took three cautious steps and then began a slow jog back to her mother. Within a minute, Ginny saw Wanda's body crumpled in the street. She stopped twenty feet from the body and stared at it.

On her twelfth birthday, Ginny was told that she was adopted. She spent countless nights dreaming of what her biological mother was like. She dreamed they would have a tearful reunion and it would be a kindred spirit connection. But this reunion resulting in a broken body bleeding on a putrid street in Detroit was leading Ginny into shock.

The lights started to blur and she began to see the body glow in her hazy vision. She shivered in the ninety-degree heat as she unsteadily stepped closer.

The doorman from The Blue Monk, Winston, walked out of the bar, saw a body on the ground and ran out into the street. He kneeled down and stopped Ginny just as she was about to reach down to touch Wanda's face. He held Ginny's hand and quickly surmised Wanda's fate.

"She's dead. You saw it?" Winston said.

Ginny nodded yes. She couldn't speak. The shock was in full control. Winston stood up, took his suit jacket off and swung it around Ginny's clammy skin.

A man with a drink in his hand looked out of the small front window in The Blue Monk and saw the body down in the street. He looked closer—he recognized the woman. He backed away quickly from the window unnoticed.

Winston turned to the sound of a car speeding toward them. He scooted Ginny out of the way of the headlights. A black 2001 Camaro drove up and squealed to a stop. Gabe Flynn, off duty from his Detroit police detective shift, ran over to the scene. Gabe gave a familiar nod to Winston.

"Winston," said Gabe. "You two witness this?"

"She did," said Winston.

Ginny looked at Gabe blankly.

"Who is she?" asked Gabe, pointing at Ginny.

Winston shrugged his shoulders.

"Her daughter," answered Ginny with careful articulation, the best she could muster at this point, and a slight southern accent.

"Wanda's daughter?" questioned Winston as he stepped back.

"I came in from Nashville on a late flight," said Ginny in a barely audible tone.

"Oh, fuck," said Gabe as he walked in a circle around Wanda's body.

Police lights swirled in the distance but their sirens were turned off.

"Did you call the police, Winston?" asked Gabe.

"Not me," said Winston.

Gabe looked at Ginny, who shook her head no.

"Christ," said Gabe. He grabbed Ginny's shoulder and started leading her to his car. "Get lost, Winston, you know what I mean?"

"Got'cha, Gabe." Winston ran back to The Blue Monk.

"Keep it to yourself. All of it!" yelled Gabe.

"I got that story down cold," said Winston as he ran into the bar.

"Wait, where are you taking me?" asked Ginny weakly.

"To my place," answered Gabe.

She jerked away from him.

"It's not like that." He took her arm and politely led her into the back seat. "Get down."

"But the police are coming, we got to tell them about the limousine," protested Ginny.

5

"Sweetie, not this time. It's hard to tell the good guys from the bad in this city. If you're a stranger that is. Now get down. Put this blanket over you."

Gabe jumped into the front seat and looked in his rear view mirror. *Shit, they're here. Fuck. What are the odds I would be here tonight?* Gabe deliberated for a split second, and popped a peppermint Certs in his mouth before bolting out of the car.

A Detroit city police car pulled up behind Gabe. The blue and red police lights swirled, illuminating the street. No street pedestrians or patrons from the bar came out to see what the commotion was—they never did. This is a city where the inhabitants know better. Minding your own business will add years to your life.

Jackson Billings, a black, forty-year old police sergeant, got out of the passenger side. With him was a young black novice police patrolman, Burt Stevens, who was busy checking out the scene.

"What the hell are you doing here, Gabe?" spouted Billings.

"Did you hear our call?" asked Stevens.

"Nope," said Gabe.

"Good, 'cause there was none. Kavanaugh called this one in," replied Billings.

"Kavanaugh? Why?"

"You think he's going to tell us or we're going to ask? Now, what's your story?"

Billings walked up close to Gabe and smelled the peppermint. The sergeant enjoyed screwing with his reputation any chance that it was served up to him. Gabe had been on Billings' shit list ever since his short career with the Internal Affair department. In his third month with IA, Gabe brought up bribery charges against one of Billings' best friends.

"Been drinking, Gabe? That's a no-no since you got reinstated from your suspension."

"Just one. I was inside the bar seeing some old friends. When I walked out I saw this mess. I was about to call it in from my car when I saw your bubble gum lights."

Billings looked into Gabe's brown eyes. Damn. He couldn't read this guy. Any criminal he could read but a cop was tough. They study lying every day. They work and hunt liars. It could go either way on this one. Billings decided he had to drop it for now, and would come back to it later if this scene became a problem.

"You didn't see anything?" asked Billings.

"Nothing."

"Okay," Billings said. "Any witnesses see it from the bar? A bouncer?"

"They have a doorman but he was inside and didn't see anything. I already asked him."

"What were you doing in your car?" asked Billings as he peered into the Camaro.

"I left my cell phone in it. I was about to call an ambulance and squad car," replied Gabe. He started walking to Wanda's body, hoping that Billings would follow, which he did.

Stevens tried in vain to feel a pulse on Wanda. Her body was losing its warmth. He found her purse nearby and rummaged through it. He pulled out a Michigan identification card from her wallet. The young officer smirked as he surmised she didn't have a driver's license due to possible DUI's.

"Wanda Doppkowski," yelled Stevens as he tossed her purse to Billings.

"Probably has relatives in Poletown with that name," said Billings.

"She does," said Gabe.

Billings threw the purse at his patrol car, irritated with Gabe's familiarity with the crime scene and victim.

"You know her?" asked Billings.

Gabe ran his hands through his brown hair and nodded.

"Don't tell me. Doppkowski. Any relation to Detective Deanna Dopp?"

"Her mother."

"Oh, shit," Billings muttered. "And you just happened to be here? This is quite a coincidence, Gabe."

"She's a singer. Been performing at The Blue Monk for years. She knew lots of people and a lot of people knew her."

"This city is too small," said Billings.

"Damn, Billings. You think I'm thrilled about this? I'm the one that has to call Deanna."

"Who's Deanna Dopp?" asked Stevens.

Billings gave Gabe a nod to go ahead and tell him.

"My ex-partner," said Gabe.

CHAPTER 2 – DETROIT RECALL

Ring! Ring! Ring! The sound of the phone by her ear made Deanna jump up from a dead sleep. She sat straight up in bed. Nerves tingled down her legs to her toes, which always happened when she was scared. It was just after midnight, west coast time.

There are only two types of calls that come in at this time of night, drunk dials from ex-boyfriends or the other bad news from hospitals, relatives or cops.

Deanna didn't have any ex-boyfriends that had this new phone number since she moved to Portland, Oregon nine months ago.

Ring! Ring! Ring!

Shit, she didn't want to pick up. She slowly grabbed the phone, hit the on button, and brought it to her ear.

"Hello?"

"Hey, kiddo," said Gabe.

She recognized the voice. It made a different kind of signal go through her body, warming her.

"Gabe?"

"Yeah. Hey, Deanna. Sorry for waking you."

"Wow, it only took nine months for you to call. What, are you drunk?"

Deanna leaned back in bed, glad that this was a drunk dial, not from an ex-boyfriend but an ex-partner from the Detroit police force. Her lonely heart needed a nice long conversation with a friend.

"You call to tell me that I got reinstated? Or did Commander Kavanaugh keel over from a stroke, that fat bastard," she said with a laugh.

"No, no. It's not Kavanaugh. Listen, I've got some bad news."

Uh-oh. This phone call was turning into one of those bad ones. One name entered Deanna's head.

"Wanda?" she said.

"She's…she's dead, Deanna. I'm sorry kid."

Deanna had expected these words since she was fifteen years old, but they still knocked a blow to her stomach. She doubled over in bed, holding her gut. She bit down hard on her lip. It started to bleed. Gabe thought he heard her cry out but couldn't verify it.

"Deanna?"

"I'm here."

"You coming back home?"

Fuck. Detroit. Home.

Deanna straightened up and began to compose herself. A laugh came up from her chest as an emotional relief to the moment.

"Christ…Gabe, how did she die? Let me guess, she OD'd."

"Hit and run."

The words sent images into Deanna's mind. The hit, the pain, a street, her mother's body.

"Oh, God. Did you catch them?" she asked.

"No."

"Witnesses?"

"You know Detroit," he reminded her.

"Yeah, big surprise," said Deanna.

"Maybe some clues will come from the autopsy. Shit, how I hate this," said Gabe.

Deanna stopped talking. Her mind began to wander. Of course they were going to do an autopsy. The actual mention of it made Deanna double over again. She'd seen bodies after an autopsy and before the cosmetologists at the funeral homes could work their magic. Lord knows what her mother looked like after a hit and run. Deanna forced herself to lie down again.

"Where was she?"

"Outside The Blue Monk. She had a gig. She was walking out to her car, I suspect. Shit, Deanna, it's been hotter than hell here the last two weeks. You know how this town gets in the heat. Everyone goes nuts. Weird shit happens."

Deanna was trying to absorb the details as Gabe said them, but her mind uncontrollably started playing flashbacks of her and Wanda over the past twenty-eight years.

Picking a drunk Wanda up from their bathroom floor, making dinner for Wanda at the age of eight because that was the only way they were going to eat anything hot that night. At thirteen, driving an intoxicated Wanda home after a family party in their broken down Chevy. The fond memories went on and on.

"Were you working tonight?" Deanna asked.

"No, I was in the bar."

Shit. Gabe was back drinking.

Deanna's silence made Gabe feel guilty on the other end of the line.

"You know, I can call your Aunt Helen and Uncle Roman for you. I can even take care of the funeral arrangements if you can't come back. It's a long way from Portland. You must be really busy with your life," he said.

Deanna rubbed her stomach. When she left Detroit she vowed never to go back. But in her heart she knew between funerals and the unlawful firing civil lawsuit her Uncle Roman, a third–rate, night–school lawyer, was trying to fight for her, she would have to fly back some day. Wanda didn't just die from her own hands, but from someone else's. A stranger, she reasoned, had killed her. Deanna stood up and looked out her window on the quiet Portland neighborhood. It was raining. Again.

"No, I'm coming home. I'm going to find the son of a bitch that was driving that car," said Deanna.

"Damn, well, I assumed you would, so I booked you a flight with Northwest. It gets into the city at 4:45 this afternoon."

"Thanks."

"There's something else," Gabe said. He put down his whiskey and looked over at Ginny shivering on his living room couch.

"What?" said Deanna.

Gabe reconsidered and rubbed his unshaven face.

"Never mind. We'll talk when you get here. Try to get some sleep, sweetie."

Gabe hung up softly and looked over at his visitor on the couch. Deanna's half-sister slept fitfully. He didn't know how Deanna would take it. A black sister that she never knew existed. What other secrets did Wanda have that now would creep out of the closet? They always do. Every cop knew that. It's hard to keep secrets because there are always two involved—unless the other one ends up dead. Lord knows Wanda wasn't the smartest lady in the world, he remembered, but damn, she could sing.

3:15 in the morning, Detroit time. He needed sleep. He walked to his bedroom on the first floor and crashed down on the bed. No use in changing clothes, he had to be at work in four hours. He closed his eyes and blocked out the night.

Deanna paced in her bedroom. She tried to push away the painful memories of Wanda. The good times. Try to remember those. She tried hard. They all came with bittersweet endings. Wait, she had one. The time Wanda took her to Boblo Island, the amusement park on the Detroit River. Wanda had come ahead on her paycheck that month and since it was Deanna's ninth birthday she decided on an outing. She was sober too—that was worth the memory right there.

Deanna shut her eyes tight, remembering going around the tilt-a-twirl with Wanda and then down the big hundred-foot slide. Wanda's blonde hair blowing away from her face, showing off those Polish features. Deanna had her father's hair, brown and straight. She loved looking at Wanda when she laughed, probably as much as the male admirers did walking by them that day.

All was well until Wanda drove them home. She stopped at The Blue Monk to pick up a sweater that she had left there the night before. Deanna waited in the car. And waited and waited, for two hours.

Finally, Deanna went into the bar, knowing she would find a loaded Wanda. But she was wrong, she didn't find Wanda at the bar. She found her in the back office. Specifically in the back office cot, naked, sleeping with Julian Cassidy, the assistant manager, who was also passed out. Deanna walked home. Christ, her mom was a head case.

Deanna started packing. She didn't have to notify her employer because she had lost her last two jobs. Lack of enthusiasm was a resounding theme in her bosses' departure speeches. She only had a few thousand left from the severance package she was forced to take from the Detroit Police Department, after they canned her on a bogus charge of entering a premise without a warrant, her first and only violation that was a matter of interpretation on a timing technicality.

No one had ever heard of the police union not being able to defend, or at least lessen a punishment for a minor infraction. Her union steward, Lonnie Monroe, and her precinct leader, Commander Dan Kavanaugh, were often in her dreams as she took them both down with her Glock G21SF automatic pistol—the one they confiscated from her when she left the precinct building. Damn, she missed that gun.

Deanna looked around her apartment. She picked up the clothes that were lying on the floor and started a load of laundry. There were no animals she had to take care of in her life. Maybe she could get a dog when she returned. The idea made her feel good for about five minutes.

She walked down to her kitchen and looked at her dog calendar hanging on the refrigerator. Deanna never had a dog, but she felt by buying the calendar it got her one step closer to taking the step toward pet ownership.

Deanna opened the freezer, grabbed a pint of Haagen-Dazs coffee ice cream and a spoon and began to stress-eat. It was a coping mechanism she started when she was hired into the police force. It didn't do too much damage to her 5'4" petite frame, her daily run kept her body in balance.

She glanced at the date, July 23rd, and then glanced to Saturday, July 25th. From her experience as a cop, Deanna knew she had to optimize the next twenty-four to forty-eight hours to find the driver. Clues, evidence and memories fade after two days. Leads go cold, people move on and cars get repaired and fixed undercover.

Deanna drove to the Portland International Airport, went through security uneventfully, and boarded a plane headed to Detroit. She took a window seat and put on her sunglasses. She didn't look forward to the five-hour flight. Too much time for thinking.

She ordered two Bloody Marys. By the time the flight attendant had swung around with the snack cart she had ordered two more drinks. As the plane crossed over the Continental Divide she was in a restless sleep. Any kind of sleep was okay with Deanna and all her sleeps were disturbed anyway.

CHAPTER 3 – MAYOR OF HARD TIMES

Hank Jenkins squeezed ahead of his classmates to get a glimpse of his final law class grades posted in Mayers Hall at Wayne State University in downtown Detroit. He scanned the list down to his name.

Jenkins, Henry—93%.

He clenched his hand in a fist and shook it with pride. Yes, A minus. He had kept his A average for three years and his rank of being fifth out of two hundred and fifty classmates in the graduating Class of '73.

Hank pushed his way out of the crowd, sharing high-fives and a few laughs with his classmates. He then strode down the hallway feeling good. Real good. He was on the right path. Arrow straight. Quite an accomplishment for the son of a garbage man.

Now he just needed to pass the bar exam, land at the best firm in Detroit, and find a mentor to help him secure a partner position in four years—five years tops. Glancing down a hallway he saw Professor Samuelsohn. Hank ran down the hall after him.

"Professor Samuelsohn, sir."

The seventy-year-old Jewish professor slowly turned around, his bow-tie perfectly centered and wearing his best houndstooth jacket.

"Mr. Jenkins, yes?"

"Professor, I was wondering if the law firms have gotten back to you yet on their top draft picks."

"Yes, we completed those yesterday. Wondering where you are landing? You know all of the law firms we deal with are equally good."

Hank knew that was a lie.

"Professor, with all due respect, you were the one that taught me that not everything that is stated equal is really equal."

"God, I hate third-year students," Samuelsohn said with a slight smirk.

"Can you tell me who has inquired about me?" asked Hank.

Professor Samuelsohn took out a piece of paper from his folder and perused it.

"Jenkins, Henry...the law office of Creery and Feiner. Good firm. Solid."

Hank's face fell. Not the firm he wanted. Professor Samuelsohn sensed his disappointment.

"That's not the one that was first on my list, sir," said Hank.

"And you were not first in your class. There is a pecking order for these placements. You know how this works."

"Yes, I know how this works. My whole life."

"Are you insinuating something, Mr. Jenkins? Because that is beneath you. And flat wrong."

"I want to be with a firm that has a principle tied to politics and social reform," said Hank.

"They all are one way or another," explained Samuelsohn.

"I mean in the heart of things. Helping make the change. Creery and Feiner represent the automobile companies. They don't even litigate in court."

"Smart lawyers don't want to go to court. Juries are too risky. Did I fail to teach you anything? The Big Three auto companies have a huge influence on this town. Jobs, unions, you name it."

"I want to be closer to the action rather than buried in union contracts. The revolution is happening on the street and in City Hall," said Hank.

"You want it all too fast, Hank. Revolutions are settled behind closed doors usually by those that can provide jobs and stabilize the economy—that would be the auto industry," reasoned Samuelsohn.

Hank stopped. He shouldn't burn a bridge with a professor that showed him much faith and encouragement for the past three years. He may need Samuelsohn in the future. He smiled and shook the professor's hand good-naturedly.

"I'm sure I will learn a lot from the gentlemen at Creery and Feiner."

"And they from you. You will be the first black man on their staff. That is quite an accomplishment, young man," beamed Samuelsohn.

The compliment stung Hank. He didn't think it was an accomplishment but a travesty. And he didn't feel like celebrating Creery and Feiner's ignorance for the past hundred years. The sons of bitches should burn—not be congratulated.

"Yes, thank you, Professor," Hank struggled to say.

Professor Samuelsohn was proud and satisfied that his student decided to look upon this as a great opportunity. He had thought highly of Hank Jenkins during his three years in law school and saw promise in the young black man.

This is what the city needed, especially a city whose population was quickly changing in demographics. The whites were beginning to flee the city for the grassy suburbs and pot-holed highways. The remaining black people will need someone to lead them and form their future.

Hank Jenkins had potential to be their leader, believed Professor Samuelsohn as he walked back to his book-filled office. He just required another ten years of maturing under the right mentorship.

Creery and Feiner may not be the cutting edge politico revolutionary firm that Hank deemed he needed, but they were strategic, behind the scenes movers that the young Jenkins was too naïve to understand.

"Goodbye, Professor."

"Good luck to you, Hank. Keep in touch."

"Yes, sir. I will. Thank you for your encouragement."

Hank turned and began to walk away, simmering inside.

"Hank," called out the professor.

Hank turned.

"Learn how this city operates. It's a complicated place. Make friends, feel it out. Take your time, son."

Hank took in Samuelsohn's words and walked away. He liked the professor but the old man didn't know what it was like to wait and wait. Hank wanted action. Now.

Hank glanced down at his watch. Five o'clock. He better get moving if he wanted to get ready for his date tonight with his girlfriend. Hank ran home to the apartment he shared with his parents, Marietta and George Jenkins, and his three other siblings.

Their apartment was in the Brewster-Douglass Housing Projects on the east side of the city. The neighborhood was tough and Hank escorted his two sisters to the store when they needed him. They didn't venture far off by themselves. It just wasn't considered.

Hank got out of the shower and began to shave. Marietta walked into the steamed-filled bathroom.

"Mom, I could've been naked," snapped Hank.

"Nothing I haven't seen before, son. Probably hasn't grown much since then anyway."

Hank smiled. He loved his mother and her sense of humor.

"Did you hear which firm wants you?" asked Marietta.

"Yes. It's a good firm," said Hank as he tapped his razor on the sink.

"Good? But not great?"

"I'll be their first black lawyer."

"So what? There are black law firms you could join right now. Where you wouldn't be the token black. Our people need some help now, son. Why don't you go down to the Muslim center with your brother? You should hear about all their plans for the city."

"I'm not going down there. We need more blacks in city government not burning down City Hall."

Marietta walked up and put her hands on Hank's back.

"I knew when you were born you were going to accomplish great things."

Hank sighed heavily with the weight of his mother's words.

"You are going to save us like Moses and part that Red Sea," said Marietta as she lifted her hands up to the ceiling and brought them to her chest.

"I'll try my best, Momma," said Hank.

"That's all I ask," said Marietta as she walked into the hallway. She looked back at her son. "You going out with her again?"

"She has a name, Mom. It's Wanda."

"Ah, yes, Miss Wanda," said Marietta softly. It pained her to think her son was seeing a white woman. How a smart boy could be so dumb was beyond her. "I don't have anything against her. I just don't want you both to get hurt."

"Love is love," said Hank as he put shaving cream on his face.

Marietta chuckled.

"Uh-huh. Especially when you are young. That's all you see. When you get older it's just one of those things that clutter relationships, like drugs or gambling. Find someone you like first, that has your same background, interests. You hear me, son?"

"Mom, look beyond her being white. I love her."

"Hank, I can't look beyond it if the world doesn't look beyond it. You are headed for hard times if you keep this relationship going. And I just don't want you or her going through the pain. That's all."

"And what about the love?"

"Lot's of people don't get what they want in life. Lord knows that. But they still have good lives. Look at all that you've accomplished. And there is more in your future."

Marietta grabbed Hank's arm.

"And you're getting out, son. Out. You got the best chance out of anyone in this neighborhood."

She squeezed Hank's arm until it hurt and he pushed her hand away.

"Mom, I'm late. And I don't want to hear this," said Hank as he slapped on aftershave.

Marietta wiped the foggy mirror with the cloth in her housecoat. Hank stared in the mirror. His mother walked slowly out of the bathroom.

"Be safe tonight, son."

"I will, Momma." Hank stepped out into the hallway, irritated. "And stop worrying about me."

"Oh, a mother never stops that. That's her job," said Marietta with her voice trailing off into the apartment.

Wanda Doppkowski entered her parents' kitchen. Their modest brick home, off Seven Mile road, sat in Detroit's Polish-dominated neighborhood. Wanda's mother, Pauline, and her father, Borys, were eating a modest meal of ham sandwiches in their cramped kitchen. Wanda grabbed a piece of ham off her father's plate and then ran upstairs to her bedroom in preparation for her date.

"Wanda! Sit down and eat. And don't steal off my plate!" bellowed Borys.

"Thanks, Pop," yelled Wanda from the top of the staircase.

Wanda's beauty had made her popular with the neighborhood boys since she was twelve years old. Her blonde hair touched her shoulders and was smooth with just the right amount of curl and bounce. Not much make-up was needed on such a delicate face with green eyes.

Borys often wondered where those eyes came from. There were no green eyes in his family that he remembered as a boy in Krakow, Poland. Blue and brown were the color of his mother and father's eyes. They both perished in WWII concentration camps because they were assisting Jews. Caught hiding their next door neighbors and best friends, Howard and Vivianna Berkowicz, in their attic, they were taken away one day while thirteen-year-old Borys was at school.

Borys's Uncle Ulysses and Aunt Clara picked him up from school that day before the Nazis got a hold of him, and smuggled him out of the country to live with his older cousin, Felix Petroski, who lived in Detroit in 1944.

This left Borys with both a profound sense of responsibility to assist those being persecuted and an equally profound fear of anything that could leave him or his family vulnerable to persecution. They balanced each other out, leaving a most nervous man.

Wanda came bouncing down the stairs and into the kitchen.

"It's not proper for you to go out with this young man without us meeting him," said Pauline between bites of her sandwich.

Wanda had kept her boyfriend, Hank, from meeting her parents for four months. But she guessed correctly that the neighborhood rumors would soon reach them.

"He's picking you up?" asked Borys.

Buzz…the doorbell sounded off.

Borys pointed his shaking finger at Wanda. "Let me get it. You wait here with your mother."

Wanda hid a smile, knowing that her father was about to get the shock of his lifetime. Not his first. She had given him many small quakes over her high school years. It pleased her a bit when she was caught being mischievous. Her father wouldn't listen to her, so she believed these little turbulences would grant him insight into his overprotective nature.

It didn't work. Borys became more bewildered by his daughter's behavior. Pauline hoped that Wanda wouldn't end up pregnant out-of-wedlock, or worse, pregnant out-of-wedlock *and* dating a black man.

Borys opened the door. Hank Jenkins stood before him holding flowers. A confused look crossed Borys's face.

"Can I help you?" Borys politely but curtly asked.

"I'm here for Wanda," explained Hank.

"You're here for…" Borys was trying to put together the puzzle. Wanda—date—boyfriend—flowers—black man. Stop.

"Wanda!"

Pauline was the first to drop her ham sandwich and rush out of the kitchen to the aid of Borys. Wanda relished the moment as she doubled-over in the pantry and held two hands to her mouth to suppress her giggles. She then realized she needed to rescue Hank. She bolted into the front room.

"Mom and Dad, this is Hank Jenkins."

Hank awkwardly smiled at the stunned Borys. He leaned over and grabbed Borys's hand and shook it swiftly.

"Nice home you have here," Hank said, not knowing what else to say. "You look nice, Wanda. These are for you." Hank handed Wanda the flowers.

"Oh, how beautiful. Look, Mom. Mom? Can you put these in a vase?"

Wanda handed the flowers to Pauline who stared at the flowers as if she had never seen a bouquet. Wanda took a quick glance at her watch.

"Oh, Hank, we're running late. We better get going."

"Nice to meet you Mr. and Mrs. Dopp."

"It's Doppkowski," Borys answered.

Hank's face soured in confusion. He looked to Wanda, who grimaced.

"Wanda started telling her friends in high school that her last name was Dopp and not Doppkowski. Too hard to spell, she said. What's that saying? Wanda marches to the beat of her own drum," Pauline said, proud of her ability to quote a popular phrase.

"That means she can be hard-headed and disrespectful," said Borys.

"Free-spirited," said Pauline, defending her daughter in front of the stranger.

Hank smiled and walked backward to the door, laughing congenially.

"Doppkowski is a fine name. I think you should reconsider, Wanda. Nice to meet you both."

Wanda furled her eyebrow at Hank. She knew he was trying to make points with her parents by his last comments. She didn't need any of that.

Wanda kissed her mother and father on the cheek. Hank opened the door and held it open for Wanda. They walked down the porch steps and Hank wiped his sweaty brow.

"Bye, don't stay up," Wanda shouted back to Borys and Pauline.

"He likes Doppkowski," commented Pauline.

"Sure, who wouldn't? It's a great name," yelled Borys. "My sandwich is getting cold."

Borys stormed back into the kitchen. Pauline watched the young couple walk down to the sidewalk and made the sign of the cross on her chest.

"Please watch over them tonight God," prayed Pauline.

Hank studied Wanda as they rode in his '65 blue Plymouth Fury. He checked out her short skirt, long legs, and beautiful face. He breathed in and smelled her. Hank was proud to have her on his arm. He had never dated a white woman.

They had met at The Blue Monk having bumped into each other on the dance floor. Hank apologized to Wanda even though she had crashed into him. She smiled and he expected her to turn around and move a few feet away—a white boundary zone he was used to and comfortable with, as well. She didn't though. She continued to dance toward Hank and completely ignored the man she was formerly dancing with, which amused Hank immensely and boosted his ego.

Hank drew up close to see how far this white woman would take it. He had a few drinks in him and proceeded with the somewhat dangerous move. The Blue Monk was a race-friendly club and he had a group of friends who would rescue him if a fight broke out with some frustrated white boy.

Wanda knew she was hard to ignore and she found Hank extremely attractive for a black man. She liked to do what she wasn't supposed to do and started to mirror her moves to his. They both found it extremely pleasurable and sexy. Both groups of friends took notice and nudged each other and shook their heads to the *playing with fire* judgments that swirled in-between whispered conversations.

That night ended with Hank and Wanda making-out in his car, that was farther than each other had gone before with a person of a different color. It might have charged their curiosity, but the attraction was real and over a few weeks it turned into an appreciation and then love.

Wanda was all Hank was not—a risk taker, a dreamer and she trusted people. Hank was the thoughtful goal-maker, reserved, levelheaded and guarded. He never contemplated he would find himself in this situation and at times it did worry him. His personal view that people should be colorblind made him hopeful that this relationship could work in the long term and could be a role model for others to overcome their racism.

For Wanda's part, dating a black man was never out of the question, it just never came up before now. She simply lived day-to-day, open to all possibilities. There was only one thing she was sure of—she wasn't going to marry a nice Polish boy from her parish and push out four or five kids. No way. She didn't know what kind of life she exactly wanted but she knew she didn't want a boring one. She craved to be special and this didn't include living two blocks away from her childhood home.

Hank drove Wanda home and ended the night that opened a door for both of them. Every following week on their dates, they pushed it farther and did things that both their parents would be very, very frightened about if they ever found out. And that thrilled Wanda and Hank even more. They were together and there was more to explore, more to shock people with, more to dig deeper into each other.

Hank forced his eyes back onto the street.

"You really think I should use Doppkowski?" asked Wanda.

"Yes, that's your God-given name. Be proud of it."

Wanda smiled. She loved this man. He was stubborn, proud and right.

"Okay, I will."

"You didn't tell them, did you?"

"What?"

"That I was black," said Hank.

"Oh, I think they figured that out for themselves," she said, giggling.

"I mean ahead of time. They don't deserve the shock, Wanda."

"Sweetheart, they don't understand and never will. Pull the band-aid off slow or fast. They are who they are."

"Why would you let me walk into a situation like that?"

"That was the best way. If my dad knew about it earlier he would have locked me in my room. This way you got to shake his hand. Meet him head-on." Wanda touched up her lipstick.

"It was uncomfortable."

Wanda finished with her lips then rolled down the window and lit up a cigarette.

"Uncomfortable, I can take. Christ, I should have been born with the balls."

Hank slammed on the brakes.

Wanda got charged from Hank's anger.

"Calm down, I just meant that sometimes it stinks being a woman. I should be able to date anyone I want. I don't want anyone telling me what I should do. My poor parents…they need a vacation from me."

"What does that mean?"

Wanda looked out into the street. The wind cooled her neck. "I don't know. I would hate to be the parent of me. Sometimes I hate the way I act, but I can't stop myself. And I hate the way they are but I know they love me. It's fucked up."

"Then is dating me a way to get back at them?" asked Hank.

"No, no…we are real. I love you. It's just too bad, the grief we cause because of our colors."

"It's not our fault."

"I know. It's just unfortunate," Wanda responded.

"Do you want to stop seeing each other?" asked Hank.

"No, I don't. Do you?"

"No."

Hank grabbed Wanda by the shoulder and pulled her close.

"I think we can make this work," Hank whispered into her ear. "I want to make this work."

"Me, too."

Wanda laid her head on Hank's shoulder as they drove down the street. People on the sidewalk stared and then turned away as they watched the couple drive by. One elderly white man spit at the car, and his young grandson picked up a rock and threw it once his grandfather gave him the go-ahead wink.

The rock didn't hit the car but Hank saw the action in the rear view mirror. He didn't bother telling Wanda. It would just set her off and she would make him stop the car and then she would likely run after the pair of disgruntled neighbors. No, they were going to have a good time tonight, together, and forget the world and its hang-ups.

The Blue Monk was packed that night. Wanda and Hank's friends, the ones who accepted their relationship, welcomed them to their table. Hank's best friend, Terry Cone, saved them seats.

Terry was just back from his time served in Vietnam. He hadn't been able to have his draft deferred by college like his friend Hank. He had let his grades sink one quarter at school and that was all that was needed for the draft board to snap him up in '71. They had acquired most of the black males in his neighborhood during the draft years.

Terry had left the army physically sound. But he was still assimilating to home life and was quieter than normal, most friends and family observed. But there was one person who always made Terry feel good and that was Wanda. She was clean and sparkling. Hank noticed this and always invited Terry out with him and Wanda. Terry was never a third wheel to Hank. They were friends for life.

"Hi, Terry," said Wanda as she gave him a kiss. Terry blushed. She knew he had a small crush on her, about which Hank was oblivious. She liked Terry the most out of all of Hank's friends, he was kind and gazed at her with admiring eyes.

"You look beautiful, Wanda," said Terry.

"Hey, how about me?" joked Hank as he pulled Wanda tight.

"You look like shit," said Terry as he drank his whiskey and Coke. Hank bumped Terry's hand so his drink spilled onto his pants. Hank let out a laugh.

"Damn it, Hank," said Terry.

"Oh, that looks real good, Terry. The women will find you very attractive tonight," said Hank as he ordered a round of drinks.

"It will dry, Terry. Any girl would be lucky to dance with you tonight," said Wanda with a wink.

"Thanks," said Terry with another blushing smile.

The dance floor opened up at eight p.m. and before that it was open mic night. Any ambitious singers could perform with the house blues band, Ronnie Charbonneau and the Cleftones.

Wanda had often sung for Hank while they rode in his car listening to the radio. As the dance floor filled with people, Ronnie scanned the room looking for the last brave, un-found talent to arrive on stage, Hank pulled Wanda near him.

"You should go up there," stated Hank.

"No way," retorted Wanda.

"Yes, you can sing. You're good."

Wanda and Hank's friends heard their conversation and encouraged Wanda to take the stage.

"Really? Me?" she questioned them, being unusually shy.

"Go for it, Wanda," encouraged Terry.

Wanda always held the ambition of being famous, she just hadn't figured the *how* part out yet. She knew she could carry a tune but had never performed before any group larger than her high school drama department. Once she asked her parents for singing lessons but her father laughed the suggestion and himself all the way to the backyard alley.

Wanda slowly stood up. Hank started waving his hand to Ronnie Charbonneau.

"Right here, right here," yelled Hank.

Ronnie spotted the beautiful blonde cutting through the crowd toward him. If she could sing half as good as she looked then this young lady could knock out the crowd, Ronnie hoped. He helped Wanda onto the stage and looked deep into her green eyes and fell hard for the young woman.

Wanda was nervous but her desire for being center stage overcame that feeling. She grabbed the microphone and whispered into Ronnie's ear. He smiled and cued the band.

At that moment, in The Blue Monk that night, people stopped laughing, stopped talking and even stopped drinking. On stage was a beauty that was fresh and wild.

Her pretty mouth opened and out came a sultry deep sound, the sound of a woman much older and seasoned, out came the sound of an untrained but meaningful voice. Wanda started slowly and then built up steam singing 'I Found a Love', the Etta James hit from '72.

Hank beamed with pride as his friends ribbed him in a congratulatory way. This felt good to him, he liked receiving his friend's praises, he liked being the 'it' couple if only for a few minutes. We *can* rise above it all, he dreamed.

Terry leaned into Hank to talk, "Hank, you know my cousin John Floyd, is working for Coleman Young, you heard of him?"

Hank's attention was fully on Wanda.

Wanda glanced at Hank and sexily smiled at him.

"Who?" asked Hank.

"Coleman Young. He's up and coming. Worked for the unions. He's going to run for Mayor of Detroit. My cousin John is working for him. He's running Coleman's campaign."

Hank's attention turned to Terry on hearing the word campaign.

"Does Coleman have a chance of winning?"

"Some say he does. My cousin thinks so. I know you like politics and all. Here's my cousin's card. I talked you up to him. You should call him," said Terry.

Hank took the card, read it and put it safely into his top pocket.

"Thanks Terry. I appreciate it, bro'." They clink their glasses in a toast.

"Just remember the little people," Terry said with a laugh.

"Always," responded Hank.

Hank turned back to Wanda on stage. She held the room and she knew it. The song ended and the crowd came to their feet clapping and whistling.

Ronnie kissed her on the cheek and as he embraced Wanda, whispered, "Come back anytime, Miss. I can use you." She felt a rush of enthusiasm and hugged him back.

Ronnie gently guided her down the stage. Wanda ran into Hank's arms and kissed him. Only a few in the crowd raised their eyebrows when they saw the embrace but the majority of the crowd began to clap harder when they saw it.

Wanda turned to her gin and tonic, and drank it down in one gulp. She wrung her hands in excitement.

"I need another. I'm shaking like a leaf!" she exclaimed.

The waitress brought her another drink and she downed that one also. Hank laughed at this response but attributed it to her nerves. It takes guts to get on stage. For the rest of the evening they danced and clung close.

That night Hank asked her to move in with him. They could find an apartment close to the University where mostly students lived. They could have a fresh start. He would be working in a few weeks and she could, well, find out what she wanted to do for a living, work, go to school, or even sing. She relished a life of freedom and that night she agreed.

Hank arrived at the office of announced mayoral candidate, Coleman Young, two days later. He had researched the energetic candidate for mayor after Terry had given him the lead with his cousin John Floyd. The office was abuzz with campaign volunteers surrounded with campaign posters of Coleman. The air was electric and this was not lost on Hank. John met him at the front desk.

"Hank, nice to meet you," said John.

John Floyd was tall and bearded. He had studied political science at the University of Michigan and was smooth and confident. He would never be in the forefront but a behind-the-scenes man that orchestrated every move of the number one man. He enjoyed it and knew this was a position he would play his whole career.

John had met Coleman Young during a black union leader's conference where John was hawking his services as a public relations man. John had endeared himself to Coleman by his slick appearance and his go-for-the-throat attack on any union suppression.

John was what every politician needed but would never admit to, a PR man who would align the candidate with the people and the press and do the dirty work for them. John felt that was fair, as did Coleman. Play fair first, but if someone crossed you then the gauntlet is thrown down.

"Likewise, thank you for meeting," said Hank.

"My cousin speaks highly of you. Fifth in your law class? Well done," said John.

"Thank you."

John led Hank to a desk right in the heart of the room's activities.

"Sorry, we don't have much space. But that will change soon. The word is getting out and we have some large endorsements coming in. So, you are interested in politics?" asked John.

"Yes, sir," replied Hank enthusiastically.

"Why the hell for?" John said looking over Hank.

"I want to be part of the change, it's exciting," Hank said nervously.

John studied the young man in front of him. He had potential, was smart, good-looking. He may just take this one on, he thought.

See if he could hold up under the pressure. See how smart he is and how stupid. Vet out his Achilles' heel. All political junkies had Achilles' heels. Hopefully this young man had a small one.

"When do you take the bar?"

Staff rushed papers in and out of John's hands as they talked.

"Next week."

"The job doesn't pay much."

"That's okay."

"You'll be one of a fleet of young legal aids we've hired."

"I have no problem standing out."

John laughed at Hank's confidence.

"Do you want to meet him?" asked John.

Hank didn't understand his question. "Meet who?"

"Coleman. Coleman Young," said John, laughing.

"Yes, absolutely," said Hank.

John guided Hank to a small back room filled with phones manned by young and old black volunteers making campaign calls. With his back turned toward them, Coleman Young stood talking on the phone. His voice was irritated but he was trying to keep cool.

"Now, you tell the Captain that he better release that young boy by tonight five p.m. Or he will see a neighborhood on fire the likes of '68 never saw unless he releases that innocent kid. Weed? What? Give me a break. We got gangs out raping and burning down houses. Let the fifteen-year-old kid go. Weed? Why don't you smoke some and get this into perspective? What? Well I…"

John tapped Coleman on the shoulder and whispered in his ear.

"Coleman, I want you to meet one of your new legal aids, Hank Jenkins. Let me take care of this for you." John gently took the phone and started talking calmly to the person on the end receiver. Coleman threw up his hands.

"That's why I like John so much. He handles all the messes. Now who are you?"

Hank stuck out his hand to Coleman. "Hank Jenkins, I'm a friend of John's cousin. I'm graduating from law school this week."

"University of Michigan?" asked Coleman.

"No, Wayne State," said Hank defensively.

"Good, I can't stand those candy-ass Michigan types, besides John, of course. I was supposed to go there but I got screwed out of a scholarship."

Hank didn't know what to say, he finally mustered up, "I'm sorry, sir."

"That's all right. To hell with those motherfuckers. Each of us has faced discrimination one way or another. All of it made me who I am today. I'm sure you have your own stories," Coleman said as he eyed Hank up and down.

"Yes, sir," responded Hank as he flashed back to racial fights he tried to steer clear of in high school and the scared eyes of white women he passed on the street.

Hank looked at John, still on the phone, sheepishly.

"Oh, John, well he slipped into U of M when their admissions board wasn't looking," said Coleman with a belly laugh.

Coleman slapped Hank on the back.

"A lawyer, huh? Good for you, brother. Minister, lawyer or funeral director, whatever way you can get out of the ghetto. Education is the key for our people. Welcome aboard," said Coleman as he guided Hank out to the main office. "What neighborhood are you from?" asked Coleman.

"Brewster-Douglass," responded Hank.

"Shit. Tough neighborhood. I need some good voter turn out there. I may have you knocking on your neighbors' doors," Coleman said rubbing his chin.

"Sure. Whatever we need to do," responded Hank too seriously. Coleman leaned in closer to his young future legal aid. He smelled Hank's youth, his hopes and his naiveté.

"Feel that?" asked Coleman.

Hank surveyed the room. He felt it.

"That's pure energy. People connecting to a common cause. They won't be able to stop us. We need to keep the dream alive. Detroit is ripe for a black mayor. Get me elected, Hank, and things will be better for you, for your family, for your children."

"I want that," replied Hank.

"You married?" asked Coleman.

"No, just dating."

"What neighborhood is she from? Yours?"

"No, East side. Seven Mile."

"Seven Mile...white girl?" Coleman ripped a big whooping laugh that filled the room.

Hank was caught off-guard and nervously laughed with Coleman as he wondered if it was true that behind every joke was a piece of truthful sentiment the mayoral candidate harbored.

"Must be upscale. Hmmm...Seven Mile. That's not a heavily mixed neighborhood."

"Umm, no, not yet." Hank smiled.

Coleman started to laugh. "You're right Hank. Not yet." Coleman stopped laughing and stared at Hank.

"You didn't answer my question."

Hank stared into Coleman Young's eyes and stayed mute. Coleman nodded his head, understanding that his new young legal aid may be venturing in dangerous waters.

"Let me give you some advice. Date women from your own neighborhood. You know each other's history. Anything else will surely shoot your political career and mine in the foot," said Coleman quietly. "You understand me, son?"

"Yes, yes, sir," Hank managed to get out of his frozen mind and lips.

"Good. I promise you'll learn more in the next few months than you did in all your years in law school. The way life really works in this city. All these people working so hard not just for me but for themselves—for a future. Once you get a taste of politics and victory you'll never want anything else," said Coleman with a large cackle as he slapped a passing volunteer on their back.

Coleman continued to laugh as he left Hank alone in the center of the buzzing room. Hank took a deep breath, looked around at all the people working diligently for one man. He closed his eyes and felt the energy pulse through his body. A volunteer ran into Hank's shoulder, pulling him out of his dream state. He stood there for a few moments feeling proud that he was going to be a part of this operation and then quietly left the office.

As he walked down the street he analyzed that this was the first time he had to navigate around the topic of Wanda being white. He never hid it from his friends or his mother. Hank had always been upfront to his family and friends regarding her color and his commitment to her.

Hank stopped in front of a vacant store window and stared at his reflection in the mirror. He felt a shift inside himself. He was on the threshold of a whole new world. The door was opening and Coleman Young was letting him in. All the hopes he had been set-up to accomplish by his mother and community could happen if he kept moving forward…without Wanda. That was made clear.

Hank struggled with the thought of calling off his relationship with her. If word ever got back to Coleman or the press that one of his legal aids was dating a white woman it could cause distraction and bad publicity. Hank didn't want to screw up the incredible opportunity he was given or Coleman's future.

Perhaps his mother was right, Hank thought, as he walked past the black-owned stores in his neighborhood. Breaking up with Wanda would be for the greater good of his people. It also could satisfy his desire of that sensual feeling of energy that overcame him in the campaign room. It was more delirious to him than anything he had felt with Wanda. At that moment Hank was resolute that his relationship with Wanda would end—he just didn't know when.

CHAPTER 4 – ROUNDABOUTS

Deanna's plane touched down in Detroit Metro airport half an hour late. That meant half an hour more containment in her seat. Any place was a prison for Deanna if she was pinned down and unable to move. When she was a kid, she was constantly in motion. As an eastside Detroit student at Pershing High School, she took up every sport that was offered for girls, excelling in them all.

Her body was sinewy and compact, the perfect size for a point guard or shortstop. Combined with her scrappy and competitive nature, she enjoyed winning and proving herself, but to whom, she didn't really know. Deanna only knew the enjoyment of being out front, in the lead, being the best. It made her feel good.

Deanna graduated near the top of her high school class in 1990. She became a runner, not a jogger, later after high school. She never felt better than at the end of a ten-mile run. The endorphins slid in as she sprinted against imaginary competitors.

Wanda and Deanna's father, Ronnie Charbonneau, didn't join the mass exodus to the suburbs that the majority of other white families took part in during the seventies. All they knew was Detroit—its bars, restaurants and neighborhoods and a house with a small mortgage payment was exactly what their budget could afford.

Borys and Pauline died during Deanna's senior year in high school. They both went quickly, one after the other within months. It was a hard blow to Deanna since her grandparents were the only ones that paid her much attention. Wanda decided to move Deanna and Ronnie into her parent's old home on Klinger Street. Ronnie used to joke that nothing could stop them living a better life—nothing but a bottle of booze, Deanna said under her breath.

After high school graduation, Deanna decided to join the Detroit police department after her pragmatic side realized there was no college fund in sight or any way to secure a loan. She easily passed the physical fitness and academic tests for the police department. The hardest part of it all was the overt attention she received from the male police candidates due to her angel-like face, petite physique and the green eyes she inherited from Wanda.

Some fellow police candidates came on to her soft, others very hard—too hard. She never admitted feeling fearful of her own classmates but she was surprised future law abiding officers would outwardly cross the line without fear of retribution.

Deanna took it in stride, cut the men down with a quip that made the men a joke to their classmates, but in the dark of the night at home in bed, she knew she would have to choose wisely when trusting a fellow officer. She would still have to watch out for herself. Nothing she hadn't done her whole life. A rush of shame came upon her.

Was that the real reason she joined the force, to surround herself with men that would protect her? She almost quit after a sleepless night wrestling with those demons.

No, Deanna determined, she joined to delineate between right and wrong, to keep some peace, if not in the city, at least in someone's household. Too many times the cops were called to her house as Wanda and her father Ronnie went at it. She remembered running to the door as a kid and being thankful when she saw the cop car pull up in front of their home.

Thank God they arrived before Wanda and Ronnie killed one another, she prayed as the officers patted her on the head when they entered the door. Later in her teen years, the sight of cops in her home only embarrassed her, although gratefulness lay at the bottom of her hidden heart.

Deanna was readily accepted on the police force. She was a Detroit girl. And her fellow officers knew that meant something. Her brothers-in-arms still hit upon her, that didn't change, but they didn't make fun of her ability. Many hoped they would get partnered up with Deanna in hopes of scoring with her. After five years of riding in a squad car, she finally made detective.

Now transferred and on her first day on the force at the 7th Precinct, Deanna shook Commander Dan Kavanaugh's hand and looked him dead in the eye. She was relieved she didn't catch him glancing at her breasts.

Kavanaugh was only one of two remaining white commanders on the Detroit force and known for his old school demeanor. He let her pass in front of him to descend the precinct staircase—and checked out her ass. She turned around and caught him staring at her behind—things never change, she sighed.

"If any of these palookas give you any shit let me know," he said, quickly diverting his eyes to hers.

"Thanks, Commander, I'm sure everything will be fine," replied Deanna.

"You don't know them like I do, sugar. They're a bunch of sexist assholes, sweetheart," said Kavanaugh.

Deanna laughed to herself at the total unawareness of the commander's own remarks.

Kavanaugh knew it was a delicate procedure pairing up women and men partners. In the forty plus years that Kavanaugh worked for the City of Detroit he had seen a lot of change. He was on duty during the '67 and '68 riots. His inexperience at the time told him that was just a few bad years. But the next decade brought just as much tension as gun battles were taking place on the street between his officers and its unsettled citizens.

Then there were the Coleman Young years. Those were tough, political, just plain bad for everyone all around—black, white, the cops, the people of the city. There had been some good police chiefs, some bad ones, great police work along with sloppy work but all in all he got through every year only a bit more cynical than the last.

This was Kavanaugh's last year on the force, by Christmas he would be enjoying his retirement on Marco Island in Florida. He didn't have to put in the forty plus years towards his pension. But, as he explained to the boys at the precinct, the difference between putting thirty years in and putting forty years in was the difference in having a condo three miles from the beach or ocean side. He was going for ocean side with his wife Betty.

Kavanaugh had to pair up his little Polish Princess, Deanna, with someone he could trust, a veteran, someone that wasn't macho, that wasn't his best cop, not his worst, not a Dudley Do-Right but someone who he didn't suspect of being dirty. He had one guy that fit that bill.

Gabe Flynn. A fellow Irishman from his neighborhood on the west side of Detroit, which made Kavanaugh feel even better.

Gabe was a fifteen-year veteran. He had just left Internal Affairs after realizing they were as corrupt as the cops they were investigating. He didn't have many friends at the 7th Precinct force or with IA. He was a loner, 36 years old, divorced ten years back, bad luck with women, drank too much on his off hours, but who didn't?

Kavanaugh informed Gabe of his new partner. He received the news with a roll of his eyes. Great, that's just what I need. But once he met Deanna and saw that she was different he took a shine and protective nature to Deanna, thirteen years his junior, that first year they worked together.

The third week on the job being Gabe's partner, Deanna knew he was special when he started a fistfight with three other officers for blatant sexual remarks they had made about her in the policemen's locker room. Gabe came out of it with two black eyes and a warning from Kavanaugh. She heard the story through Kavanaugh's secretary, Marie. Deanna remembered the ride in his car after his warning from the commander.

"I got some green eye shadow you can borrow to cover up those shiners," said Deanna.

"No thanks. Blue is my color. I'm a winter you know," said Gabe.

"I would have guessed you were a summer."

"No, definitely a winter. The Avon lady told me so."

"You know, you don't have to go around defending my honor. I can hold my own."

"I know you can. I got these by defending Mickey Lolich's honor, not yours. They said after the '68 series he was washed up.

That is totally false. '71 and '72 were his best years. Those guys don't know jack about baseball."

"Really?" said Deanna, not buying his story.

"Yeah, if they really knew him. Well…they would never say bad things about him," said Gabe quietly as he turned his car into a roundabout, one of his favorite things to do.

"Here we go," said Gabe.

Deanna slid into her car door and laughed as they swirled in the circle three times. She knew he would always defend her and she would do the same for him. He wasn't dirty like the other cops. He wasn't shaking down any pimps, prostitutes or gamblers. He was a straight shooter. She trusted him—completely. Five years went by and they became one of the strongest detective partner teams on the force.

Their partnership could have gone on longer but the leaders of the Detroit Police Department fired Deanna nine months ago. They were out to get her. God knows why. The firing baffled Gabe and the whole precinct. The order came from high up, higher than their commander, possibly higher than the Police Chief. They said they were making an example out of her. That didn't add up for anyone. Since then, Gabe worked solo and was back drinking.

Kavanaugh didn't know who to pair Gabe up with after Deanna left the city. Gabe was spitting up venom due to his third time found drunk on the job, he was walking a fine line on his probation period.

In reality, Kavanaugh didn't have the heart to pair anyone up with Gabe—he looked like he was sliding downhill without Deanna. A shame too, sympathized Kavanaugh, just ten more years until he hit his twenty-fifth year on the force. Gabe could have joined him on Marco Island—not in a beachside house, of course.

Deanna looked out of the plane window as it circled Detroit on its landing pattern. Flat land, a sea of highways, neighborhood after neighborhood, and the cars. Look at all the cars. The heart of Detroit. The Motor City. Her stomach clenched. Damn it. This city. She was part of it, and it was a part of her. How could you hate what bore you?

Easy. But if anyone said one word against Detroit, Deanna would go nose-to-nose defending it. Like defending your parents even though they are shitty. They're your blood.

Deanna walked off the flight. She grabbed her luggage and searched outside on the curb for Gabe. The heat and humidity immediately hit her. She spotted a sign that flashed: 5:33pm 102F degrees.

The sky was overcast and she breathed deeply. It smelled like home. It was an odd combination of diesel fumes, cut grass and grilled hot dogs. Hot dogs? She looked around and saw a hot dog vendor hawking his food to hungry travelers. She smiled. The vegan friends she had made in Portland would not appreciate this scene. She searched for Gabe.

Deanna spotted him. Gabe drove his black Camaro up slowly. He had suped-up the engine and carburetor so that it purred like a kitten. She missed that damn car. She missed the man that drove that car. She couldn't help thinking that this would be the most ridiculous scene in Portland. It would be laughable. But in Detroit it was all too real.

Maybe Detroit is real and all other places aren't, or the other way around. Deanna started confusing herself but shook herself out of it. All she knew was that she was home, and real or unreal, this is just how it was. Detroit became a character in a bad gangster movie or blacksploitation movie. She waved. Gabe smiled and stopped the car. She threw her bag in the backseat and they took off.

Gabe drove out of the airport onto the highway. He drove fast. Deanna liked that. He didn't use air conditioning but had all the windows rolled down. She looked him over. A bit more gray in his brown hair.

He looked at her and locked eyes. Oh, those eyes he had missed so many nights.

"How was your flight?" Gabe asked.

He gave one of his killer smiles to her. She started to laugh.

"Wonderful. I got drunk and slept the whole way," Deanna answered.

"I'd say it was a good flight then. Now you just sit back. Time for a drive."

His eyes went back to the road. She leaned over to her window and laid her head down on the car door, closed her eyes and let the wind sweep over her face and into her hair, drying off the sweat on the back of her neck.

It felt good to have Deanna in his car again, Gabe mused. He liked her, shit, he loved her. For her strength, her wit, and she was a damn good detective. He even admired her, and he had never admired many people in his life. And more amazingly he never wanted to fuck it up by screwing her. Their friendship was more important, they never discussed it, they just put their trust and friendship first.

Wives and boyfriends would come and go but they would always have each other if they didn't sleep together—they both knew that instinctively.

Gabe turned up the radio that was parked on his favorite rock station WRIF. He drove her into the heart of the city. For visitors, Detroit is a hard town to navigate in and it can cause any visitor to go crazy. The city planners in decades past had built four main roundabouts that any European would embrace. But Detroiters have never fully embraced roundabouts, nor visitors to the city, but the natives learned to live with them.

Both Gabe and Deanna learned if a criminal was being chased in a car, most would head for the roundabouts, the surest way to lose someone chasing you, due to their nerves. Gabe and Deanna never lost a car chase.

Gabe knew these streets better than anyone and Deanna loved driving with him. She smiled as she saw he was taking her on a tour of all the roundabouts before he dropped her off at her aunt and uncle's home.

Deanna waved at some of the old familiar junkies on the corner.

"Just a welcome home tour," shouted Gabe.

"Thanks, I feel like the homecoming queen."

Gabe squealed the tires as he tightened the turn. Why did she feel more alive here than anywhere else? Soon, they were in her old neighborhood. Deanna looked out the window like she was watching an episode of 'This Is Your Life'. It all passed by in flashes—the bakery, St. Florian's, the baseball yard, grocery store, deli, movie theatre, strip bars, pubs, second hand stores, music shops—in a montage that summed up her twenty-eight years in fifteen minutes flat. Humbling.

The place sickened her, saddened her, but electrified the inside of her stomach where danger and comfort kept each other in balance. But on these streets her intuitive danger signals sounded off a bit more. This city kept you on your toes and Deanna's heightened cop skills played on it even more. She felt like a drug addict getting her last hit. Only the fall came quicker than the high.

Deanna let out a deep sigh.

Maybe this is where she belonged, it was a part of her. Portland was never going to work, she would be a stranger there her whole life. She couldn't relate to the think-green, re-useable energy, salmon-eating, oops no-salmon eating due to the mercury levels, granola crunching, Birkenstock-wearing residents. Nice as they were…maybe that's what it was. They were too nice. And try as she might, Deanna couldn't go there because it frightened her to reveal herself to anyone but a few trusted souls. Really, just one soul. Gabe.

Why did Gabe buy her a one-way ticket home? Maybe he wanted her to stay. If she wasn't on the force anymore, they could finally pursue each other. Make love wildly and try to make a go of a relationship. She looked at him, was that what he was thinking?

Uncle Roman was always bugging Deanna to come back to Detroit. He had gone to night school to finish a law degree and, bless his heart, he promised her he could win a big lawsuit against the police force for unlawful firing and get her some big bucks. She could set up a private detective agency, he suggested. At the time, she could think of nothing worse. But after being away from the city for a while, maybe it could work.

Gabe pulled up slowly to a row of brick houses in the small city of Hamtramck that is surrounded completely by Detroit. From the 1910 until the '70's it was a stronghold of the Polish community in the Detroit area. Two Polish parishes with supportive grades and high schools, Polish restaurants and stores. The neighborhood had changed over to artists and other poor ethnicities, not exclusive to the Poles anymore. But there was still a stronghold of Polish families and its elder population that could never live anywhere else.

Gabe stopped in front of Deanna's Aunt Helen and Uncle Roman's home. Aunt Helen was her Grandmother Pauline's youngest sister, the baby of the family, now seventy-five.

Gabe let the engine idle and turned down the radio.

"Coming in?" Deanna asked.

Gabe smiled and looked at Deanna with a sly look that she had missed for nine months.

"Why did I even ask?" Deanna replied to her own question. "I have a lot of questions. I want to start investigating tonight."

"Go spend time with your family," advised Gabe.

She started to slide out of the car angrily and Gabe grabbed her arm to pull her back.

"Tomorrow, I'll pick you up in the morning. Then we can talk about it," he said.

Deanna knew Gabe would only talk when he was ready, so she knew better than to push it, even if it involved the murder of her own mother.

"Okay...any suggestion on where I should start looking around?"

"Please, Deanna."

Deanna sat thinking, frustrated playing at Gabe's speed and not her own.

"Gabe, I appreciate the ride, and your help, but this is my mother. No one's going to stop me. I have nothing to lose anymore. We only have a day or two, tops, to find who did this. You know that better than anyone."

Gabe was silent. There was no talking to Deanna on going slow. Christ, who was he to tell her what to do. It was her mother lying dead in the street yesterday night.

"You'll think clearer in the morning. Your aunt and uncle are hurting, too." Gabe turned off the radio. "Shit, I liked your mom."

"She was a train wreck."

"I liked the way she sang," said Gabe.

"The one thing she was good at, but she fucked that up too, for the most part."

Gabe turned to his steering wheel. He didn't like to hear Deanna trash Wanda and Deanna didn't like doing it either—it was a hard habit to break. Now it didn't sit well in her stomach either.

"See you tomorrow," said Deanna as she got out and pulled her bag out of Gabe's car. She walked up to the front porch and rang the doorbell and then impatiently knocked on the door. She heard a commotion of her aunt and uncle rising from their seats inside.

She saw an eye in the peephole and then a shout from her Aunt Helen, "It's Deanna. Open up Roman, open up."

Uncle Roman opened the door, and looked up and down the street before locking eyes with Deanna and scooting her inside the house.

Uncle Roman's 6'3" figure smothered her with a hug. Aunt Helen pried her husband's hands off Deanna and she wrapped her arms around Deanna's waist and rocked her. Deanna hugged her back. Her aunt looked liked a miniature version of her Grandmother Pauline.

After Grandpa Borys and Grandma Pauline died, Uncle Roman and Aunt Helen did their best to keep in touch, but Deanna kept out of reach, only coming by around the holidays.

After two minutes of holding Deanna, Aunt Helen let her go and started to cry. Back into her niece's arms she crumpled. Roman took Helen out of Deanna's arms and held his wife.

"She has fits of crying ever since we got the call about your mother," said Roman.

Deanna nodded. They got 'the call', too, from Gabe.

"Who did this, Deanna? What do your cop friends say?" asked Roman.

"I haven't talked to anyone on the case yet. I'm going to the precinct tomorrow."

"What about Gabe? What does he think?" asked Roman.

"He doesn't have anything either," Deanna lied. "I'm pretty tired. Can I put my bags upstairs?"

"Yes, go. Rest. I'll cook you some supper. Roman, help with the bags," said Aunt Helen as she grabbed a hanky out of her brassiere, blew her nose, re-inserted the hanky and straightened her housecoat.

Roman grabbed Deanna's bag and carried it upstairs. Deanna took a glance around the living room as she was led by Roman. Various old photos of grandpa, grandma, Wanda and Deanna, and Helen and Roman lined the wall.

Aunt Helen's shrine to the Lady of Czestochowa caught Deanna's eye and she stopped. She watched as her aunt lit a votive candle underneath the picture of the woman the Poles call The Black Madonna.

Deanna looked closely at the face of the Virgin Mary. The painting hung originally in her grandparents' home. She had stared at it many times and often in her youth would pray to Mary but that stopped after all her prayers went unanswered.

In grade school, Deanna had heard the story many times from the nuns and her own grandmother about the miracles the Lady had performed. But Deanna felt abandoned by her as a child and embarrassed that she wasn't more lovable to incur help.

Deanna looked deep into the Lady's eyes. So round and full of love, a perfect mother. She must have felt a mother's pain just as every mother feels the pain her children go through. At that moment, for a split second, Deanna wished she could be cradled, like Jesus, in the Lady's arms.

She couldn't remember being held in the past. Often she felt protective of Wanda, as if their roles were reversed, typical of a child of an alcoholic. She looked into baby Jesus' eyes. Deanna was much better as the parent—that was what she was trained to do and she was excellent in the role.

Deanna made a sign of the cross and followed her uncle upstairs. Roman scooted their cat off the spare bed and set Deanna's bag down.

"Deanna, both you and I know that Wanda had her problems. But no one deserves the way her life was taken, in the street that way. No one. Now, I still know some of the old boys in the neighborhood. They could help us track these people down."

"Who do you know, Uncle Roman?" asked a tired Deanna.

"Remember your Great Uncle Felix. Ever hear of the Pope of Hamtramck?"

"Felix Petroski? Christ, how old is he? A hundred?"

Deanna fell on the bed exhausted and a little delirious as she laughed. She didn't mean to put down her uncle, she just couldn't contain her police professionalism since she wasn't an official cop anymore.

"Smart ass, he came to your confirmation," countered Uncle Roman.

"That was the last time I saw him," said Deanna.

"Your grandfather tried to keep him distanced from you and your mother. He looked out for his family but still was involved with some bad things and bad people," confessed Roman. "Even though he is retired, he still has his fingers in things."

"I used to hear his name now and then on the streets when I first started on the force. What does he run now? The bingo session down at St. Florian's?" Deanna giggled some more.

She realized she was pissing off her uncle more than she should. Uncle Roman was familiar with Deanna's sense of humor, which was why he was so fond of her. But he began to feel his face turn red. He wanted to help.

"Deanna, listen to me." Roman stood over her by the bed. "He's close to St. Peter's gate, granted. But his organization is connected up and down, left and right, into everything, the casinos downtown, the strip clubs, drugs, prostitutes, you name it."

"Lovely," grimaced Deanna.

"He owes me a favor, remember?" Uncle Roman was getting charged up.

Deanna pushed her head into the pillow. Yes, she did remember. In 1997, Uncle Roman and Aunt Helen hosted a barbecue for his bowling team in their backyard, which bordered on an alley that was shared with Felix Petroski's son, Michael Petroski, a small time drug dealer. Michael was a scuzz-bag but he only sold his crap drugs to blacks so his father let him do it.

As the party was wrapping up, Roman emptied the garbage into the alley. He heard a commotion coming his way into the alley from

Michael's house. Two black guys busted into the alley, beating the shit out of Michael who was covered in blood and crying bloody murder by now.

One of the black guys saw 6'3" Uncle Roman and took out his gun. Uncle Roman took the top of the garbage lid and used it as a shield like Captain America as the black guy shot at him three times. Luckily the perp wasn't a good shot. Uncle Roman reached the one with the gun and knocked him to the ground with one swoop of the garbage can lid. The other black guy ran and never looked back.

Roman carried Michael into his house, cleaned him up and put some barbecue ribs on his kitchen table. Michael never said thank you but two weeks later there was a delivery of four hams, four pounds of bacon and four pounds of polish sausage on Uncle Roman's front door. Felix didn't leave a calling card with the meat, Uncle Roman said, but he had put two and two together and apparently that equaled four in a very significant way. Nothing was said, nothing had to be said. Just family taking care of family.

Deanna dreamily said, "Captain America."

"That's right, yours truly. He owes us."

"He paid you off in meat," countered Deanna.

"I saved his son's life, that's more than a ham," retorted Uncle Roman

"For Michael? I don't know about that," said Deanna about her cousin.

"I'm going to talk with Felix tomorrow," stated Uncle Roman.

"Uncle Roman, hold on. Let me first talk to the police," pleaded Deanna.

"I'm not doing anything but talking, too." Roman took some papers out of his back pocket and handed them to Deanna with a pen.

"I need you to sign these," he said.

"What are they?" she asked.

"We're suing the Detroit Police department for your wrongful termination. You're not going to take being fired lying down, are you?" said Uncle Roman forcefully.

Deanna looked at herself lying down.

"Of course not." She started signing the papers. "You still practicing law?"

"I came out of retirement for you," said Roman. He took the papers and happily rolled them back up.

"What do you think our chances are? The union isn't even backing me," she asked.

"Slim. But we got to try. If we don't then they already won."

Uncle Roman hit her playfully with the papers and started to walk out of the bedroom.

"Then you can open a detective agency. It's good to own your own business. Smart. Cut out the middle man."

Deanna pushed her head into the pillow at the sound of getting career advice from her uncle. As much as she loved him, she had sunk pretty low at this point, she realized, with her future in her uncle's hands.

A faint sound of rock and roll music wafted through the bedroom walls. Deanna picked up her head. The Rolling Stones. 'Wild Horses', she guessed.

"What's that? Neighbors?" asked Deanna.

"Your cousin, Stanley."

"He's living here?"

"Yep, again. Down in the basement."

"How's he doing? He clean?" inquired Deanna.

"I think so. I don't know. So many times I was wrong." Uncle Roman shrugged his shoulders and gave a hopeful smile and walked down the staircase.

Deanna loved her Uncle Roman. That was the one stable thing in her life. If he wasn't the smartest man on the block he was the sturdiest. And that's all Deanna needed, she had enough smarts and it hadn't gotten her too far, what she needed was consistency and the solidness her uncle represented so well.

"Go down and visit him," Uncle Roman called up to Deanna from the bottom of the staircase.

Deanna pushed herself up from the bed. Her second cousin Stanley. She hadn't seen him for a year. He was Uncle Roman and Aunt Helen's only child. At 38, he was ten years older than Deanna.

She remembers him as a cute, curly-haired teenager always quick to greet her with a smile and kiss at family gatherings. That smile seemed to slip away as he entered his thirties. His parents contributed it to being unsettled in his career, not having a girlfriend, not going to college. But Deanna saw it in his eyes earlier than that.

Stanley had started experimenting with drugs in his late twenties after a few failed business attempts. He went through the drugs of choice—cocaine, pot and speed. When he moved in with some buddies that he worked with in the kitchen of a casino restaurant he started the harder stuff—heroin, meth and crack.

He got busted twice. Deanna had him released two more times. Every cop did it. Christ, try to find a cop that doesn't have a family member messed up on drugs, she rationalized. He continued to get thrown in jail a few times and was sentenced to drug rehab and a halfway house. Now he was back to where his drug abuse all began - in the basement of his parents' house.

Deanna's footsteps creaked on the wood staircase leading down into the unfinished basement. The Rolling Stones music stopped. U2, the old stuff from the album Boy, began at a lower volume.

"Mom, I'm turning it down," Stanley yelled out.

"I was going to ask you to turn it up, man," Deanna yelled back.

Stanley stumbled out of his room with a smile.

"Deanna!"

Stanley ran over and scooped her up in his arms and swung her around.

"Hey, cuz," she said as she landed a kiss on his cheek.

"I'm sorry about Wanda," he said as he put her down. "I loved her, she was a free spirit."

Out of all the relatives, and even Deanna, Stanley appreciated and understood Wanda the best. During family parties he and Wanda would end up smoking cigarettes in the back yard, even on the coldest nights, drinking beer and talking. Deanna realized how much he and Wanda had in common the last time she saw Stanley. He was in bad shape and she had to drop him off at rehab—handcuffed. Then it all made sense.

One addict to another, Stanley and Wanda related to each other. They could smell each other out in a party and see it in each other's eyes and the disappointed eyes of their relatives. They weren't arrogant or boastful of their addictions. They just understood the craziness that drove them to do it and the craving itself. They laughed. It was an inside joke. Sometimes Deanna was jealous of the insider knowledge he shared with Wanda, but when she dropped Stanley off a year ago she wasn't jealous anymore. That was one joke that she didn't have to get or be on the inside track with...better to be on the outside.

"She certainly was," Deanna agreed.

"You got some leads?" he asked dragging on a cigarette.

"No, not yet."

"How's Portland?"

"It's beautiful, lots of jobs, it's clean."

"Sounds like Detroit," Stanley cracked a smile. "You love it?"

"It rains a lot," she said avoiding his question. "How long have you been living here?" Deanna asked as they both flopped on an old couch in the main room of the basement near the water heater.

"Four weeks, it's not that bad...no, it really sucks." They both shared a laugh. "Hey, I never thanked you for dropping me off at rehab that night," said Stanley.

"Anytime," kidded Deanna. "Glad to see you clean," she added seriously.

"Good to be alive." Stanley looked up into her eyes, this time straight into them, something he hadn't done in years. "I can finally say that."

Deanna smiled. It was good to have Stanley back.

"Where you working?" she asked.

"Back at the casino."

"Yeah?" she questioned.

"Hey, I already heard it from Roman and Helen. I can't run away from drugs. They're everywhere. I have friends in the kitchen. They respect that I'm clean. Plus, the money is pretty good. Next subject. Did Gabe drop you off?"

"Yeah."

"Damn, I wanted to say hello to him. How's he doing?" asked Stanley.

"Same. Gabe never changes. He's got ten more years on the force then he's retiring."

"Good for him. He's cool. One of the few cool cops I've known. Have you guys fucked yet?"

Deanna hit Stanley square in the face with a pillow. Stanley started to laugh, swiped the pillow away from her and threw it across the room and put his now crumpled cigarette back into his mouth.

"Christ, little tough Detroit chicks. God help us." Stanley scratched his head. His hair was a mess but seemed to be a controlled mess like a rock and roll singer. They both listened to the music for a minute.

"You going to get them, Deanna?" Stanley asked slowly.

Deanna stopped and felt the question. She had blocked out the image of Wanda laying dead on the street for the whole plane trip. She knew she wouldn't be able to block it out tonight, as she stayed awake in her bed. Was she going to get *them*? The bad guys, was it bad guys? Or was it a drunk driver, better yet, an underage high school student driving home drunk to the suburbs after drinking all night in Windsor?

But something in Deanna's gut told her that there was a *them*. Gabe seemed to know, too. He would have told her if he knew it was just a drunk that didn't see Wanda on that dark street. *Them* seemed to have shadowed her and Wanda their whole lives. And *they* started to reveal themselves, as of late, with Deanna's firing, and now this.

"Yes. I am."

Stanley blew a long line of smoke out of his lungs.

"Good. If you weren't, I would."

Stanley got up from the couch and headed back to his bedroom. He threw Deanna his cigarettes and lighter. "Here, you may need these." He knew Deanna didn't smoke. "Time for me to blow into my phone."

"What?"

"Come look."

Deanna followed Stanley into his bedroom strewn with his old high school rock and roll posters of Prince, U2 and Elvis Costello. Next to his bed was a court-ordered landline phone with a DUI blower attached to it. Deanna had heard of these phones for repeat DUI offenders but hadn't seen one in-person, least of all at one of her family member's homes.

Stanley grabbed the blower. "I'll take two whoppers with cheese, one fry and two cokes." He laughed and jumped onto his bed. "God, who would think it would come to this?"

Deanna threw up her hands to support his question.

"Good to have you home, even if the reason is shitty," Stanley confessed.

Deanna couldn't make herself say that she was glad to be home, she wasn't, even if it would have been under better circumstances.

"Good night," said Deanna as she turned off the basement lights and walked upstairs.

Uncle Roman and Aunt Helen were in bed and all the lights were off but the light over the kitchen sink and the outside porch lights. Deanna walked quietly into the living room and stopped as she was about to walk up the stairs.

The Black Madonna was lit up by the streetlight. Deanna could see the whip marks on her face. Deanna was drawn to the painting.

Deanna walked closer to the Lady. She took one of Stanley's matches and lit it. The small sound seemed too loud at that time of night. She lit one of the votives and the Madonna's face was a chestnut brown in the light. Deanna stared at her without blinking.

She was lost in the painting, the face, and the eyes. She took her hand and gently tried to feel the whip marks with her finger. She pulled it away quickly when she realized she was touching just a cheap print. She was embarrassed for her action. She started to back away and then quickly stepped forward and blew out the votive. The Madonna was in the dark again.

"Goodnight," she whispered.

Deanna retreated to the spare bedroom where she would try to sleep. Tomorrow she would get out on the street, get talking to people. Damn, six hours of being in that bedroom with nothing but her restless mind. She dreaded it.

She looked in the direction of her aunt and uncle's liquor cabinet. A hand-carved chestnut cabinet held bottles of vodka, whiskey and rum. She remembered the same cabinet sitting in her grandparents' home. Her grandfather, Borys, loved being the bartender at family gatherings.

Deanna walked over and pulled out a bottle of Canadian Club scotch whiskey. Lord knows how old this is, she wondered. She opened the bottle and took a whiff. Smelled okay. She brought the bottle to her lips and took a long swig. She shook her head and swallowed. It burned its way down her throat. She opened her eyes, wiped away a tear, turned to the Black Madonna and lifted the bottle in a toast.

"Here's looking at you, kid."

She took two more long drinks and gently put the bottle away. She crept upstairs as quietly as she could, crawled into bed and stared at the ceiling with songs by the Rolling Stones swirling in her head.

CHAPTER 5 – BACK ON THE STREETS

Deanna woke up to the smell of eggs and ham at eight a.m. She dragged herself out of bed and ran her hands through her hair trying to adjust to the East Coast three-hour time difference. She was never a morning person and stopped apologizing for it since she was sixteen. She threw on a t-shirt over her tank top and headed downstairs.

She could hear her uncle and aunt bickering about the garbage pickup, city schools, weather, whatever—the subject was inconsequential. Did it matter what the topic was? In fifty years of marriage they have bickered about the same issues and annoyances thousands of times. Probably switching sides in the arguments just to keep it new.

Deanna stood in the front room and looked out the window. Kids were already in the street, having been kicked out of their house, trying to find something to do. She checked out the thermometer on the front porch. Already, 85 degrees. It's going to be a hot one. She closed the door and stared at the Madonna.

Deanna gave the painting a nod of recognition and whispered, "Anything you can do to relieve the heat would be appreciated," and walked into the kitchen.

"Morning, Deanna. Sit right here. I got some eggs cooking for you," said Aunt Helen.

"Morning," Deanna managed to pull off before her cup of coffee was poured by Uncle Roman.

"What are you up to today?" Roman inquired.

"Go see some friends."

"At the police station?" asked Helen.

Deanna knew they were fishing. She quickly assessed that she would have to keep her uncle engaged enough so he wouldn't step-in, but she would have to slightly point him in the wrong direction to keep him off her real leads, whatever those were. Deanna ate her eggs and picked at the ham.

"I'll get the police report and start there," she said.

"What about funeral arrangements?" asked Aunt Helen.

"Crap. Um, I'll figure that out tomorrow," said Deanna.

"What did Wanda want at her funeral? Did she ever mention anything?" questioned Aunt Helen.

Deanna leaned back and tried to remember. Of all the nuances of their conversations she never recalled any comments from Wanda on the subject of her funeral.

"Nothing," said Deanna wiping sand out of her eyes.

"Well then, I guess we can't disappoint her. Are you going to see Gabe again? What a nice man," Aunt Helen said as she sat down to gossip. "Has he been married? I bet he likes ham."

"Stanley! Wake up," Uncle Roman yelled down the stairs. "Boy, can that kid sleep."

"He's picking me up this morning," answered Deanna.

With perfect timing there was a *knock* at the door. "Shit, that's him. I got to run." Deanna ran upstairs to get dressed.

Aunt Helen combed her hair to the side and scurried to the door. She welcomed Gabe in as he gave his condolences to her and Uncle Roman.

"How many years until you retire Gabe?" Uncle Roman asked.

"Ten more."

"Ask for a desk job for the remainder," implored Aunt Helen.

Gabe laughed, "I'd rather take my chances."

Deanna came down the stairs dressed in a short skirt and silk tank top. Gabe felt relief when he saw her. Too much family always made him uncomfortable.

Uncle Roman shook Gabe's hand. "I know Deanna's safe with you."

Deanna kissed Uncle Roman and Aunt Helen goodbye, grabbed Gabe's arm and pulled him out the door. "Uncle Roman, we aren't back on patrol again. Just asking some questions."

"Bye, Gabe. We'll see you at the funeral then." Aunt Helen waved goodbye.

"Why didn't she ever marry him?" asked Uncle Roman.

Stanley walked up and stared out the window as Deanna hopped into Gabe's car as he held the door open for her.

"Maybe she will," said Stanley as he blew smoke out the window.

Ah, freedom again. Deanna felt it immediately. Gabe pulled out of the neighborhood and hit Conant Street to catch the highway back into the city. She looked over at him. He had just showered but sweat was already forming on his shirt and forehead.

She smelled his aftershave, Armani Black Code, and it brought back memories of riding with him on patrol. It made her feel warm, safe and that she belonged there with him. Her mind reeled back to Wanda. She imagined Wanda's face feeling the cement street. She shook her head and focused on Gabe.

"So spill it. Tell me everything you know," said Deanna.

"Jackson Billings and his partner, Burt Stevens, showed up a few minutes after it happened. Strange part was that the accident hadn't been called in yet. They were tipped off. I was the first cop at the scene."

"How did you show up so fast?"

"I told you that I liked the way your mother sang. I was at The Blue Monk that night. I was in the parking lot around the back when it happened. When I pulled out in front of the bar I saw her in the street."

"Any witnesses?"

Gabe pulled up to his home. It was located on the west side, in an old Irish neighborhood. His yard hadn't been mowed in weeks and the house was in serious need of a new paint job. But he owned it outright. The mortgage was paid off two years ago.

"Why are we at your house?" inquired Deanna.

"Follow me."

Gabe unlocked his screen door and the two locks on the front door. He walked into the darkened house. The shades were all drawn closed. The house was stuffy. He let Deanna in and she slowly looked around his living room.

Books, videos and clothes were shoveled onto one chair—a hasty cleanup she ascertained. Deanna had been in Gabe's home before, a few times, but her gut called out warning signals. Deanna grabbed Gabe by his shirt and pulled him around.

"Gabe, what's going on?"

"This may take you for a surprise."

"I don't like surprises," said Deanna cautiously.

"I'm afraid you don't have a choice."

"God, what now?" said Deanna.

"It's okay. I brought her," Gabe whispered out into the darkened home.

Deanna took a few paces backward to situate her back against a wall.

"Talk to me, Gabe," said Deanna cautiously, knowing someone was in the house besides her and Gabe.

"There was one witness that night," said Gabe.

Gabe walked into the kitchen and turned on a single light.

"It's okay, you can come out," he coaxed. "Ginny…it's okay."

Ginny walked out of the bathroom, shaking, with a screwdriver in her hands. Gabe slowly grabbed the tool out of her hand and guided her to the living room couch.

Deanna checked out the African American woman before her. She was obviously a freaked-out witness. Shit, why didn't Gabe just drive her back home that night and tell her to lay low, criticized Deanna, whose stomach twinged with a small bit of jealousy in the way Gabe was gingerly handling the woman. She was pretty and Gabe was being so gentle with her.

"Deanna, I want you to meet Ginny," said Gabe. Deanna nodded at the woman.

"Ginny, this is Deanna…my old partner and…Wanda's daughter."

Ginny's eyes filled with tears, she buried her head into her hands and cried. Gabe sat down on the couch with Ginny and held her.

Deanna searched for answers in her head. Is this Gabe's girlfriend, a scared stranger, a...

"Who is she?" Deanna asked gently.

"Wanda and Ginny were supposed to meet that night."

"Why?"

"They had been arranging it for months."

"Why?" she said again.

"No one knew, Deanna," said Gabe.

"Knew what?"

"Wanda had given up a baby for adoption, before you were born."

Deanna's mind stalled. She tried to repeat Gabe's words in her head. *Baby, adoption, before you were born.*

"She's my..."

"Sister. Half-sister," said Gabe finishing Deanna's sentence.

Ginny looked up with her brown skin and green eyes. Deanna looked into those eyes—they were her mother's, they were her own eyes. *My sister.*

Ginny wiped away her tears and stood up.

"I was going to meet her, finally. She was right in front of me, I was about to cross the street, a car sped up and I stopped," explained Ginny. She began to walk closer to Deanna. "I can't get the sound out of my head."

Ginny put her hands to her ears and began to scratch at them violently. Gabe pulled down her hands to stop more damage.

Deanna was shell-shocked. Her mother had a child before her. No one knew? No one in the family ever said anything to her. These types of things always come out. Secrets can never be kept too long, especially after the dead have been buried. But Wanda hadn't even been buried yet.

Ginny turned into Deanna's arms and collapsed. Deanna slowly patted her sister awkwardly on the back. She didn't know what to say or do with this woman. She looked at Gabe who was now pacing the apartment with a whiskey in his hands.

"I didn't know I had a sister," said Ginny.

Deanna pulled Ginny away slowly and set her in a chair gently.

"She must have been very proud of you," said Ginny.

"She never told me she had another child either," Deanna said softly. "How do I know this is true?"

Gabe shrugged her shoulders. They both had interrogated countless thieves, drug pushers and abusers and could smell a lie.

"It's true. You know it," stated Gabe.

And she did. She felt it in her gut and she saw it in Ginny's green eyes.

Ginny started to cry again. Deanna went to the other side of the room to sit in the Lazy Boy chair.

"It was a limousine," said Gabe.

"A limo? We can track that down easy enough," said Deanna. "Does anyone know about...I'm sorry, what's her name?" she whispered to Gabe.

"Ginny," he whispered back. "Winston saw her. He's cool, though."

"I was supposed to go home tomorrow," said Ginny.

"Where's home?" asked Deanna.

"Nashville," said Ginny.

"Are you married?" asked Deanna.

"Engaged."

"We'll have you home soon," promised Gabe.

"I want to help find who did this," said Ginny.

"Did you see any faces?" questioned Deanna.

"Yes, the limo driver," replied Ginny.

"Call your fiancé. Tell him you are meeting all sorts of relatives and you want to extend your trip. Will he buy it?" asked Deanna.

"Yes, I'm a good actress," Ginny said, trying to smile.

"Must have got that from Wanda," cracked Deanna.

"Can I leave the house?" asked Ginny.

Gabe approached Ginny tenderly, "I'm afraid this is the safest place for you right now. Stay tight. Deanna, I'll be in the car."

Gabe left the house to give the two women some time alone. They stared at each other.

"Who's your father?" asked Deanna.

"I was hoping Wanda would tell me that. You don't know?"

"No."

"Who's your father?" asked Ginny.

"Ronnie Charbonneau. He was a local blues band leader," said Deanna.

"Uncle Ronnie?" asked Ginny. "He visited Nashville on and off for years. He knows my adoptive parents. My father worked in a recording studio. Sometimes he would give Ronnie some studio gigs as a backup session player."

"He split town when I was twelve," said Deanna flatly.

"He's living in Nashville," said Ginny.

This information hit Deanna like a truck. She dredged up the past and remembered Ronnie leaving for weeks on end. He said he was cutting records. Deanna didn't like any of this. She prided herself on knowing everything about Wanda and Ronnie. They weren't smart or sober enough to keep anything from her since she was eight-years old. But they could keep this from her? She felt liked she didn't even know herself at this moment.

"Are you sure you don't know who my father is? A musician, neighbor, old friend? Any black man that she was close to? Any old photos?" asked Ginny.

"I don't know. The Blue Monk was a mixing pot. Black, white, Italian, Irish. She had a lot of friends—bar friends. I assume she had a lot of boyfriends before Ronnie just like she did after he split. She never talked about the past."

Deanna sat down near the window and pulled the curtain to the side to look out at Gabe sitting in his car.

"You can't hide a child. Someone must know. They're out there. You think this is related to her death?" said Ginny grasping for reasons.

"I have no idea. I have to start at the beginning."

"Which beginning? The night of her death or my birth?" asked Ginny.

"Her death. That's why I flew back to Detroit. Not to meet a sister. Sorry. I'll be back later. Try not to go stir crazy here."

"Is there anything I can do to help?" asked Ginny quietly.

"No. I just want you to stay safe before we get you back home," stated Deanna.

"Find the driver...and the person in back," directed Ginny.

"You saw someone?"

"Just a shadow behind the tinted glass. I think it was a man."

Deanna walked to the door. "You can call your fiancé. Do you have a cell phone?"

"Yes," responded Ginny.

"Use it, not Gabe's home phone."

"Okay."

"Do you think anyone saw you witness the hit and run?" asked Deanna.

Ginny shook her head. "No, I don't think so. I wasn't in the light. But I'm not certain...you think someone could be looking for me?"

"I'm not sure who knows what at this point."

"Gabe didn't trust the policemen that showed up afterwards."

"Gabe knows which cops he can trust. We'll be back in a few hours. Don't go near the windows," said Deanna as she walked to the door. "It's okay, Ginny. We'll get you back to Nashville in no time."

Ginny sat on the couch and curled her feet to her chest. She nodded but didn't say anything more as Deanna left the house.

Deanna went outside to Gabe waiting in the car. The air conditioning was on full blast and Deanna used it to cool her face. She sat back.

"Think she can hold it together?" asked Deanna.

Gabe grunted. "Long shot. She's a wreck."

"Ah, she did inherit something from Wanda besides her eyes."

Deanna didn't feel bad about how she sounded. Gabe understood. Most cops used dark humor and off-color jokes to deal with the stress and situations they find themselves in. He grinned.

"Where first?" asked Gabe.

"The only criminals up at this time are cops. Let's go visit Kavanaugh."

Deanna turned off the air conditioner and rolled down her window. Gabe took Deanna's hand, squeezed it and let go. Deanna took a deep breath. Today she had to find answers.

Deanna let the wind curl her hair. A sister. A half-sister. Wanda could keep a secret. She had always felt like the second act in Wanda's life and now it made sense. She was a footnote, the postscript, the second bow to the crowd.

Wanda's drugging and drinking had to have a centering somewhere. That center must have been Ginny. But why give her away? Wanda was ballsy enough to raise an illegitimate child. It wouldn't have shocked her parents or extended family. Why did she give her up? And how did Deanna's dad, Ronnie, get involved with finding adoptive parents. She turned to Gabe.

"Did you know?"

"I didn't. But it didn't surprise me. Nothing Wanda did surprised me."

"Did you talk to her that night?" asked Deanna.

"She stopped by my table before her first set and we chatted. She was dolled up a bit more than usual. She was in a good mood. Excited. That's what I noticed. Like if there was a talent scout in the audience or a bigwig she wanted to impress."

"Was she drunk?"

"She had a few, but she wasn't drunk."

Gabe pulled up to the 7th Precinct police station. They hopped out of his car. It was their precinct, one of the busiest in the city with the toughest surrounding neighborhood. The police station was a four story brick building that has been the sight of more bribes, busts, back-room deals, snitch trade-offs and double-crosses than any other precinct building. It was the culmination of the best and worst of law enforcement. That's why most of the cops that worked there loved it and were devoted to it. The good and bad balanced themselves out— but just barely.

They climbed the staircase to the front doors.

"What's your plan?" Gabe asked.

"Don't have one."

"Oh, just like the old days."

Deanna felt her detective juices flowing again. She never did make complicated plans but just went in head-on.

Deanna walked into the precinct she was fired from only nine months earlier. Old faces passed by her. Fellow police officers greeted her with a smile and condolences. She felt some of them were genuine. She walked up to the records officer, Louis Crisculo, a third generation Greek cop.

"Louis, hey there, the Greek God that you are," said Deanna.

"Deanna, hello honey. Oh, what a sight you are. Sorry to hear about your mother. I saw her once play at Hart Plaza. She was a gem."

"Thanks, Louis."

"How can I help you?" asked Louis.

"Her police report should be filed at this precinct. Can I get a copy?"

"I wish I could accommodate you, sweetheart."

"Come on, Lou, give us the goddamn report," Gabe said as he leaned over the counter.

"Gabe, I don't got it. They pulled it the night it arrived."

"Who?"

"Some suits from downtown. City Hall."

The word that Deanna Dopp was in the building had started to spread as soon as one of the officers had spotted her getting out of Gabe's car. The news had flown up four flights of stairs by the time they had reached the entrance of the building.

Commander Kavanaugh was in the john having his daily private time to catch up on the Detroit News when his administrative assistant, Marie, burst into the bathroom. She used her hand to cover her nose.

"Commander?"

"This better be damn important, Marie!" answered Commander Kavanaugh.

"It is, Commander. Deanna Dopp is in the building."

There was a loud flush of the toilet.

"Shit. Does she want to see me?"

"She was headed to records."

Kavanaugh tried to get up off the porcelain seat. "That's even worse. Try to stall her."

Marie, who had worked for Commander Kavanaugh for the last fifteen years, only entered the bathroom and disturbed him twice in those long years. The first was when reporters were about to storm his office wanting information on two detectives swiping coke in the holding room scandal that rocked his precinct ten years ago.

The second was when the current mayor of Detroit, Hank Jenkins appeared, unannounced, to shoot some publicity photos with the commander. Neither time was Commander Kavanaugh pleased Marie had rushed him through his morning ritual. But he was pleased this time. He wanted to talk with Deanna and stall her. He hadn't seen her since he was forced to fire her.

Marie rushed down the steps and caught Deanna and Gabe leaving.

"Deanna!" Marie threw her arms around her. Deanna was caught off guard and almost fell down with the weight of Marie. Gabe steadied them both.

"Marie, I'm jealous, you never greet me with a hug," said Gabe.

"Gabe, you dog. I would love to greet you that way—only after working hours. But somehow I think I'm twenty years too old, and fifty pounds to heavy too make that happen," said Marie as she hit Gabe playfully and turned to Deanna.

"How are you, Deanna? Sorry to hear about your mother. So is the commander. He feels bad about everything."

"He *feels*?" Gabe cracked.

"Sure, he does. He…" Just then Kavanaugh barreled over to them and interrupted Marie.

"Here we go," whispered Deanna.

"Deanna," said Kavanaugh as he patted her shoulder awkwardly and pushed Gabe out of the way.

"Sorry to hear the news. How can I help you?" asked Kavanaugh.

Deanna shoved his arm off of her.

"Get me the police record for one thing," said Deanna.

"We can get you a copy, sure."

63

"If it was here," Deanna countered.

Kavanaugh rolled his eyes. "Deanna, this town is rotten to its core. After the funeral, go back to Portland and forget about this place."

"Why is the record at City Hall, Commander?" Deanna demanded.

Kavanaugh was quiet. Deanna grunted in disgust.

"I can't believe I stomached this place for five years." Deanna stormed out of the building.

Kavanaugh grabbed Gabe's arm. "Gabe, she'll listen to you. Pack her up and escort her to the airport. Get her out of here."

"You know Deanna, she's hard-headed. She left the first time totally confused. Didn't know why she was fired and no one would help her. The next time she leaves this city, she's going to have some answers or else she's never leaving."

"You're not assigned to this case, Gabe. You're on those Conner Avenue auto thefts. You better watch yourself, while you're at it. Hear me?" threatened Kavanaugh.

"Just putting in some overtime, that's all." Gabe pulled up close to Kavanaugh. "Why in the hell is City Hall messing with Deanna and her family?"

"I don't know. Details are never shared this far down," said Kavanaugh.

"If we can't find out why, at least we can find out who is doing this."

"Gabe, leave it alone, you stupid Irishman. Just fuck her and get it over with."

Gabe got in Kavanaugh's face, "Screw you. I regret that I didn't bash your head in when you fired her."

"I doubt you would risk your whole retirement on that piece of Polish ass."

Gabe's hands were about to grab Kavanaugh's shirt collar but he stopped himself just in time and smoothed out the commander's sweaty shirt wrinkles instead. The mad look in Gabe's eyes scared Kavanaugh.

"I'm glad you're re-thinking your actions. Christ, we're from the same neighborhood. Remember that," said Kavanaugh.

Gabe cooled down.

"You left the neighborhood fifteen years ago with your promotion. Being Irish isn't enough for a friendship. You're a disgrace," stated Gabe.

"I'm not a sell-out Gabe. I've got Betty to think about. I'm just playing the game until I retire."

"Christ, Dan." Gabe sniffed his nose twice toward Kavanaugh. "You smell like shit. Are you sure you wiped your ass good enough this morning?" said Gabe as he left his commander alone on the staircase. Kavanaugh sniffed the air around him and headed back to the john as he called out for Marie.

"Marie," yelled Kavanaugh.

"Yes, Commander?"

"Get me Jackson Billings on the phone in fifteen minutes."

"You got it," said Marie.

"Make that twenty," said Kavanaugh.

Marie rolled her eyes and headed back to her desk.

Gabe pulled himself together before entering his car. His face was flush which he could blame on the heat. Deanna figured he must have had words with some of the cops in the building. Riding him like they always did about their friendship. Wanting him to dish on details of sex in the backseat with his partner. He never complained to her, he never let on, but she knew they razzed him behind her back.

"Let's get a drink," suggested Gabe.

"Not this early. Take me to the morgue."

"I'll definitely need a drink then." Gabe reached his hand under his seat and pulled out a pint of Captain Morgan's spiced rum.

"How long has that been there?" asked Deanna.

"A few months," Gabe answered. Deanna shook her head and rolled down the window.

He opened the bottle, downed a swig, closed it up and put it back in its place.

They pulled into the Wayne County Medical Examiner's morgue parking lot. The morgue was housed in a state of the art facility.

The Chief Medical Examiner, Dr. Max Schwartz, led the department with a fiery temper but never followed through after his tantrums. The staff was disobedient, lazy and many were taking bribes for inappropriate side deals from the public and police, such as slight alterations made on autopsy reports and shoddy, trumped-up forensic evidence.

Max tried to clean up the staff, but occasionally he was known to bend the rules himself. He was tied up politically with the mayor and he knew where future favors could come from if he was good to those that had power. The other assistant medical examiners kept their moonlighting exams low key and kept the night shift Assistant Medical Examiner, Jerry Swift, compensated well for not reporting any oddities to their boss.

There was an assembly line of bodies coming through this facility, one of the busiest morgues in the country. For medical examiners this was the big leagues, the most exciting, fast-paced action one could hope for if you were into studying the results of trauma-induced deaths in every possible way—drug overdoses, beatings, shootings, knife wounds, blunt force trauma, child abuse, and of course, death by fire.

From time to time, Gabe and Deanna had leaned on Jerry Swift when it was needed. Only pressing him for time or information, never to alter any documentation their fellow officers requested. They both rationalized that a pair of tickets for Jerry to see the Pistons or Red Wings was worth it when they had a hunch and needed something fast for the D.A.'s Office.

Gabe knocked twice on Jerry's office door and opened it without waiting for a response. Deanna walked in first and plopped down on Jerry's leather couch. He was in the middle of a meatball sandwich that smothered his mouth and tie.

"Hey, I didn't say come in," Jerry muffled.

"Nice coronary breakfast, Jerry," replied Deanna. Jerry wiped up his mouth and desk once he took notice of Deanna, who he had a serious crush on from the minute he met her.

"Deanna, oh, you got here quick," replied Jerry with a nervous tone.

"Expecting me?" she asked.

"Well...yeah. I got word that your mother came in. I'm sorry. My condolences. I wanted to do her autopsy but Max stepped in rather quickly to take it over. That damn hog."

Jerry leaned toward Deanna and whispered, "But I reviewed his work on her, and had a look-over on the body when he went home. I theorized you would want me to do that."

Deanna nodded at his twisted favor. "Thanks, Jerry."

"What are you doing here this morning? You should be gone by now," said Gabe.

"I've been pulling a few double shifts to finance a trip to Vegas in the fall. Hey, Deanna that's not too far from Portland," implied Jerry.

"Far enough," said Deanna, denying him.

Jerry started to review Deanna's bodily attributes—her hair, her breasts, those shapely calves, her eyes. He wanted to...

Deanna jumped up off the couch as she could tell that Jerry was undressing her mentally. Jerry had always creeped her out. She used his crush on her to influence the favors she asked of him, but at times she couldn't even stomach doing that.

"Take me to her," she told Jerry who then stopped his fantasy mid-stream and abruptly turned to his computer, typed and searched for the information he needed.

"Doppkowski. Not a lot of those in the system, just two," said Jerry.

"One of advantages of not having a common name," commented Deanna.

"She's in cooler 34," said Jerry.

Deanna winced at the word *cooler*.

"Sorry, Deanna. I meant unit number 34," restated Jerry.

Jerry grabbed his keys and led the way into the storage room. Earlier he had felt it was an honor to be touching Deanna's mother. Knowing the body shared the same DNA as Deanna was tantalizing to him and Jerry found it sexually stimulating to examine Wanda.

They reached the morgue room. Jerry went right to the freezer and began to unlock the door.

"Afraid she's going to run away?" kidded Gabe.

Jerry laughed nervously. "No, just following the rules."

"When did you start doing that?" asked Gabe.

"New rules come down every day from Max. A lot of heat is on him," said Jerry.

"From where?" asked Gabe.

"Where it is always coming from—the Mayor's Office. Saying we're slopping at this and that. I'd like to see the mayor slog through three thousand autopsies a year with five pathologists. Hmmph...I'll start sending the bodies to the Manoogian Mansion. How would he like that?" Jerry realized his words could be insensitive to Deanna.

"Deanna, I'm sorry. I wouldn't send your mother there."

"My mother never liked Detroit politics. But she would have liked to go to a party at the mansion. You're all right, Jerry. Go on."

Gabe helped Jerry bring out Wanda's body. Deanna froze in her tracks. She never froze. *Was she really ready for this? To see her mother on a slab?* She took a deep breath. Gabe noticed and walked over to her and put his arm around her shoulder.

"We can wait on this," he whispered.

"No, I'm okay," lied Deanna.

Jerry spun Wanda out of the cooler and pushed the cart out under the lights into the adjoining exam room. He donned a mask, gloves and a gown, walked over to a computer station and brought up Wanda's file. He reviewed it quickly, reminding himself of the nuances of the case.

Deanna walked into the examination room, staring at the blue sheet covering her mother. Everything will change once the sheet is pulled and she sees Wanda's face, the hair, the fingers...her eyes. She won't be able to see her green eyes, the eyes that they shared. She needed to see those eyes.

"Pull it," she commanded.

Jerry pulled the sheet in one tug as if he was a grand magician. The sheet floated for a second in the air on a ripple of imagined wind in the autopsy room. Jerry's second tug drew it into his arms.

There was Wanda, dead.

And it did all change.

Deanna felt it inside her.

Deanna looked upon Wanda. She started at the face, it was white-blue but the bruises were apparent. Deanna walked around the table. One side of Wanda's face looked crazed and the other seemed at peace. Fitting for the bi-polar pained life she led, reflected Deanna.

"Start," said Deanna quietly.

"Speculated time of death was between one and two a.m. outside The Blue Monk bar," Jerry reported.

Between 12:50am and 1am, Sherlock, Gabe corrected Jerry in his head.

"She had numerous broken bones, her right hand and wrist, left femur and hip bone, broken ribs, skull, pelvis...you get the point. Internal injuries include damage to the liver, lungs and bowel. She died due to internal bleeding. She went quickly, matter of a minute or two."

"Where did she land? How far did she fly?" asked Deanna.

"I, I don't know," answered Jerry.

"What? Why? Didn't you examine the crime scene?"

"No...no one did. I got a call from Max to report down here and check the body in and that he was going to do the exam."

"Did Max go to the crime scene?" asked Deanna.

"If he did, he didn't tell me. There aren't any notes added to this file. It's pretty sparse."

"What the hell, Jerry?" growled Gabe.

"I don't know...sometimes calls get made. Things get taken care of out of the normal routine. Not all the rules are followed."

"But now we are locking up bodies so they don't walk out the door? We follow those rules?" asked Gabe.

"I don't know what's going on. What was your mother into?" yelled Jerry nervously. "I was told not to even show you the body."
He did it, he let out the secret he promised Max he wouldn't. Shit.

"What?" hissed Deanna.

Jerry contemplated his next words. He knew Deanna and Gabe could smell a liar. He considered his contempt for Max and his craving for Deanna.

"Max said if you came by that I was supposed to call him and not show you the body. I wasn't going to do that, Deanna. I had every intention of reviewing the body with you if you showed up…and you did," explained Jerry.

"Thank you, Jerry. But did you bother asking Max about a forensic investigation? Was there any evidence?" she asked.

"I didn't want to push it. He had a funny look in his eye. He was deadly serious. But Max did mention something about when your mom got hit."

"What?" asked Deanna.

"She wasn't hit just once."

"What do you mean?"

"Twice. They hit her twice. Head on and then they backed up and hit her again. I found some windshield glass imbedded near a large contusion. She must have rolled over the top of the car the first time. Then see here are the tracks for the second pass they made. I'm sorry," said Jerry as he pointed out the tire tread marks on Wanda's thighs.

Deanna had to register his words. *Twice…those sons of bitches.* The tracks were imprinted red on Wanda's skin. She took out her cell phone and took a picture of Wanda's legs and slowly put her phone away in her purse.

"It was a hit," said Deanna.

"There's something else. Max didn't write it down on the report but there were microscopic paint chips on her dress. The car was black. It would have major damage to the front. Not sure from which side. I have the paint chips stored in my desk."

Gabe saw that Deanna was processing the information and it was beginning to overload her.

"Thanks, Jerry. We'll be in touch," said Gabe as he guided Deanna out of the room.

Jerry stared down at Wanda's body and whisked the sheet over her. Deanna shook off Gabe's arm and started walking slowly down the hallway and then picked up speed.

"We didn't get a copy of the autopsy report," said Gabe as he ran after Deanna.

"It's just shit anyway," said Deanna.

Deanna strode out of the building. Gabe could hardly keep up with her pace. She was an animal about to go rabid. She was free, free of Wanda, free of those alcoholic rampages and phone calls, no more manic-depressive highs and lows that she would have to pull Wanda out of, no more fear of calls at midnight. The call had come.

She had what she always wanted—total freedom from Wanda. No more burdens, no more responsibility. No more Wanda. She was gone. Forever.

Deanna yanked open Gabe's car door and plunked down.

Gabe got in, closed his door, sat behind the wheel and waited. Deanna looked up at the sky through the windshield. It started slowly. First the trembling, then shaking, her eyes began watering, a yell was starting to form, she threw her hands in front of her mouth to stop it. If she came undone, she might not be able to pull it together for hours.

Her brain pressed on her skull. The emotions overcame her...the tears rolled down her cheeks, her mouth watered and the low muffled scream from down deep came to the surface.

She began to cry uncontrollably. Gabe moved over and grabbed both of her shoulders not to stop her but to steady her body. She turned into him and cried. An hour passed. By the time her cries turned into deep breathing Gabe was drenched to the bone in tears and sweat.

"I got you, I got you," soothed Gabe. "We can sit here for as long as we need."

She didn't answer. She didn't and couldn't make any decisions. Deanna hated how she was feeling, but for the moment, this was bigger than her. She let it be. But she knew in the far distant remnants of her cop mind that after she pulled together, she would be tracking the killers. She would find them, God help them, and kill them. She knew this absolutely.

CHAPTER 6 – HALLS OF STONE

The Mayor of Detroit finished his breakfast every morning on the back porch of the Manoogian Mansion before he went to his office at City Hall. The mansion had been a sore spot for generations of Detroiters. Halls of stone built to keep the public an arm length away. Some mayors had refused to live in it—to be exact only one. But for the most part it was forgotten when Hank Jenkins took office. Hank was an educated black man, a lawyer, had roots in the neighborhoods and the churches—and he was going to live in the mansion and enjoy its stature and view on the Detroit River.

Hank had done well over the nineteen years working for Mayor Coleman Young from 1973 to 1994. He took eight years off to establish his presence on multiple corporate boards in the community before launching his successful bid for mayor in 2002 after Mayor Dennis Archer. He easily won his re-election four years later. Another re-election bid was fast approaching. Coleman had enjoyed the fact that Detroit didn't have any mayor term limits, a benefit that Hank now appreciated also.

Over the years, Hank had led policy efforts to improve the hotel and convention business in Detroit as well as leading the improvement in the riverfront revitalization and brokering with executive leaders to bring businesses and job opportunities into the city.

Education was Hank's passion and he was currently working with the Detroit Education Board on charter schools and budget reforms. No one could say that Hank didn't work hard for the people of Detroit. He loved this city.

Hank was well-respected by both sides, the white and the black, and he had been able to walk this delicate line without the perception that he was walking the line ever since his law school days in the early seventies.

Of all the gifts that Hank Jenkins had, the ability to relate and be favored by both blacks and whites was his greatest gift, the one that only he celebrated quietly with a drink of champagne the night he first won the mayoral race in 2002. As he was making the rounds in the hotel banquet room that night, he spotted a mirror and winked, raised his glass and toasted himself. Hank imagined what Coleman would think of him now, a slight shiver went down his spine, he shook it off and joined his celebrating supporters.

This morning at seven, Hank's cell phone rang after breakfast while he was getting dressed for the day. Only three people had his cell phone number—Joe Dempsey his limousine driver, the Harbor Steward who oversaw his yacht, and his Chief of Staff, the distinguished John Floyd, who had ushered him into the adult world of politics.

"Yes?" answered Hank.

"Good Morning," said John Floyd.

"Morning. How can I help you?"

"I want you to work at home today."

"And why would you want that?"

"I got a call from the 7th Precinct's Commander Kavanaugh. They are missing the police report for Wanda Doppkowski. A woman that died on the east side. Hit and run. He said someone from City Hall requested the record get sent over here. I don't know what he's talking about, do you?" asked John.

"Let me think," said Hank as he finished perfecting his tie.

John had to internalize a chuckle. The arrogance that this position created never ceased to amuse him.

"Her daughter, Deanna Dopp was looking for her mother's police report. Name ring a bell? She may turn up at City Hall and I don't want to chance a run-in between you and her."

"John, look over my desk. If the report is there—then get that damn piece of paper back to the precinct. I'm sure that records office was just having a bad day and misplaced it—emphasize that's what he should say, at least. No woman is going to keep me away from my City Hall."

Hank hung up the phone and grabbed his suit jacket. His butler called for Joe to retrieve the limousine. He pulled up-front in a tricked out GMC Yukon. The dented and bruised limousine that hit Wanda was in the mansion garage, out of view. If anyone asked where it was, Joe was prepared to start a long-winded discussion of rotator valves, belts and electrical panels.

Joe parked, jumped out of the SUV and opened the door for the mayor.

"Thank you," said Hank.

"Morning, Mayor," responded Joe, who already was sweating through his uniform in the eighty-five degree heat that the weathermen promised would hit the triple digits.

"How are you this morning?" asked Hank.

"Fine, sir," said Joe even though he was feeling scared and disgusted with himself. "And you, sir?"

"Fantastic," said Hank and he meant it, without a whistle of sweat on his body.

Joe closed the door softly and looked across the lawn. How he wished he could walk toward it and lay down under a tree and sleep. Sleep all morning into the afternoon until it cooled off at night. How had he gotten here? He walked to the front and climbed into the car. He felt his hand start the engine but his mind was off in a daydream, thinking back on who led him to be the mayor's chauffer. It was John Floyd.

John Floyd and Joe Dempsey were from the same neighborhood off Hastings Street, a center of black-owned nightclubs, stores and hair salons. John was one of the kids that was doing well and had gotten into University of Michigan on an academic scholarship. John's mother, Georgia, was a neighbor to Joe and his mother, Bess.

Bess Dempsey knew her son, Joe, wasn't as bright as Georgia's, and she also knew he would never go to college. But Joe was a good follower and minded himself even when playing with a younger set of children in the neighborhood. She wasn't afraid of him becoming a thief or drug addict, she was afraid of him being lost in the world and taken advantage of by those of less than good character. Bess's son was simple and it was her main goal to have him hired into a compatible job that he could hold onto until his retirement.

One day back in 1990, Bess had heard that John was in the neighborhood, visiting his family, when she took it upon herself to drop in and plant a seed. She slipped on her best dress and looked for her good earrings, the one that her dead husband, Bertram, had given her. As hard as she tried she could only find one of the earrings, but there was no stopping her. Bess put the one earring on and hid the other naked earlobe with her hair. She walked out onto the porch, slapped Joe on the knee as he sat by himself eating an ice cream sandwich.

"Come with me, Joe. We're going visiting," announced Bess.

Joe continued eating his ice cream as he hopped down from the cement step and followed her down the block.

"Where we going, Mama?" he asked.

"To get you a job."

"I take care of you. That's my job."

"And you do a fine job, angel. But mama's not always going to be here and we need you to take care of someone else and bring in some money."

Joe stopped in his tracks, thinking of what his mother just said.

"What can I do, Mama?" he asked.

Bess stopped and straightened Joe's shirt collar. "You can do lots of things, son. You can help in all sorts of ways. Um, I can't think of any off the top of my head but let the Lord open a door and we will figure out the rest."

Bess and Joe walked up to Georgia's front porch and found her sitting with John and three of her other grown children all visiting on a nice summer day.

"Afternoon, Bess…good to see you Joe," announced Georgia glowing in the company of her son, John, and the monthly check he had just dropped off to her.

Joe fidgeted with his collar. Bess hit his hand to stop his fussing. John stood up to give Bess his seat.

"John, kids, nice to see you all. Just wanted to say, hey. I don't think you all have seen Joe for ages. Look how grown up he is," said Bess.

John was accustomed to the neighbors coming over when he was visiting his mother. Everyone wanted to hear about life at City Hall or needed favors. John surmised that Bess was angling to find Joe a job with the city.

"Hello there, Joe. How are you?" said John as he offered his hand.

Joe smiled nervously and shook John's hand.

"John, hello. Mama says you have season tickets to the Tigers, that true?" asked Joe.

"Sure is, right behind home plate. Are you a big Tiger fan?"

"Never miss a game…on t.v. or the radio that is. I've never been to a game, in the stadium," said Joe.

John sometime forgot about the abject poverty back in his old neighborhood. This poor son of a bitch had never been to a game. Every man deserves to go to a baseball game in person. John loved those season tickets and the thrill of seeing the green grass on the field when you walk out of the stadium tunnel.

It struck John that the green grass was probably why he loved going to those games so much, it was something that you never saw in the ghetto. He suddenly felt sympathetic toward Joe and his pathetic mother. He decided he would help this plain but harmless man.

"I'll have my secretary send you over a pair of tickets for an upcoming game. You and your mother can go," John offered.

Joe let out a squeal and jumped over to shake John's hand again. Everyone on the porch started to clap their hands and laugh at the excitement that John had brought Joe.

"Thank you, John. Boy, oh, boy. I'll bring my mitt, catch me a fly ball," said Joe enthusiastically. "Isn't that great, Mama?"

"It is mighty generous of John," said Bess as she twirled her one shiny earring.

Georgia beamed with pride. Her son was generous and righteous and that reflected on her and her family name.

"Sure, maybe one the players will sign it. Joe, what are you up to? Do you have a job?" asked John.

"No. Just living with Mama."

"Oh, he's been busy going to night school, going to get his GED next spring, and volunteering at church. He's busy," countered Bess. "But he's looking for opportunities...someone that needs a dependable, honest, hardworking soul."

Georgia nodded in approval, "John, do you know anyone that needs some help?"

John scratched his head and looked Joe up and down—what in the world could he have this man, a simpleton, do?

"There's lots of city jobs, right John?" asked Georgia.

"Oh, that would be fine, John, just fine," replied Bess.

John remembered that Mayor Coleman Young's limousine driver was retiring in a few weeks and needed to be replaced.

"You have a driver's license?" asked John.

Joe started shaking his head no when his mother leaped up from her chair.

"Yes—yes he does!" proclaimed Bess. "Got it last summer."

John looked slowly from Bess to Joe.

"That right?" asked John to Joe.

"Mama's always right. I got one, sure," confirmed Joe, who knew better than to correct his mother in public.

"And he knows them streets. He used to ride shotgun on his father's old milk route," explained Bess.

"I know every alley and street in this town. No one knows them better than me. I swear by that," said Joe as he put his hand over his heart.

John laughed. Maybe he could use him. He's dumb as an ox but trainable. John could tell him to never breathe a word to the press on the comings and goings of the Mayor of Detroit. Meetings in restaurants, hotels, a mistress's apartment, across the bridge to Canada—all things that he could trust Joe to keep quiet about and not worry that the press would find out. He could rule over Joe, that was apparent.

"I need a chauffer for the Mayor of Detroit," stated John.

Joe's mouth dropped open. Bess let out a small scream. Georgia and the kids clapped their hands again in appreciation for the second time.

"Oh, Coleman Young," cried out Bess.

"How about it Joe?" asked John.

"It would be an honor. Thank you. How can I repay you 'bro?" asked Joe.

"Don't worry about that. Just keep him safe, out of trouble and not trapped by the press, hear me?" John said seriously.

Joe nodded his head and John shook his hand again and his family joined in with chatter.

Later, walking home from visiting Georgia and her family, Bess was wiping tears of gratitude from her face.

"Thank you, Lord. And God bless John Floyd. God bless him all his days."

Joe was happy when his mother was happy. And he hadn't seen Bess this happy since his father died and she received three thousand dollars of life insurance money.

"Mama, do I have a license?" Joe asked.

"No, but that don't matter. You got a job!"

"I better get a license," Joe said nervously.

"We'll have your Uncle Duke take you driving this weekend. You'll be fine. Just fine. Boy, you are set. Set for life. Let's pray a word of thanks to the Lord," exclaimed Bess.

When they had walked up the four flights to their apartment they got down on their knees and prayed. Bess prayed for blessings to be given to John Floyd. And Joe prayed that he would never ever get in a car accident, especially with the Mayor of Detroit in the car.

In the nineteen years that have passed since Joe Dempsey took the job as driver for three different mayors, he never had a car accident, received a ticket or a driver's license. The oversight of Joe not having a driver's license, a small technicality for a highly dysfunctional City Hall, was typical for a society that regularly overlooks an unforgettable man in an unforgettable job.

Joe faded into the background. He was blurred in the newspaper photographs and none of the reporters bothered to even remember his name once they first tried, unsuccessfully, to get him to report to them any activity that seemed out of the ordinary for the mayor. Joe flatly said he wouldn't be saying anything to anyone. He simply drove the mayor from city hall to the Manoogian Mansion, and the numerous social functions.

Oh, the mansion, the reporters crooned. *What is happening in that mansion?* It's just a large stone hall, Joe would say. Quiet, boring, nothing happening there. His bland responses frustrated the press corps and they labeled Joe either brilliant in his role of the naïve driver or a few bricks short of a load, which was closer to the truth.

Either way, they left Joe alone, and he kept them away from the mayor. Joe took his job very seriously and became the best chauffer anyone could employ.

When Joe became Hank Jenkins' limousine driver he felt different around him than the other mayors he had driven for. He respected Hank, but he feared him also.

He heard all of Hank's phone conversations in the limousine. Especially the ones between Hank and John Floyd that sounded backstabbing. With most of the discussions, Joe didn't understand the details but he knew they were trying to lean heavily on people for favors, which Joe could understand from his experience with thugs in his neighborhood.

Hank was always curt with Joe, and at times he would hear Hank sneer at some poor drunk or drug addict they passed by in the limousine. Sometimes adults had to do that, at least that is what Bess would say when he would tell her what he heard and saw. She would remind him of all the great work that Hank was doing in the city— better schools, more jobs, and the beauty of the riverfront projects.

Bess never told anyone what Joe told her. She was the neighborhood gossiper but knew better than to gossip about powerful men who could squash her pathetic world in an instant.

Joe snapped back to his current duty of driving Hank Jenkins to his office at City Hall. He glanced in the rear view mirror to get a glimpse of the mayor. He saw the mayor staring out of his passenger side window.

Hank sat rubbing his index finger under his chin. His razor was dull and his usual close shave was missing. He remembered how he enjoyed shaving before a date with Wanda.

Hank Jenkins was running ten minutes late picking up Wanda. He wiped the last bit of shaving cream off his face, looked into the steamy mirror and approved of his shave. He looked at his watch. *Shit.* He considered calling Wanda but decided to hurry and ask forgiveness later. Hank ran down the hallway to his room to quickly dress.

Wanda paced upstairs in her bedroom waiting. At the beginning of their romance Hank was never late, always early, but his extended talk with his mother, Marietta, overlapped into his grooming time.

Wanda felt her chest tightening. A doubt crossed her mind— what if he didn't show up? What if he had met someone else? Ten other questions flew into her mind and her heart raced. Wanda was experiencing the first of many anxiety attacks that would plague her for years to come. She sat down on the bed. If he shows up tonight, I will do something special, she bargained with herself.

Hank's car pulled up in front of Wanda's house. She knew the sound of the engine. Wanda sat down on her bed and took a deep breath and wrung her hands. She nervously laughed and made fun of herself. *Why did she worry so much?* She quietly walked from the bed to the window and watched Hank climb out of the car. Wanda walked over to her vanity set, looked in the mirror, and combed her silky hair one last time and smoothed out her dress. It was new. She looked good in red. It showed off her blonde hair. She breathed in to fill her lungs with confidence.

After two months of dating, Wanda could feel them both being anxious at the end of each date. All things need to move forward. They both wanted to move forward each night.

The doorbell rang.

Borys called out, "Deanna! He's here."

She walked down the stairs. Click, click, click went every heel as it hit the wood stairs. She put on her smile and walked into the front room.

"Hi, sorry I'm late," apologized Hank.

"Oh, are you late? I just got finished dressing," said Wanda.

She saw him brighten up when she walked in with her new dress. He wanted her and she knew it. Her heart melted when she saw his dark cream skin, his broad shoulders, and his brown eyes. His confidence and intelligence would glide her through the night. *Tonight, we will sleep together and you don't even know it, yet. But it will make you so happy.* She smiled back with her secret.

Hank looked Wanda up and down. *God she was beautiful. Like an angel.* He wanted to hold her and never let go whenever she walked into a room. *How did he get so lucky?* There aren't many black men in his situation. He must be special, he concluded. He started to get nervous. She seemed bigger than life, more than he could handle in that red dress. He started reassuring himself in his mind, I can handle this. It's big but I'm in control.

"Bye Mom, bye Dad," said Wanda.

She kissed Borys on the cheek as he watched television with a Pabst Blue Ribbon beer in his hand. Borys didn't flinch, he kept watching the Lawrence Welk show.

"Wait, Wanda." Pauline ran into the room with her apron on, "Here, take this." It was a broach pin of a butterfly. Wanda knew it was given to Pauline from her mother.

"Mom, I can't, that's yours," protested Wanda.

"Just take it, you need something sparkly."

Pauline pinned it on Wanda who was startled by the gift of such a memento when she was about to go out with a man that turned her and Borys's worlds upside down. They did love her. And she was wild and had hurt them in so many ways, for so many years. Wanda started to cry and turned and kissed Pauline and walked out of the house quickly.

Hank opened the car door, Wanda slid in. He watched her long legs curl into the front. She felt his eyes on her body. He ran around the car, got in, started the engine and slowly took off down her street.

He let out a breath. It was always nice to get out of Wanda's neighborhood. He felt some big Polack brothers, who didn't like the fact that Wanda was dating a black guy, could jump him at any moment.

They were out now on Six Mile and heading downtown. He looked over to Wanda and pulled her into his arms. She smiled and slid over to him. He kissed her forehead. She looked at him, their eyes locked. He could fall into those eyes, going deep and deeper, into those green pools. He wanted to possess those eyes, tame them and have them forever looking upon only him.

Hank pulled into the lot next to The Blue Monk. He parked the car. They began to kiss softly then stronger.

"We better go in," Hank said, feeling himself get hard and knowing he didn't want to start something he couldn't finish. He straightened out his jackets and adjusted his pants.

"Hank, let's not go in."

"Why? Terry and the whole gang are already there."

Wanda looked out her window. "I think we need some alone time."

"Alone time?"

"Tonight."

"Are you sure?" he asked.

"Yes."

She put out her hand. He grabbed it and squeezed. She turned to him and smiled confidently.

"I love you," he said.

"I love you, too. Where should we go?" she asked.

"I know a place," said Hank.

Hank pulled into a parking lot near a pharmacy off of Gratiot Avenue. He stopped and ran into the store to buy a packet of condoms. Then he crossed the street to enter a liquor store and left carrying a bottle of pink champagne. She was glad he thought of the condoms. She hadn't gotten that far in the plan.

Hank pulled into the Melody Inn Hotel just a few blocks up the street. It was a sleepy hotel that had seen better days when people vacationed in Detroit in the thirties and forties. Its pool hadn't been used in ten years and it needed a paint job. Hank parked the car, told Wanda to lock the doors, and he walked into the front check-in office.

The manager, an older black man named Stewart, chomped on his cigar while he watched a Tiger baseball game on his beat up black and white television.

"Can I help you?" Stewart struggled to say due to a bad case of emphysema.

"I need a room," said Hank.

"How many nights?" asked Stewart.

"Just one. How much?"

"How many people?"

"Two," Hank answered defensively.

Stewart pulled out a registration card. Checked a box and handed it to Hank to fill out. This is the moment when Stewart frequently checked out the car that the hotel guest had parked in front of the check-in office. It gave Stewart at least fifteen seconds to get the make, model and to see if anything looked suspicious. And something usually did.

Stewart stole a glance at Hank's vehicle. Nice car. He saw an outline of a woman in the passenger seat. He squinted and looked closer. The lights from the parking lot shined into the car. Wanda's blonde hair reflected in the light. She moved in front of the rear view mirror to put on some lipstick and Stewart could clearly see she was white.

Stewart took it in and didn't make a judgment, just an observation. He had seen white woman come in with black gentlemen before. He just didn't like it, since it could cause trouble.

Some white husband, boyfriend or father banging on doors trying to find their little princess. He would keep an eye on their room tonight in case that happened. He didn't want any trouble. He just wanted a quiet night.

Stewart had been on duty at the front desk the week of the '68 riots. He kept his hotel open. Some people had run up to his office seeking shelter. He rented every room he had, if people didn't have money he let them stay anyway. That week all normal business functions were put on hold. Stewart tried to keep people calm, and keep the hotel from burning down, and he proudly accomplished both in that brutal week.

Hank finished filling out the registration card. He handed it to Stewart who noticed he hadn't signed it.

"You didn't sign it," Stewart pointed out.

Hank hesitated for a moment and then signed his name with his flamboyant style that always got him into trouble in grade school. Showing off was what his fifth grade teacher called it. Stewart handed him the key.

"Thank you," Hank said as he turned toward the door.

"I want no trouble tonight," growled Stewart.

Hank's hand on the doorknob stopped. He felt like he was breaking the law. He didn't turn around.

"No trouble, here."

"All right then," said Stewart as he felt for his baseball bat under the desk counter.

Hank turned the knob and controlled his temper and a bit of fear as he walked back to the car. Wanda looked at him, trying to read his face. He smiled and showed her the key. Hank drove the car to the front of the hotel room door and walked around to open Wanda's door.

Hank nervously tried to put the key into the door lock. Wanda put her hand on his to steady it. The lock clicked open and they walked into the dark room. It was deathly hot.

Hank turned on a bathroom light and went to open the windows but changed his mind when he realized he might not want to hear the streets and want the streets to hear them. There was a fan on the desk, he flicked it on and the white noise filled the air.

Hank grabbed the champagne bottle. The bag from the pharmacy fell off the table to the floor with the forgotten condoms inside. He opened the bottle with a pop. They both nervously laughed as it bubbled all over Hank's shirt.

Wanda grabbed two glasses from the bathroom and held them as Hank poured. They clinked glasses and drank deeply. Champagne dripped down both their chins. Wanda looked around the room over the rim of her glass as she drank. Not too bad. Bed, dresser, and a velvet painting of Jesus, dressed in thorns, hanging on the wall. It didn't matter.

They weren't virgins, either one of them. Hank had never slept with a white woman and Wanda had never slept with a black man. They knew they were breaking a taboo. To even call this a taboo was wrong, but the term had been around a lot longer than both of them. They had to give some recognition to what they were about to do even if it was a racist cliché.

Hank eyed Wanda in her red dress, her body outline, already dreaming what it would feel like to have her skin touch his from head to toe. He wanted her body on his. Just to feel all of her would take him to the top. He grabbed her drink and put their glasses down on the desk. He put his hands around her waist and pulled her close.

"This will change everything," said Hank.

"This will change nothing," she said with a smile.

He knew what she meant. They loved each other now and they will love each other tomorrow. He grabbed her tighter and their lips met with a hunger. They needed to satisfy the desire that had been building since they first met.

Their slow kissing became deeper and deeper, each other's hands caressing every curve and corner of their limbs and body parts. They kissed faster, their lips parted and they began to strip each other's clothes off.

Hank could see Wanda's fair skin in the light from the bathroom. So white, so white…he had to touch all of it. He ran his hands over her whole body. She swooned as he caressed her crotch and then grabbed it firmly. She felt his hardness and led him to the bed. She lay down and he crawled on top of her. *It is going to happen. I cannot get enough of her.* She felt herself allowing him into her body, she spread her legs and pulled him into her.

They made love for hours. She on top of him, on the desk, on the sink, on the floor. They could not help keeping their skin touching. It is all they wanted. They were all each other had.

They curled into each other's arms afterwards, drained. Just before Hank fell asleep he swept his hand down Wanda's shoulder, breasts, legs and back to her flat stomach. He sighed inside his heart and slept a contented man.

Down deep within Wanda's uterus life had started. Cells frantically began to duplicate for two embryos. Neither knew that this night would change everything.

Hank gently woke Wanda at two a.m.

"Wanda, time to go home."

She slowly rose. He watched her dress as he did the same. He was wondering when the next time they would be together would be.

They were both quiet as he drove her home. The streets were quiet. It was hot. The windows were rolled down. Wanda let the wind dry the back of her neck. He touched her neck and felt her sweat. She smiled and sat back.

He pulled up quietly in front of her house. They walked up to her front porch and silently kissed, exhausted. She opened the door and waved goodbye. He watched her disappear. Her living room was dark with the streetlights streaming, it was just enough light for her to see the outline of the furniture.

This time Wanda did something out of the ordinary. She turned to the holy water bowl near the front door and dabbed her two fingers in it, she made the sign of the cross and prayed in front of her mother's painting of the Black Madonna.

Wanda prayed for herself and Hank. That they could be married and raise a family. She prayed that they could live peacefully together and no one would harm them. She made another sign of the cross and crept upstairs past her parent's bedroom.

Borys had been lying in bed for two hours awake. He heard Wanda's footsteps and looked toward the door. He let her pass. He rubbed his forehead, sighed and turned over in bed.

He could never control Wanda. He could only watch as a bystander, something as a father he never imagined would happen, but he was learning that was what parenthood would consist of from now until his or her death.

BAM!

The SUV that Joe was driving halted to a stop. He had been watching Mayor Hank Jenkins too long in the rear view mirror and had bumped the cement-parking block. Joe put the car in park and jumped out of the car. They had arrived at City Hall.

"Damn, Joe. Almost gave me whiplash," said Hank as he rose out of the limousine. Then Hank decided to comfort his driver. He had, after all, been through a traumatic event two days ago.

"Sorry, Mayor," said Joe sheepishly.

"No bother." Hank let out a laugh. "It woke me out of a daydream."

Hank slapped Joe on the shoulder and jogged up the steps with his guards.

John Floyd looked out of the window of Hank Jenkins's office. The city of Detroit was awakening. He felt proud as he looked out upon each section of the city that he helped build over the past thirty years.

John felt the buzz of the staff and secretaries floating in and out of the office with papers and hot discussions. Hank must be getting closer, felt John. He heard the office door slam and didn't turn around to greet the mayor.

"John, look, I made it with no run-ins with a five foot four Polish ex-cop," said Hank as he walked up to the window.

Hank also admired the view. It was his city, and no one was going to take it away. Hank strode over to his desk to settle in and began sorting through the neatly stacked pile of paperwork.

"We need to talk about this situation," said John.

"I'm listening. Oh, first, are you coming to the fundraiser at the mansion tonight?" asked Hank.

"Of course, have I ever missed one of your events?"

"I always count on you and your deft ability to talk to the deep pockets in the room," said Hank warmly to John.

"Hank, we need to talk about Detective Dopp. When you asked me to help you ferret out this detective and lean on the union steward, I took care of it. You said you wanted to make an example of sloppy police work. You chose an up and coming officer to scare the department straight. But now her mother was killed in a hit and run a few days ago, and with your request to see the police report, I have to ask you what the hell is going on?" John was now pacing the office in anger.

"Just an unfortunate accident," explained Hank.

"There are few accidents in this city. This city thrives on pre-meditation," countered John. "What's the correlation, Hank?"

Hank reviewed the options he had at this point. One, he could tell John everything. John was still the best PR man in the city and had connections to cleaners that could help him with the limousine damage and an alibi. But he would have to tell John about Wanda getting pregnant, the baby boy, everything.

Two, he could give John just half the story and own up to trying to get rid of Deanna by wiping the scourge of Doppkowski from being any place near him or the city but not confess to Wanda's murder, he could blame her drug habit and a revengeful drug dealer on that action.

Third, he could deny any and all connections. John was too smart for the last option and the other options were too risky in Hank's eyes. He could still pull this off he told himself.

Hank's pride began to well up in side of his chest. He had been listening to John Floyd for the past three decades and he was tired of it. But more than being tired of listening to John like the eternal student, he felt fear that John would recoil and never agree to help a man who killed his own son. Only a monster would do such a thing. If Wanda had kept the pregnancy from all her friends and family, and the baby's death from them, too—then only she knew of the monster that lived inside of him.

Hank's own knowledge of his dark capacity was kept deep within for thirty-five years and only came out when he had heard of a detective named Dopp who had shortened her name from Doppkowski. This young detective was on her way to being a future star on the force if she kept up her stellar performance. The name reminded him of the devil that lived inside his chest and that pain made him unable to eat, sleep and function. He had to fire her to get her out of his system and after she left Detroit he slept soundly every night.

The only reason Hank had let Wanda live all those years was that she kept her side of the bargain, she never leaked a word of the murder of her son to her family, friends or the press.

A week ago Hank had gotten a call from Julius, the old assistant manager at The Blue Monk, and now the manager, that he had eavesdropped on a phone call that Wanda had made from his office phone. Julius picked up the same phone line at the front bar and heard Wanda make arrangements with Ginny and relayed the mother and child reunion to the mayor.

Hank had kept Julius quiet about his inquiries regarding Wanda by having all liquor violations against The Blue Monk quietly disappear in the court system. The local beat cops in the neighborhood didn't know who was protecting the owner of The Blue Monk but he had special powers and they basically left Julius alone.

After Julius gave him this last piece of information Hank knew it was time to step in and take action. Wanda's alcoholism and drug abuse had gotten worse over the years. Even though she had kept their secret hidden he couldn't trust when a drug-infused fog would loosen her tongue.

As he entered his fifties, Hank felt that Wanda would rethink their deal. Her relatives were dying off quickly, her daughter Deanna was out of the city, and now, she didn't have much to lose if she came forward to report his murderous past.

His next election was coming up, and too much was riding on his success over the next four years and a possible opportunity to one day be in Barack Obama's Administration in Washington D.C. Wanda had to go down for good Hank anxiously decided as he paced his office.

Hank didn't need John anymore he deliberated as he looked up from his paperwork. Hank had everything under control, especially the monster within.

"Families go through tough times, a string of bad events. That's all you're witnessing. You saw plenty of that in the old neighborhood, right?" asked Hank.

"Yeah, we both saw plenty of that."

John contemplated Hank's response. Hank was lost to him now. Whatever he was up to—Hank would now have to fend for himself. John went back to the window. He could see people walk slowly on the sidewalks in the rising heat of the day.

"Hank, we've known each for a long time," said John.

Hank looked up and studied the outline of his old friend against the backdrop of the city.

"And, I have tried to serve all the mayors and this city the best I could," finished John.

"You've done an outstanding job, John."

"I remember back, when you first came into Coleman's campaign headquarters the first day we met. Remember that? You were all green and anxious."

Both men laughed. Hank started to rub the scar on his chin, remembering back to working late into the night accompanying Coleman and John Floyd to neighborhood meetings, union rallies and political fundraising dinners. He spent hours visiting any black-owned store, funeral home, barbershop, church and restaurant in the city. Hank began to know Detroit like never before.

He learned every nuance of every street, he saw the up and comers, those in desperate situations, and he saw the fallout and rise of hope that came from the '68 riot. He could smell which community leader was going to make it and who was just kidding themselves.

"We were so alive, making changes, it felt good to be the underdog knowing you had a chance to win. Make things better," said John.

"Amen," confirmed Hank.

"And I also remember…there were rumors you had a white girlfriend," said John as he turned to face Hank who stopped rubbing his scar. "That you ended the relationship once the campaign heated up. Why was that?"

John walked up to Hank who looked up blankly at his mentor.

"Got busy with the campaign. It was nothing. We just dated a few months," said Hank.

"Really?" asked John looking deep into Hank's eyes.

Hank searched for an answer as he gazed out the window and then back to John. Hank heard the scores of advice that came to him over the years from his mother, from John, and from Coleman. The voices became louder in his head. His brain began to pound in his skull. He pressed his hands to his head. The voices stopped.

"It was Coleman," said Hank quietly. "He said I wouldn't go far with a white wife."

Hank felt a stab go through his stomach. Regret burned in his heart that he had listened to the former Mayor of Detroit, that he was so impressionable as to take that man's advice. He was ashamed.

John felt the name of the former mayor like a slap against his face. *Damn, Coleman. How could he say such a thing to the young man?* John reflected, he could understand how *that* man could say *that* in *that* time in the city's and the country's history.

Maybe Coleman was right, but damn politics and a future if you couldn't marry a woman that you loved. John shook his head.

"He said that?" asked John.

"In so many words," said Hank trying to sort out all the pressured voices that he heard back thirty-five years ago.

"Hank, you're a lawyer for Christ's sake. Did he say it or not? Exactly."

"He meant it, he meant that I shouldn't be dating a white woman!" yelled Hank who pushed himself away from his desk with force. "Everyone was saying it, Coleman, my mother, my sisters, and her goddamn family. And our people. The very ones we were trying to get a vote from would never have accepted the situation."

"And would have never accepted...you?" added John calmly.

Hank choked back his emotions in his throat and didn't answer.

"I knew Coleman better than most and I can't believe he would say that to anyone. I'm sorry, son, if he really did say that to you. And

I'm sorrier that you took his advice as an order. I wish I could have talked to you that day," said John as he began to leave the office. He could do no more for Hank Jenkins. He suspected that bad things were lurking in Hank's past and present and he wouldn't be able to give guidance anymore to his old friend.

Hank rose up and shouted, "You mean, you, the greatest Detroit soothsayer and political pit dog, wouldn't have said the same thing to me back then?"

John turned to face Hank.

"No, I wouldn't have. I do have a line that I don't cross. That line is drawn when it comes to matters of family and I'm sure as hell not going to tell a man who he can love or not."

"Bullshit. Love? Jesus, you make me sick. You and Coleman were all about telling me and this whole goddamn city about who they were supposed to be for and against and how all of us black brothers and sisters better mobilize and stop the white man from telling us what and how to live our lives. Shit, you've been telling me what to do for years. I've made decisions and I'm all right with them, damnit." Hank smoothed out his tie, took a deep breath and sat down.

"Maybe it's time for you to finally retire, John. I never heard you utter such sentimental crap in all the years we've known each other," said Hank calmly.

"Maybe it is. And maybe we really don't know each other like we assumed we did. I just remembered, Mayor, I have a previous engagement tonight and won't be able to attend the party at the mansion. My apologies. Oh, and Hank, God have mercy on you," said John as he walked out of Hank's office and closed the door.

Hank looked blankly across his room looking over the city. John Floyd had never denied any of his requests. It was an odd feeling, like floating in space. His phone rang and it shocked him back into the moment.

"Jenkins, here," he growled.

"Mayor, it's Max Schwartz down at the morgue. We've had a visitor this morning. A Detective Deanna Dopp."

"There was no information for her, right?" asked Hank.

"Correct. Nothing but a banal autopsy report. No details. No forensic investigation. You know how understaffed and sloppy we are down here, I just forgot to send someone out to the site," said Max sarcastically.

"Good work, Max. Keep me informed," said Hank. "Did she give you an inclination of where she was going next?"

"She was talking with one of my assistant examiners," answered Max.

"What the hell does he know?" asked Hank.

"Nothing. He has a crush on Ms. Dopp. I warned him to not show her the body, but he did anyway. I plan on disciplining him right now."

"Hell, fire him!" shouted Hank.

"Um…but he's been a good examiner overall," sputtered Max.

"Fire his ass, or else," threatened Hank.

"Yes, sir, right away," said Max as he manipulated the leveraging of a need. "So if I am letting go of poor Jerry, when could I expect some budgetary funds to acquire two more pathologists and to be able to attend the next Medical Examiner's convention in Maui?" asked Max.

"I'll get the funds transferred by next week," said Hank.

"Thank you, Mayor, have a good day."

"Keep in touch, if anything else comes up," ordered Hank.

"Yes, sir."

Hank slammed down the phone. He had everything under control as best he could knowing that Kavanaugh had officers Billings and Stevens watching over Detective Dopp. He turned back to his mountainous paperwork and began reviewing his briefings. He had a new school reform he wanted to push through the next city council meeting. It was good for the kids and he knew that education was their ticket to a better life. He looked down and concentrated his mind on the reform and away from John Floyd, Wanda and Coleman Young.

Max walked into the autopsy exam room expecting to find Jerry but he was gone. Max had been executing on all of Hank Jenkins's

94

requests ever since his Medical Examiner's Office was almost shut down by the city five years ago.

Hank had given Max a second lifeline for his department and kept him out of jail on charges of false and inaccurate evidence being presented in court by him and his assistant medical examiners and bribery allegations coming from the police department's Internal Affairs. Ever since Hank had the allegations quieted and funding sent to Max's department to reach modest quality control levels—he owned Max.

Max yelled out Jerry's name. Luke, a forensic pathologist, walked up to Max.

"He's not here, sir," said Luke.

"Where is he?" asked Max.

"His double shift ended. He went home. He'll be back tonight."

"Thank you, Luke. Go about your business," said Max. Luke walked off. He could be his next assistant medical examiner, proposed Max. Luke's a suck-up, which is always a good attribute for someone on his team.

Max wiped a bead of sweat forming on his lip. Damn, the mayor will have his ass for this one. He could find Jerry's home address and swing by there right now but then again he didn't have anyone to cover the night shift. The firing could wait one more day.

Max tapped his hand on the exam room computer as he weighed his options. The screen came alive from the motion of his fingers. He looked down at the screen. Wanda's morgue file was still open. He reviewed it to see if had been altered and then closed it. The complete morgue list was revealed, with Wanda's file being the last highlighted name. He looked at it. His eyes drifted down the morgue list.

He saw two Doppkowskis. *Two?* He hadn't noticed that before.

He double-clicked on the name and quickly opened the second file.

Male. Four months old.

Mother: Wanda Doppkowski.

Father: *It was blank.*

Birth date: February 10, 1974.

Date of Death: June 17, 1974.

Reason for Death: *Another blank spot.*

Sloppy pathology was Max's first thought. His second was sadness that Wanda had lost a young child. His third thought was that this stunk to high heaven and he knew it must tie to the mayor.

Max made a copy of the file and emailed it to his personal email address. His stomach growled. After a quick bite to eat it would be time for a nap in his office. Max would take the afternoon to consider his options now that he had the death certificate in his possession. He wanted to think through his approach and review the list of forensic conferences coming up in Fiji. This type of opportunity didn't come up often and he planned on taking full advantage of it.

CHAPTER 7 – THE POPE OF HAMTRAMCK

Deanna's body swayed to every turn that Gabe's car made in the streets, highway, and roundabouts. Her clothes were drying from the air blowing through the windows. Gabe turned on the radio. Remedy, a song by The Black Crowes, came on and sent her back to her youth. She grappled with the reality that she had no parents to take care of anymore.

Deanna's father, Ronnie Charbonneau, had left her and Wanda sixteen years ago. Deanna was twelve years old. There was no note, no telephone number to reach him at, and no dramatic fight that triggered his departure. It was a slow push. Like a hypodermic needle injecting the heroin that Deanna secretly saw Ronnie take one night in their basement.

One more drunken fight with Wanda, one more push, one more lover Wanda cheated on him with, one more push, one more lost gig due to Wanda's absenteeism, one more push.

Ronnie had left behind a vintage collection of jazz and blues records. Before Wanda got her hands on them and sold them all to pay the rent, Deanna snuck into the boxes and took his Miles Davis live at Amsterdam record. She hid it under her bed and at times would take it out and feel the grooves in the record. It was the only way she could still feel Ronnie, like when he would rub his stubbly chin on her face to make her laugh.

It wasn't that Ronnie treated Deanna so terrible; there just wasn't room in his life for her. He was wrapped tightly into the existence of Wanda and that was all encompassing. Without Ronnie, Deanna knew that Wanda was now her full responsibility and she hated Ronnie for leaving her with that mess.

Deanna stopped asking about Ronnie after two months and accepted that he wasn't coming back—ever. Sometimes her anger toward him swayed into envy when she picked Wanda off the kitchen floor after a hard bender. Deanna rationalized that Ronnie had to save himself and that's why he left, not wanting to broach the subject that he didn't love her that loomed in dark passages within her.

Deanna realized Wanda must have known that Ronnie went back to Nashville for work and to start a new life. She had to give Wanda credit for keeping another secret, never telling her where Ronnie was, perhaps, to protect and keep her away from a dangerous past.

Ronnie and Wanda never did marry and Wanda refused to have his last name put on Deanna's birth certificate. Deanna had always liked the last name Charbonneau, and when she was young she would make Wanda cry when she yelled in anger after a fight that she was changing her last name to Ronnie's.

Deanna never meant to do it. It was the only way she knew how to lash back at Wanda who desperately wanted Deanna to hang on to her Polish surname. For all the years of pain she had caused her parents, Wanda felt the only payback and homage to them would be to have Deanna carry on the family name.

But Deanna wasn't willing to oblige and she decided to shorten her name to Dopp when she was out of high school. After years of disappointment she felt no need to be connected to the name or Wanda. Now that Wanda was dead, the family name of Doppkowski had ended, Deanna pondered. No more Doppkowskis in the Detroit city phone book. Only two Doppkowskis in the city morgue file log.

Two.

The number popped in Deanna's head again. Only *two* Doppkowskis Jerry had said. *Two* in his morgue file log. How could that be? Was there another Doppkowski family in Detroit? Both her Doppkowski grandparents had died in their home of natural causes and were sent directly to the funeral home. Deanna tried to evoke details from her past.

Grandpa Borys had died of a heart attack from all the damn cigarettes he smoked and Grandma Pauline had died of a stroke. Neither required an autopsy at the time. They had services on the east side at Jarzembowski Funeral Home on Warren Avenue with wakes at the Polish Century Club where Wanda got stinking drunk at both. Who could blame her or expect anything different, maybe that was a better way to view it, Deanna rationalized. She certainly wasn't expecting anything differently from Wanda on those mournful days. Deanna had the usual responsibility of peeling Wanda away from the bar and any ogling men to drive her home. Still *two...*

"Gabe."

"Yeah?" Gabe pulled up in front of his home and turned off the engine.

"My grandparents were the only Doppkowskis in town, them and Wanda."

"So?"

"When both my grandparents died their bodies went directly to the funeral home. They weren't involved in any crime scene or unexpected illness. When Larry was searching for my mom's file he said there were two Doppkowskis in the system. How could that be?"

"Sure another Polack didn't slip in from Krakow?" Gabe asked with a grin.

"As a kid, I checked the phone book religiously. Even up until I left Detroit. Just a habit. Not sure why."

"Maybe he didn't have a phone," Gabe said, deadpan.

Deanna always got pissed when Gabe didn't latch on to one of her theories.

Deanna and Gabe got out of his car and headed up to the porch. She hadn't had time to think of her newly found half-sister Ginny. Lose a mother, gain a sister. That's the last thing I need now.

Damn, a rise of venom came up from Deanna's throat. *Damn you, Wanda. How could you keep a daughter hidden from me? You spilled your guts to me on everything. Told me too much. Never treating me like a daughter but a girlfriend—utterly inappropriate. You were incompetent as a mother, a wife...I could have helped you.*

Deanna's mind flipped back to Ginny. She would have to start interviewing her. She was family, don't make this so cold, she told herself. But Deanna wasn't quite ready, if ever, to open her heart and gab on the couch about all the fun she had been having with Wanda and her fucked up life for the past twenty-eight years.

There weren't any cute Wanda anecdotes, habits or stories that didn't end with puking and the hospital. Deanna would have to keep it sterile. That would be best for Ginny, who may have orphan fantasies bouncing in her head. Although not many orphan fantasies end with your birth mother being run over by a car—not once, but twice. Damn it, that's infuriating, right in front of you.

Gabe unlocked the screen door to his home that was really a wrought iron security door that most Detroit residents owned. Most tried to buy the most decorative security door, the kind that looked like it belonged in a regal castle from the fourteenth century, but really it was an ugly attempt to decorate the bars of steel. Gabe went for the 'don't even try it' style of door. It must have worked, since he never had a break-in in the fifteen years he lived there. Or everyone knew he was a cop, which everyone did in the three-block circumference.

He then unlocked the two deadbolt locks on the inside front door. Deanna could tell he was opening it softly enough not to unnerve Ginny but loud enough so that she wouldn't be totally surprised when they walked in the door. He was much more considerate than she was, Deanna observed. In fact, he was just all around nicer. God, she missed being around him.

Gabe put his hand on his gun as he entered. Deanna reached for her side, but she didn't carry her gun anymore, she caught herself in the automatic reflex. Gabe prepared himself for anything they might find in the house as they walked in. It was dark inside. Gabe had closed all the curtains and shades.

Outside, a black Jeep appeared around the corner and slowly stopped three houses down from Gabe's home. Inside the Jeep, policeman Burt Stevens put the car into park. Alongside Burt was Sergeant Jackson Billings.

"How long does Kavanaugh want us to tail them?" asked Stevens.

"Until Detective Dopp leaves town," answered Billings.

Stevens rolled down his window and sipped a warm Diet Coke.

Inside Gabe's home the air was cool. He had been kind enough to keep the air conditioning unit in the living room on since he left this morning. That was the least he could do for Ginny.

"Hello?" Gabe called out. "It's Gabe and Deanna."

Silence.

"Ginny?" Gabe called out louder.

Maybe she was upstairs. He walked up to the staircase, scanned the area and stopped, locked on something in his line of sight. Deanna could tell from his stillness he had found Ginny on the stairwell.

"It's okay. It's just us," he said reassuringly up toward the top of the stairs.

Deanna walked over and saw Ginny sitting on the staircase shivering with fright. She couldn't stop shaking. They needed to get her down on the couch. God knows if she had even eaten or drank anything all day.

"Let's get her down here," said Deanna as she walked softly up the staircase. Ginny seemed like a frightened cat that needed the local firemen to get down.

"It's okay, Ginny. Let's go downstairs and talk. You're okay," Deanna said.

Deanna purposely kept her voice low and steady. The kind of voice she used on child and adult victims of crime. Being in emotional shock for this long wasn't good for the body. Either was not being able to talk to anyone and hiding in a stranger's house in a strange town having just witnessed a murder. Deanna felt more sympathy rise up inside her. She didn't like the feeling, but she couldn't do anything to stop it. She did feel sorry for her sister. Sister. It still felt odd. *Say it, own it*, she said to herself.

Ginny let Deanna guide her down the stairs to the couch in the front living room. Gabe handed Ginny a half-filled glass of water that she tried to hold in her shaky hands. Deanna studied Ginny. She was going to take the adult tone, not the child tone with Ginny, she decided.

"Have you drank anything today?" asked Deanna.

"No," said Ginny in a low voice. She looked up into Deanna's eyes searching for answers—begging for answers. Deanna knew that look well.

"Don't worry. You're safe," said Deanna.

"Did you go see her?" asked Ginny.

"We went and saw her body," said Deanna.

"Are they searching for the killers?"

"Um, well…" mumbled Gabe.

"They need my description of the car. The limo," implored Ginny.

"No," said Deanna. "There doesn't seem to be interest in a deep investigation."

"How can that be? You just can't wipe someone off the face of the earth like that. Too many people will ask questions. Right? Right?" Ginny raged.

Gabe and Deanna looked at each other and stayed silent. It was Deanna's next move. Gabe let her have it. He certainly didn't want to try to answer all of Ginny's passionate but naïve questions.

Yes, you can wipe someone off the face of the earth and no one or perhaps not enough people will ask questions to prompt any further action by the police. This was Detroit. The only way to get things done was through the back door—grease some palms, get some answers, do some brutal paybacks and try not to leave a trail. God, we need to get this woman back to Nashville as soon as possible. Deanna took a deep breath, rubbed her forehead and began the interview process.

"Ginny, what plans did you and Wanda make for the week?"

"She was going to give me a tour of Detroit," Ginny said.

Gabe belted out a loud laugh at the comment. "Sorry, sorry, continue," he said stifling his laughter at the notion of Detroit as a tourist attraction.

"I had a late flight in from Nashville. I took a taxi from the airport to The Blue Monk. That's when…well…we were going to catch up all week. Go shopping, go out to dinner, what friends do. We were going to be friends."

"That's nice," Deanna replied in a calm manner.

Ginny's version of doing girlfriend activities led Deanna to think how much Wanda must have sugarcoated herself to Ginny. She was a good actress, that Wanda.

Deanna smirked at the mental picture of Ginny being horrified as Wanda led her from bar to bar after their 'girlfriend shopping' and getting stinking drunk in the process. Deanna shook the vision out of her head and got back to the questioning.

"Is there any information that Wanda shared with you about our family?" asked Deanna.

"She didn't tell me about anyone. Not even you."

Deanna felt a small stab in her chest that she ignored.

"Wanda was really nervous about me visiting but excited too. I had tracked her down. Some people think that isn't fair, orphans tracking down their biological parents. But people don't know how it feels. There is always a piece of the puzzle missing. You just want to find that missing piece and you believe it can make you whole. For once."

Deanna tried on her sympathetic role.

"Wanda always seemed like she had a missing piece, too," said Deanna.

Gabe shot a glance at Deanna, rolled his eyes and downed his whiskey. Deanna shot back a glance to shut-up. She was trying to get information out of Ginny, and as corny as it sounded, it was true that Deanna was gathering missing pieces to Wanda's life.

Gabe got up for a refill of his drink.

"How did you track her down?" asked Deanna.

"My parents have been in the Nashville music scene their whole lives. That's how they know your dad, Ronnie. I always felt there was some connection with Ronnie and my birth parents. When I mentioned to mom and dad that we should visit Uncle Ronnie, that's what I call him, in Detroit, they would become so nervous and change the subject. I knew I was on to something."

"Go on," said Deanna, intensely interested in hearing more about Ronnie.

"One time, when I was in my teens, Ronnie was visiting Nashville, I was alone with him for a couple of minutes and I asked him if he knew my mother, my birth mother. Ronnie is a lovely man, a drunk but a great musician. He had a few drinks in him and he let slip Wanda's name."

"You found out where Wanda lived?"

"Yes, I rifled through my parent's address book and found her name and a number. I kept it for years. Never having the courage to call. It took me twenty years. That's my biggest regret."

"Good detective work," commented Gabe with another swig of his drink.

"I surprised her and called to tell her I had bought tickets and there was no stopping me from coming up to visit. That was a week ago. She had wanted to come down to Nashville. But that's not what I wanted. I wanted to see her, in her environment, what would have been *my* environment," Ginny explained.

"Well, you certainly got a taste of it." Gabe winked.

"I wouldn't take no for an answer," said Ginny as she began to cry. "I should have let her visit me. Then this wouldn't have happened. She would be alive. Damn it. Damn that driver to hell."

Deanna smiled slightly at Ginny's anger. At least she was pissed, a good forward step out of shock. Maybe this southern belle had some of Wanda in her, something that they shared.

"She was upset at first, I guess she was worried it would shock some of her friends and family, but then she instructed me that if anyone asked who I was, I was going to pretend to be a fan of hers," said Ginny.

Gabe let out another rip-roaring laugh he couldn't hide. Deanna held it in for as long as she could too. They both enjoyed their deep belly laughs.

"God love her, that Wanda," said Gabe wiping his eyes with tears of laughter. "A fan, oh, she was in her element, always."

Deanna felt good, the first time in 24 hours. Ginny was deeply disturbed by their laughing outbreak.

"Sorry, go on. It was just funny to us. Um, how it sounded. Go on." Deanna tried to recover.

"That's all. I was going to spend time with her. But we had to stay low," said Ginny sheepishly.

Deanna stopped smirking and held on to those last words from Ginny. *Stay low.* That was so unlike Wanda. She never stayed low her whole life. She craved attention. She adored anyone who adored her—and loudly.

"How old are you?" Deanna asked suddenly.

"Thirty-five. I was born in February 1974."

Deanna starting thinking ten months from that time. May of '73. Hard years in Detroit. What weren't, though?

Ginny interrupted Deanna's processing. "Can you help me find my birth certificate?"

"How did your parents hide that from you?" asked Deanna.

"Oh, they gave me a fake one. Pretty good one, too. When I found out I was from Detroit, I started calling all the hospitals in the city limit. They didn't or couldn't find my birth certificate."

"What hospitals did you call?" asked Gabe.

"All of them, Detroit Receiving, Henry Ford, Hutzel, Sinai-Grace, Mt. Carmel, all that I could find," answered Ginny.

"I'll see what I can do." Deanna's head was processing all the information.

Who would kill Wanda? Who was Ginny's father? Who was Wanda seeing in '73? Who would have known about the pregnancy? How can you hide that? Especially Wanda, she never shut her mouth, at least that's how Deanna used to think of her. All secrets eventually come out. That is the one truth that Deanna believed in.

Ginny leaned back in the sofa. She had stopped shaking.

"You know she didn't run out of the way," said Ginny with her eyes wide, open not blinking. She was back at the crime scene.

"When I saw the limo heading toward her. I screamed. But she didn't run. She stared at it head on. Just staring. Like…like there was no way to avoid it. Isn't that strange? Why didn't she run?"

Ginny started to cry.

Deanna reached out and stroked her back. Why didn't Wanda run or at least try to get out of the way? Unless Wanda knew it was worthless to try. As if that limousine had her number, like standing in line at the butcher's shop, her number was called and she was next.

She knew them.

Deanna ran the theory again across her brain. *Wanda knew her killers.* Deanna's head sagged between her shoulders.

"Deanna?" Gabe asked, concerned.

"Have you talked to your fiancé lately?" asked Deanna, ignoring Gabe's question.

"I told him I was having a great time," said Ginny.

Good liar, another Doppkowski trait, recognized Deanna.

"But now my cell phone is dead. I didn't bring my charger," added Ginny.

"Good, I don't want you to make any more calls until you are home. Gabe, we need to find her a flight. Get her out," said Deanna.

"Let's go to the airport right now. There should be a few flights to Nashville," Gabe said as he started for the door.

"Hey, I'm not going anywhere. You think you can just pack me up and ship me out? My mother got murdered before my eyes. I want to help. I can identify the driver," yelled Ginny.

"Ginny, this may be a cold case before it even gets out of the gate. There may not be suspects or a trial," explained Deanna.

"You're a cop," said Ginny coldly.

"Ex-cop," clarified Gabe.

Deanna shot him a deathly look. Gabe raised his hands innocently and smiled at her.

"All the better, call the t.v. stations, the newspaper," said Ginny.

"That's not the way we do things here. We need evidence," said Gabe leaning back against the wall.

"Well, what way *do* you work? What are you going to *do*, Deanna, to avenge the murder of our mother? What *do* you and Hutch, here, *do* when you can't go through the normal channels?" yelled Ginny as she rose from the couch.

"We get even," Deanna whispered.

With that brief but full explanation that summed up all of her life experiences in Detroit from the time she was eight-years old to twenty-eight, Deanna got up from the couch and strode over to Gabe who was looking out the window through the shades.

"Shit, we got someone tailing us," whispered Gabe.

"What?" said Deanna.

"Check it out, the black Jeep." Gabe let her look through the window.

"Billings and Stevens," said Deanna.

"Think they know about Ginny?"

"We have no way of knowing...unless they got to Winston," said Deanna.

"Damn it, we need to get Ginny out of here," said Gabe.

Deanna started to pace and think of a plan. Ginny walked over to them.

"What's going on? Who's out there?" asked Ginny nervously.

"Some cops, they must have tailed us," said Gabe.

"If they don't know about Ginny then let's keep it that way. Gabe, you and I are going back out to the car. Let's take them on a tour of the neighborhood. You'll drop me off, I'll pick up Ginny and meet you over where Orchard hits Bentler Street. Got it?"

"Let's do it," said Gabe as he grabbed his car keys.

"What's going on?" said a terrified Ginny as she tried to strengthen her voice. "I mean tell me what the hell is going on?"

"Ginny, we need to get you out of here. We're taking you to a safer place. Gabe and I are going to leave. In five minutes you're going to hear me knock two times on the back door. Be ready to come out running. We just have to go three blocks and Gabe will pick us up free and clear. Okay?"

Ginny darted her eyes from Deanna to Gabe trying to keep up.

"Okay, okay," Ginny said bravely.

"Good girl," said Gabe.

"Loan me a gun," said Deanna.

"What kind?" asked Gabe.

"I like your Beretta M9."

"You got it."

Gabe walked over to a large picture of the '68 Detroit Tigers World Series baseball team on his living room wall.

"Excuse me, boys," Gabe said politely.

He lifted the picture that covered a safe and spun the wheel a few times. *Click.* He opened the safe and pulled the gun that Deanna requested which laid among the three other guns he had in the safe along with his high school diploma and a picture of his ex-wife. He closed up the safe and handed the gun to Deanna.

"Nice. The arsenal of democracy in the comfort of your own home," said Deanna.

"Remember Deanna, guns don't kill people…but they help," said Gabe.

Deanna ignored his humor and checked to see if the gun was loaded.

"Bullets?" asked Deanna.

"You didn't ask for bullets," he challenged.

"Damn it, Gabe."

He smiled and threw her two clips full of bullets.

She loaded the gun, put the extra clip in her purse and turned around to Ginny.

"I'm not going to let anything happen to you," Deanna said to Ginny.

Deanna opened the front door and a force of light flooded the house. She walked out into the heat. Gabe looked back at Ginny.

"Is she a good cop?" asked Ginny.

"One of the best. But not better than me." And with that, Gabe gave a wide grin and closed the door behind him. Ginny walked to the back door and slid her back down the wall so that she was on her knees waiting for Deanna.

Billings and Stevens sat waiting in their Jeep. The windows drenched in steam.

"We got some movement," said Billings wiping his brow.

Stevens spilled his soda pop and began to fumble with the car keys.

"Don't start the engine yet," warned Billings.

Gabe and Deanna entered their car. The afternoon temperature point had risen to 99 degrees. Gabe unbuttoned his shirt a notch lower.

"Shit, I'll be able to fit in my old Calvin Klein jeans again if I keep sweating like this," joked Gabe.

"You must have looked good in those," cracked Deanna.

"Oh, I was a sight. Twenty pounds lighter, less gray hair and a perm."

Deanna groaned. "No..."

"Yes."

"Oh, you just shattered any illusions I might have had about you."

"This is all that's left," said Gabe.

She smiled and looked him over slowly. He was handsome in a disheveled way. His sandy brown hair and mustache turning gray. That mustache. He should have shaved it off five years ago. But it was so Gabe. He worked out regularly and didn't have a gut. He was still hot.

"Looking good to me," observed Deanna.

They both let the awkward moment pass silently. They missed each other. And now it was different. They weren't both cops working together. They were cop and civilian. Cop and friend. Cop and a woman. It was not the same as it used to be, a bit unbalanced now. They both kept feeling the situation out. They were familiar with hiding their feelings and just being partners. They were in new territory.

Deanna felt better with the gun in her purse. She wished she could conceal it on her body but she didn't know how that would be possible in this heat where she wanted to wear as little clothes as possible.

"Ready?" asked Gabe as he revved the engine.

"Born ready," said Deanna with a smile as she reveled in the familiarity of having said this line thousands of times in their five years of riding together.

Gabe's car squealed out of the parking spot with smoking tires. Deanna's body was forced back into her seat.

"Go, go, go!" yelled Billings to Stevens who tried his best to keep up with Gabe's first turn.

Gabe's car darted down neighborhood streets and alleys trying to lose the Jeep. An elderly woman putting out her trash caught Stevens off guard as he crashed through the trashcans and braked hard to avoid hitting the woman.

Gabe peeled the corner and floored as he curved onto Lahser Road going south. He kept looking in his rear view mirror. He didn't see the Jeep.

"Feel like seeing a movie?"

"What?" yelled Deanna.

"I'm dumping you off at the Redford Theatre."

"Sure, why not?" answered Deanna as she prepared herself and grabbed the door handle.

"You've got three minutes," yelled Gabe as he veered the car in a 180 degree turn right in front of the theatre to the delight and terror of the fans waiting in line for a vintage showing of The Great Escape starring Steve McQueen.

Deanna flung her door open and jumped out of the car. After the two second stop Gabe revved his Camaro and took off going north on Lahser. Deanna pressed her purse with the gun to her side and then pushed through the crowd entering the theatre.

Deanna ran down the long hallway to the back of the theatre and busted through the doors to the back alley. Damn, that popcorn smelled good. She weaved her way through the back alleys to Gabe's home on Greydale Street. Deanna ran to his back door and knocked hard twice.

They had one minute to meet Gabe three blocks away.

Inside, Ginny opened the door cautiously. Deanna pushed the door open, grabbed Ginny's hand and pulled her down the steps. Ginny muffled a scream.

"Follow me," said Deanna as she opened the alley fence and ran down the street. She saw Gabe's car flash by at the end of the street chased by the Jeep.

"Shit, this way," directed Deanna.

Ginny furled her eyebrow and dug deep inside, more than she ever had before. She was determined to stay within one step of Deanna who opened a neighbor's fence and ran through their backyard past Burgess Street. They repeated their neighborhood visit again as they crossed over Chapel Street.

Deanna looked at her watch.

Fifteen seconds.

She didn't have to look back at Ginny, she felt the heavy breathing on her neck. She gave her half-sister credit for not freezing in the midst of this chase.

"One more street, Ginny," said Deanna as she hopped on a car to jump a high fence. Ginny followed and toppled on top of Deanna. They both hit the ground hard. Deanna could see the corner of Bentler and Orchard fifty yards away.

"You okay?" asked Deanna, pulling Ginny up.

"I ran track for three years."

"Me too."

Deanna pointed to the intersection.

"That's it," said Deanna and before she could get a start Ginny had already begun her sprint.

Damn, she is fast, judged Deanna.

The women ran through the remaining front yards as neighbors and kids watched them run past. Deanna heard Gabe's Camaro gunning down the street.

Gabe took a hard left turn onto Orchard Street and slammed on the breaks at their meeting point just as Ginny and Deanna reached it. The women threw their bodies into the Camaro, Gabe hit the gearshift and took off heading for Grand River Avenue.

"Get down, Ginny," yelled Gabe as he pushed her head down to the floor in the backseat. Ginny screamed at the sudden force of his hand.

Billings and Stevens rounded the corner too hard. Stevens skidded onto a newly watered lawn that made his tire traction useless. The Jeep slammed into the brick porch causing the owner to run out with a shotgun yelling at the police officers.

"Damn it, Stevens," yelled Billings.

"Sorry, Sergeant," sighed Stevens.

Billings got out of the car and hit his hand on the Jeep hood. The homeowner jumped down on the lawn and held the shotgun up to Billings who looked at the man coldly.

"Sir, do you know there is a city lawn watering restriction ordinance in-place?" asked Billings with as much restraint as he could find at the moment, as he flashed the man his police badge.

Deanna leaned back and gained her breath back. She looked over to Gabe who was sweating profusely.

"Nothing like jumping back into the saddle," said Gabe. "How'd she do?"

"Good. She did good," said Deanna as she looked back at Ginny crouching down in the back seat.

"Where next?" asked Gabe.

He was letting her run the show. It wasn't his mother that was murdered and he felt this was getting to feel bigger than both of them first suspected. The bad taste of a conspiracy grew in his mouth. He knew if you poked around too much, you could wind up dead or kicked off the police force. He only had ten more years left and he could retire early. That was the one big difference between him and Deanna. She could go off-the-cuff. She didn't care. But he needed his pension.

Gabe's reasoning would help balance and protect her. He will tell Deanna when they should give it up and get both her and Ginny out of town. He would try his best for Deanna—he owed that to Wanda.

"I need some information. Family information. Let's go to Hamtramck and visit Uncle Felix," said Deanna.

"Felix the cat," said Gabe as he turned the car around and headed to Poletown, the affectionate name given to Hamtramck, a city surrounded by the city of Detroit. At one time it was the most populated location of Polish people in the metro area. Now it was fashionable for struggling artists and students to rent there. But it still had a stock hold of Polish neighborhoods, restaurants, bakeries and parishes.

Felix Petroski was known as the Pope of Hamtramck, personally responsible for Pope John Paul II's visit to the Pontiac Silverdome in 1987 when he called in a few favors to the Vatican via Krakow.

Felix was Uncle Roman's first cousin, born and bred in Krakow and a veteran of WWII which he entered at the tender age of seventeen. He fought for the Polish army in their tank division, which had stopped the Germans for four days. His tank was overtaken in a battle and he and his best, friend, Dariusz Kapacinski, were taken prisoners and sent to a concentration camp in Germany. Felix and Dariusz escaped four months after their capture in the dead of the night after an air raid. They both later joined the Canadian army for two years before getting safe passage to Windsor, Canada and finally, immigrating to Detroit.

It took Felix ten months before he got himself up and running as a loan shark to the Polish community of Hamtramck. He later franchised his operations into strip joints, cigarettes and booze brought in from Canada, and one can't forget rigging the races at the old Hazel Park horse track.

Felix kept the drugs out of Hamtramck as long as possible. There are crack heads in Hamtramck, he couldn't deny that, but they have to go into Detroit to buy it. That is where Felix drew the line—drugs. And that is why his boy Michael broke his heart so much until he died from a drug overdose at the age of forty-five.

Felix was ten years older than his cousin Roman. When Roman arrived in Detroit, at the age of fifteen, he stayed with Felix for two years before he landed a job at a Chrysler car factory in the foundry. It was back breaking work but it paid Roman's portion of the apartment rent. Felix had offered Roman a job as one of his bodyguards, but Roman, although he was thankful to his cousin, didn't want to be a wise guy. Felix respected his choice and never asked Roman again. Felix kept his distance from him out of respect and only showed up when he was invited to Roman and Helen's family parties.

Felix had planned to hand over his empire to his son Michael back in the late '80's but that was impossible due to his son's dependency on a scoring crack every four hours and a penchant for a Polish hooker named Zotia, that sucked out every bit of common sense that was left in his brain.

Felix got a call one day from an Italian mob boss that one of his drug dealers had found Michael in a Detroit drug den, blue, bloated and dead. Felix felt more relief than sorrow. His son had embarrassed him countless times and the drugs had taken him away years earlier.

He held a low-key funeral for Michael and spared the life of the Detroit drug dealer due to the respect they paid him by calling to report the location of his overdosed son's body instead of dumping it in an alley. That gift wasn't lost on the Italian mob boss or the drug dealer. They did try to live by codes after all.

Felix abdicated control of his small empire to his second-in-command's son, Kasper Sobczak. He was a good kid, a good patron to St. Florian parish and tough as a rock. Kasper carried a chip on his shoulder but that was okay with Felix. Every tough guy needed to have that, and it would subside after he had a few people in town rival his turf.

Rivalry was bound to happen, had to happen, and Felix warned Kasper but it's hard to tell someone everything. They just won't believe it until they experience it themselves. So Felix stopped giving him advice and let Kasper lead with his instincts and grow into the job the hard way. Felix leaned back and enjoyed his retirement. He had skimmed off enough profit and stashed the proceeds in the basement so that he had two million dollars to last the rest of his days.

Deanna had a cooled relationship with Felix. She was asked to call him uncle out of the respect for his age and position. Deanna started calling him Felix minus the uncle pre-fix when she was fifteen at the family's Mother's Day celebration at his restaurant. It didn't go unnoticed by Felix.

Deanna felt Felix's outright prejudice against her at a young age. It showed up in small slights that hurt her—telling Deanna to act like a lady, chastising her for wearing blue jeans, or ignoring results when she would out-run her older cousins Michael and Stanley in sprinting contests at family gatherings.

Felix would never praise her, which is what Deanna craved. Instead he would give her male cousins baseball bats and gloves right in front of Deanna just to put her in her place. Later came bolder insults from Felix that criticized any trait that Deanna showed. She let those slights stew in her for years whenever she saw him.

She knew Felix was clever, and was involved in a sketchy occupation, but she was drawn to his obvious stature and power. And she knew he knew she was smart, smart as him, even as a kid.

At the Mother's Day celebration, Deanna had enough after Felix told her to go wash her dirty face in front of everyone. Deanna's face burned with embarrassment as she washed it in the women's bathroom sink. Felix was inadvertently making her tougher and tutoring her on the power of endurance.

The lessons Felix tried to teach her, knowing her place as a woman and not being boastful, backfired. She simply became as tough as him but with the added hatred and intolerance of any and all bullies. Deanna knew that being verbally assaulted by this sinful trait was bad. But the worse part was that being a victim of the bullying made it grow within her.

She could summon up rage at any point but she kept this alien in check for the most part. The abused would not become the abuser, Deanna vowed. At times she tripped in maintaining control of her anger and a venomous mouth. The goodness in Deanna won out, but at times, it could be an exhaustive fight engulfed within her.

The day Deanna graduated from the police academy Felix sent her a bouquet of flowers and a note that read 'Congratulations, Glad Detroit has you to keep its streets clean like Hamtramck.' She got the point. She had Detroit and he had Hamtramck. Stay out. Still, they were more alike than dissimilar. They wanted each other's respect.

Felix held court in a Polish restaurant called Under the Eagle off Joseph Campau Street in Hamtramck. The only place you can get stuffed cabbage and dill pickle soup that tasted like it was from the old country.

Gabe pulled up in front of the restaurant.

"Good, I'm hungry. I could go for some peirogis," said Gabe.

"God, it's sad to hear an Irishman say that," said Deanna.

"Hey, I love my people but their cooking is for shit. I should have married myself a nice Polish girl who could cook."

Deanna shot him a glance and rolled her eyes.

"No Polish woman would take you," Deanna commented.

"I beg to differ," refuted Gabe.

Ginny began to get up.

"Ginny, we can't take you in there," said Deanna.

"Where are we?" asked Ginny.

Deanna pushed her down gently.

"I'm sorry, you have to stay down. We're going to meet my uncle...I mean our uncle. Shit," said Deanna confused on how to describe common relatives with her new half-sister.

"I could get heat stroke in here," said Ginny.

"That should be the least of your worries," said Gabe as he pushed a blanket toward her. Ginny grabbed the blanket, wiped away some sweat with it, and threw it over her body.

Deanna and Gabe walked through the restaurant doors and immediately the smell of cabbage and sausage hit them. It made Gabe salivate and made Deanna shoot back twenty years into the past when she would visit her grandparents' home. She tried to shake off the feeling that she was eight-years old again and pressed the gun in her purse to her hip to reinforce her mission.

Deanna spotted Felix at a table in the back with two of his close friends, Marty Sobczak and Tommy Nowak.

Felix spotted Deanna as his right hand picked up a shot of plum vodka that he imported from Krakow. He held the chilled vodka, identified Deanna, threw his head back and swallowed his shot in one gulp. He wiped his mouth and shared a laugh with his friends.

Since Felix had heard of Wanda's death, he had been waiting for Deanna. Waiting for her to come to him. He knew she would. Deanna had a temper that he always knew lived inside her since she was a small girl. He realized he couldn't squash her confidence, and got over the jealousy that his son did not have any of the strengths that she did. That is when he decided to leave her alone. Their families were tied together through Roman and he protected Deanna from afar although she never was aware of his quiet guardianship.

The week Deanna graduated from the police academy he not only sent her flowers but he also let the word out on the Detroit streets that his niece was now a policewoman. Anybody give her a rough time and he would kill them, it was that simple.

Felix had liked and even loved Deanna's mother, Wanda, as a little girl. She was the most beautiful girl with her blonde hair and green eyes. When Felix saw her after church on the steps he would always pick her up and give her a silver dollar. Her mother Pauline would sometimes dress her in a traditional Polish dress and she would count to ten in Polish. Felix remembered helping Wanda count...jeden...dwa...trzy...cztery...

Wanda knew her place, Felix contemplated, totally unlike her daughter. Wanda was a woman, made to keep a happy home and husband. He heard she had started to rebel in high school but he minimized it and said she would grow out of it. Then when he found out she was dating a black man he intervened without her father or uncle's request.

Felix looked into Deanna's green eyes as she walked toward him without a smile. He knew the rage that was building inside her—he could see it in her eyes.

"We have visitors," said Felix in his thick Polish accent. His friends dispersed out of respect. They nodded to Deanna. She barely remembered them but they knew her.

Deanna and Gabe sat down at the table.

"Felix," she said simply. She kissed him on the cheek. This move surprised Gabe. He never saw Deanna kiss anyone. But it didn't surprise Felix. Family always kissed. Even if you were dead enemies.

"Deanna," said Felix.

"This is my partner, umm," she realized she wasn't a cop anymore. Fuck it. "This is my partner Detective Gabe Flynn," she said concretely. Her slip to the past didn't go by unnoticed by Felix who extended his hand to Gabe who was amazed at the strength of the old man. Felix knew his handshake always raised this surprise and it gave him great pleasure.

"I'm sorry about Wanda. Such a shame, such a shame," commented Felix.

"Thank you."

"When's the funeral?"

"I haven't even started the arrangements," realized Deanna.

"Let me call Jarzembowski's Funeral Home. It's the least I could do. I'll take care of it," said Felix as he poured himself another shot.

Deanna let Felix offer assistance. She couldn't be running around town trying to find Wanda's murderers and dealing with a funeral service. She hadn't returned to the task of thinking about what Wanda would have wanted. Deanna knew that Felix would do the right thing. Everything would be first class. Small, quiet, but first class. He would pick out the right casket, the catering, and flowers. Everything. For that she was grateful.

"Thank you," whispered Deanna.

Felix enjoyed hearing her say thank you. He knew he would hear it one day. He also knew she came to him in search of answers.

"Her body at Wayne County Morgue?"

"Yeah, we just got back from there," said Deanna.

Felix waited. Not offering anything.

"I came to ask you some questions. I need some information," explained Deanna.

"First. What do you know?" asked Felix.

Deanna calculated it would be foolish to hide anything from Felix. She decided to play this hand straight.

"A car hit her after one a.m. outside The Blue Monk," said Deanna.

This was not new information. Felix waited.

"They hit her twice," added Deanna.

Felix did not know this fact.

"It was a limousine," finished Deanna.

Another piece of information he didn't have. She was a good cop, he admitted.

"Sons of bitches. Twice? Christ," Felix said as he pounded his fist on the table.

This set off Felix inside. He could feel his stomach tighten. He tried to keep his face calm. Wanda, given all her faults, was still family, and he remembered her as the charming little girl he knew long ago. One of the few relatives he had left in Detroit. Now it was just he and Deanna to figure this out. A fear passed his mind—could it be one of his rival gangs settling an old score against him? Felix went back to gathering more information.

"A limo? On the east side. Hmm…" said Felix.

"What have you heard?" she asked.

Felix decided at that moment not to hold back too much either. He was going to help her.

"I have three guys that keep me informed. One scans all the police channels, one works at police headquarters and the other works in the Wayne County Medical Examiner's Office. I got a call at five a.m. in the morning from the morgue that Wanda had been identified. That it was a hit and run. No witnesses. I was saddened, but it happens. I heard Wanda was still drinking, so I assumed she had walked out drunk from a bar.

"I had my friend at HQ go down and get a copy of the police report at the 7th Precinct right when it was filed. Later that day, I talked with my friend that scans the police radio channels. He said he heard of no hit and run accident on any channels that night. I thought that was odd," said Felix.

"That report got pulled, it's now at City Hall," said Deanna.

"It didn't say shit anyway. Sons of bitches," whispered Felix. "My connection said it had no information, no witnesses. Even the ambulance report was generic. That's how they treat people who are bingers and addicts."

Deanna winced at his cold, hard words. He was accurate.

"But hit twice with a limousine. Who the hell are they protecting?" asked Felix.

"I don't know. A rich auto executive, a visiting celebrity trying to score some drugs, or a sports star in town for a game," Deanna gingerly offered up.

Deanna reviewed a string of ideas in her head. None of them felt right. Ran over twice? They wanted her dead. Felix looked at her with doubt.

"Shit, I don't believe that either," responded Deanna. "Did Wanda ever date any men you or grandpa didn't like?"

"Lately?"

"In the past."

"Well, your mom was beautiful long ago, she dated a lot of guys. Some losers, some nice, but all too boring for a girl with a wild streak."

A name popped into Felix's mind. Uncle Felix stopped fiddling with the shot glass. Deanna and Gabe noticed this small give-away. They shared a glance.

"I didn't keep track of all of your mother's suitors," said Felix.

Deanna stared him down cold. Felix knew she wasn't moving off the subject.

"Your mother could have married any nice Polish man in town. But that's not what she was attracted to." Felix looked into his shot glass then up to Deanna. "I heard she dated a black guy a few years after she was out of high school."

Felix closed his eyes and went back to '73...he had tracked Wanda's black boyfriend down through the help of his friends. Hank was walking to his car alone after leaving a Coleman Young fundraising event at the New Bethel Baptist Church.

Felix and Tommy Nowak followed Hank in their car as he walked to the bus stop. They jumped out and dragged him into the front seat. Hank wasn't a fighter. To get through this event he would have to listen, keep his cool, and be at the mercy of his captors.

Felix had just wanted to have a few words with Hank. To demonstrate to him that it wouldn't be good for his health to hang around his niece. They drove north on Woodward Avenue...Six Mile, Seven Mile, they were heading out of the city, Eight Mile, Nine Mile. They were they taking him to the country to dump his body, Hank guessed.

"You date Wanda?" asked Felix.

"Yes," replied Hank, trying to keep his voice from cracking.

"That's not a good idea," said Felix.

"Says, who?" asked Hank.

Tommy Nowak laid a punch into Hank's jaw. Hank reeled back and grunted with pain. He started to go for the door, reaching over Tommy, who out-weighed him by at least seventy-five pounds. Hank was easily put back in his seat with one shove of Tommy's arm.

"Says her Uncle Felix," replied Tommy.

Felix slowed down the car. They were in Bloomfield Hills, a wealthy suburb of Detroit, filled with auto executives, lawyers and the CEOs of suppliers to the auto business. Such connections with the automobile field went on and on in Detroit.

On a quiet road, just yards from a beautiful estate, Felix stopped the car and got out. Tommy grabbed Hank and pulled him out of the car. Hank squirmed with fear. They threw him to the ground under a large oak tree. Hank landed hard on his knees and rolled over to view Felix and Tommy standing over him.

"Listen, I don't care if you went to college, that you're a lawyer, or even if you wear a tie everyday because it don't change nothing. You and her don't belong together. Period. End of story. Got that?" threatened Felix.

"Does Wanda know you are doing this?"

Felix laughed. "Wanda's beautiful but not too smart. She's shaming the family."

"She's talented," retorted Hank.

"Oh, yeah, are you the one that got her singing in front of a bunch of drunks in clubs? Oh, that's classy. Just what her parents dreamed of. End it," demanded Felix, who now was rolling up his shirtsleeves.

"You can't force us," cried Hank. "Go ahead, beat the shit out of me, it doesn't change anything."

"If you don't stop seeing her I will make it very difficult on her parents. How long do you think her father Borys would last without a job? How long until he lost their house? Is that a weight on your shoulders you're prepared to have? I am prepared to bring down Wanda, her mother and her father if this doesn't get under control. Oh, and wait until I get a hold of your family. Your mother to be exact," said Felix.

Hank got on his feet and raised his hands to a boxer's pose.

"There'll come a day when your kind will be wiped off the earth. Coleman was right," yelled Hank.

"Well, until that day, stay out of Hamtramck, stay away from Wanda and tell Mr. Coleman Young to go to hell. You think the mayor runs this town?" Felix started laughing. "You are naïve, you son of a bitch. Between the Italians, the Poles and enough crooked cops—white, black, Irish, German, you name it—to fill up all the jail cells in the city—we got a bigger underground government than Coleman will ever have. So go elect your black mayor. He's not going to run this city," snarled Felix.

Felix laughed and walked back to his car. Tommy turned to Hank and pretended he was about to hit Hank just to watch him flinch, which he did. Tommy laughed and then hauled off and punched Hank in the stomach knocking Hank to the ground, breathless.

"Have a nice walk back to town. Don't get into any trouble," said Tommy.

Felix and Tommy took off in their car with tires squealing, blowing dirt and stones into Hank's face.

Hank dusted off his clothes. Damn Polacks. Ignorant. Plain ignorant. He looked around at his current location. Porch lights glowed in the distance. He had a few blocks to walk to get back to Woodward Avenue that led back to the city.

Hank saw a family bicycling toward him. Shit. The sight of him would scare them. Fuck'em, he screamed inside. He grappled with the option of staying quiet so as not to frighten them, and the other option of saying hello, which would scare the crap out of them. They should be scared. I just got jumped here.

Hank started walking and kept his eyes staring straight ahead. The suburban family got quiet when they saw him and his color. The white father and mother eyed Hank curiously like an animal that escaped out of the zoo walls. They scurried their children along. More cars of neighborhood homeowners drove by, returning from their cocktail parties and country clubs. They slowed their cars as they watched him walk by.

Hank Jenkins walked twelve miles home that night. He was picked up by two different suburban police units, questioned on the side of the road, frisked, had his record run through their systems and was then let go. No one wanted to investigate the men that allegedly kidnapped and drove Hank out to their part of town, and no one offered to drive Hank home.

Hank walked through the door of his apartment at two a.m. His mother, Marietta, heard him close the door quietly and she breathed a sigh of relief. He must have been out late planning Coleman's campaign or out with Wanda. She hoped for the former.

"Son? Everything okay?" asked Marietta.

"Yeah, Mama. Everything's fine. Go to sleep. I'll see you at breakfast," answered a weary Hank.

Hank's mother knew her child. Knew when he was sick, tired, lying or drunk. She heard lying in his voice. But it was a troubled lie. He was hiding something.

"Were you out with Wanda?" she asked.

"No, Mama."

He was telling the truth.

"Okay...Good night," she said.

Probably just a tough night campaigning. Working with people is hard. Politics is even tougher. She remembered her beloved JFK and MLK that were assassinated. Such lovely men they were. She prayed that Hank wouldn't ever run for office. Just be behind the scenes, son, she prayed. Better serve out of harm's way. Then she could sleep well.

Uncle Felix came back from that hot night in 1973, back to his restaurant with Deanna and Gabe.

"She dated Hank Jenkins," confessed Felix.

"The mayor?" exclaimed Deanna. Gabe shook his head in disbelief.

"Yeah, only then, he wasn't mayor. He was just out of law school working on Coleman Young's campaign," said Felix.

Deanna put her hands to her temples. Wanda never said a word after all these years. Deanna began to wonder if Uncle Felix knew about Ginny. Should she tell him? She decided to hold on and not show all her cards to protect her half-sister.

"Did he have something to do with this?" asked Deanna.

"I don't know," said Uncle Felix. He poured another shot and drank it down.

"When he was dating Wanda, me and Tommy had a run-in with him," said Felix.

"What happened?" asked Gabe.

"We took him for a ride out of town. Just tried to scare him. Wanda was bringing so much shame to her parents."

"And shame to you?" asked Deanna.

"It's not right. Black and white mixing like that."

Deanna shook her head in disgust.

"Did it work?" asked Gabe.

"They dated for awhile afterwards but eventually broke up a few months later. They knew better than disobey me."

"From what I saw, Wanda never obeyed anyone," reflected Gabe.

"If that guy had anything to do with this I will nail him. What made you ask about your mother's boyfriends?" said Felix

"Just trying to put some pieces together. Promise me you won't do anything," demanded Deanna.

"I won't. Just know I still got people. That's all," explained Felix.

"I know you have people. Just keep them at bay," requested Deanna as she got up to leave with Gabe. She turned back to Felix. "Did Wanda always live at Grandpa's house?"

"She moved out after they broke up. She was upset after getting so much heat from me, her parents, the neighborhood. She moved into an apartment in Cass Corridor and didn't talk to anyone for over a year. I had my people track her down when she first moved out of your grandparents' house. What was the name of that place? Some dump called the Davenport Apartments."

"Anything else, Uncle?" asked Deanna. His great niece was fishing. The sound of her using the word uncle felt good to him.

"No, my niece," he answered.

Deanna looked into his eyes. They were deep brown. Was he telling the truth? Did he know about Wanda birthing a child?

"Cześć," said Felix.

"Bye," replied Deanna. She didn't feel like replying goodbye in Polish. She felt a bit sickened by the visit to her uncle. What she avoided for years was served up in her face in ten minutes, Felix's corruption, prejudices, and pressuring fear on people. God, this man was related to her. No wonder she had stayed away from him for so many years.

No one ever had to tell Deanna, as a child, that Uncle Felix was a leader of a mob. By ten, Deanna had watched enough television shows and films to notice the wise guy attitude in real life. She noticed Felix's male friends always by his side, no apparent daily work, and him always having a flash of money when everyone else was struggling were all silent signs to her.

Deanna feared Felix slightly as a child, but she sensed he feared her also...her intelligence, her strength, the fact that she had his number by the age of nine. The only one of them with any brains, Felix would lament.

Damn, why did it have to be a girl and not my boy Michael? What a waste. Let the cops have her, he lamented. When word had reached him that she was joining the police force years ago it was sealed that Deanna could never work for his gang, an option that crossed his mind as he grew older. But with her new commitment she was useless to him.

Gabe and Deanna left the restaurant and went outside. It was five o'clock and the traffic was getting busy with workers coming home. They opened the door to Gabe's car. It was over one hundred degrees inside. Deanna pulled the blanket off Ginny.

"Ginny? Are you okay?"

She was in a fog.

"Thirsty," said Ginny softly.

Gabe grabbed his rum bottle under his seat and gave it to her. She took a swig and gagged.

"Don't you think water would be more appropriate, Gabe?" asked Deanna perturbed.

"I'll get a breeze going," said Gabe as he started the engine and rolled down all the windows. Ginny looked up to Deanna.

"Did he have information?" asked Ginny.

"Yeah, he's a man that can help or hurt you. But he helped us today," said Deanna.

"He liked Wanda?" asked Ginny softly.

"He loved her," answered Deanna as she turned to face the front.

Gabe drove back towards the downtown area taking the less traveled side streets, still looking out for Billings and Stevens.

"We can't get a search warrant for the Manoogian Mansion. No reasonable cause," said Gabe.

"I know."

"We can't subpoena the mayor and call him a suspect. No evidence linking him to anything."

"I know."

Deanna stopped thinking of her mother's murder and jumped to her dismissal at the police department.

"He got me fired," said Deanna as she stared at the passing burned-out buildings and homes that looked like they belonged in Beirut rather than a major metropolitan city in America.

Gabe's shoulders slumped down. He shook his head. He agreed. They had no proof, but no one else had the power to influence her firing in such a way as it went down.

Deanna had been doing well on the force. She had served five years when one day she was called up to Commander Kavanaugh's office last October. As Deanna reached his office she sensed it wasn't good news. The commander had a strained look on his face and he was reading over her file. Also in the room was Lonnie Monroe, the union steward for her department.

Lonnie was a thirty-year veteran of the force. He became a full-time steward fifteen years prior. It was a good position and it made his wife happy that he was off the streets. He just had to deal with the politics of accusations and misconducts, and negotiating early retirements for some officers caught in precarious situations.

Lonnie tried to have the outcome of every situation benefit the officer and not the city of Detroit if it wasn't too offensive. He stopped short when an officer had sexually abused someone. Other than that, he fought for his brethren.

Deanna knocked on Kavanaugh's door and was waved in. She looked at Lonnie's face, he wasn't flushed with anger or waving his finger at Kavanaugh, as was customary when they were deep in negotiations. Lonnie sat with his legs crossed and his hand cupping his chin. He was just waiting. Waiting for Deanna to come in.

"Hello, Lonnie," Deanna said and sat down.

"Hello, Deanna," Lonnie said warmly. There was bad news in his voice. A pitying voice.

"Deanna, thanks for coming up," said Kavanaugh as he looked up to Deanna and warmly smiled without showing his teeth. "I have a letter from the disciplinary board on the Falco case."

Minister Falco was a local pastor that was downloading porn pictures by the thousands. Pictures of kids as young as one were in his files. Deanna and Gabe were originally investigating Falco with selling cocaine out of his office. But when they came upon a lead regarding the minister's kiddie porn habit Deanna couldn't resist taking a look.

"We had a search warrant," stated Deanna firmly.

"It was signed at 8:30am. You entered at 8:15am," said Kavanaugh.

"I had gotten off the phone with Judge Dilworth. Falco was on his way to his office. He caught wind we were on his tail. He would have hid the computer."

"You're not on vice. What were you getting involved with porn downloads?" asked Kavanaugh.

"Just lucked out," said Deanna.

"Well, the city of Detroit isn't so lucky. The minister is suing the city of Detroit for two million dollars, claiming defamation of character, hurting his career and church expansion. We had to release his computer back to him today."

Deanna let out a large sigh and slid back in her chair. Sometimes these things came up. Not on her cases, but other officers had run into similar trouble. You catch a criminal and then have to let them go due to technicalities. It upset her.

"Okay. So we will get him some other time. Guys like him can't keep straight," said Deanna.

"Deanna, headquarters decided to make an example of this case," said Kavanaugh.

"And you," chimed in Lonnie.

"How so?"

"We're going to let you go. You're fired," said Kavanaugh.

"What? Fired? On this? Lonnie, help me out here. Check the Judge's phone record, it will show you when we talked. They can't do this. I'm protected by the union," exclaimed Deanna.

Lonnie shook his head. "Nothing I can do on this one, kid. I went up to the union leaders. They agree with the disciplinary board's stand."

"What? There are cops downstairs who are walking a thin line, beating up on suspects, missing evidence and property, taking bribes..."

"Whoa, whoa there, Deanna. Stop, right there," yelled Kavanaugh. "Every department's got some problems. But this is a clean department. Unless you want to identify those that are involved in what you just proclaimed, I'd advise you to keep your mouth shut."

"Me, too," said Lonnie, wiping his forehead.

"This is absurd. I've never had one infraction. What's behind this?" she asked, searching Kavanaugh's sweaty face for clues.

"Nothing is behind this, except all of the police commanders and HR have decided to take a stance. Too many cases have been lost. We are prepared to give you a year's salary and..." explained Kavanaugh.

Deanna was shell-shocked. Her world started closing in. This was a dream she was in. With all her concentration, she snapped back to the commander's office.

"How can you beat the union? Lonnie, I have rights."

"Deanna, if charges are heavy enough then the force has a right to fire you. This isn't a heavy charge but we have hundreds of policemen that commit this yearly. The bureau is trying to go after them. This could have a big impact on cleaning up our precinct," said Lonnie.

"So, I am a goddamn example?" asked Deanna.

"Basically," replied Lonnie.

Deanna raised herself to her feet and steadied herself.

"This is what you want, Commander? I'm one of the best cops here. You and I know it."

"You're also a loose canon," responded Kavanaugh.

Deanna laughed at his accusation.

"Who is greasing your palms on this one?" she hissed.

Kavanaugh wasn't going to take any backtalk from a detective. Especially an ex-detective.

"Deanna, close your mouth and sign here before you go too far," commanded Kavanaugh.

"I'm not signing anything." Deanna turned for the door. "This place is a den of snakes. Maybe it's for the best. I don't know how you can sleep at night. To hell with both of you. You can have these rotten streets and all the jacked-up criminals. They aren't much different from you, are they?"

Kavanaugh stuck out his hand.

Shit, Deanna sighed. She threw her badge on his desk and took her gun out of its holster and gave it to the commander.

She slammed the office door behind her. Kavanaugh felt sick. He opened a drawer, threw the gun in it, grabbed a bottle Pepto-Bismol and slugged some down. He gave the bottle to Lonnie who did the same.

"God, you owe me one, Kavanaugh," said Lonnie.

"I don't owe you nothing, Lonnie. This came from up high. There wasn't an option. We're lucky to have our jobs. The mayor has had me by the balls ever since he saved my ass during the last round of layoffs. I'm one of his last white commanders on this force and he has made me pay for it over and over and over."

"She may sue the department," said Lonnie.

"No one in town will touch this case. And I know that girl. She doesn't want to be a part of something that doesn't want her. Damn, she was a good cop," said Kavanaugh. He dropped the Pepto-Bismol bottle back in the drawer and slammed it shut.

"Get out of my office, Lonnie."

"With pleasure," responded Lonnie.

Lonnie left Kavanaugh alone with his guilt. Shit, what kind of man had he become, he thought. He rationalized. Sometimes one must be sacrificed to keep the war going. Or was the object to stop the war? He was confused. Stop thinking so much. You got four hours of paperwork to slog through before going home typically late for dinner in which you will be yelled at by Betty once again. That was okay, forty years of yelling had its place of normalcy in their lives.

Deanna put a hand on the stair rail to steady her body as she went down to the desk where Gabe was working. He looked up— something was wrong by Deanna's stunned look on her face. Someone had died, he guessed.

"What is it?" he asked.

"They fired me," said Deanna blankly, in shock.

Gabe leapt up and went to her desk. "What the hell?"

"The Falco case. My search warrant was signed fifteen minutes too late, even though I had a verbal from the judge. I entered illegally."

"So? Happens all the time. Slap you with a day or two suspension. Maybe a week without pay. But they fired you? Goddamnit."

Gabe's anger took hold of him. He turned and headed for the staircase to Kavanaugh's office.

"Gabe, no, Gabe!" Deanna shouted after him. She didn't want anything to happen to him. Gabe stormed to Kavanaugh's office. He saw Lonnie exit.

"You, come here!" He pulled Lonnie by the arm and forced him into the office. Kavanaugh tumbled back into his chair when he saw Gabe coming at him.

"Hold on, Gabe, hold on," Kavanaugh tried to say before Gabe went off.

"Dan, what the hell is going on?" Gabe yelled.

"She's going. I got the order. That's it," said Kavanaugh.

"Lonnie, come on. What are we paying you for?" asked Gabe.

"I got no power over this one, Gabe," said Lonnie.

"Who gave this order? Who's behind it?" Gabe walked behind Kavanaugh's desk and hovered over him within inches of his neck.

"Step back, Gabe, I'm warning you. Touch me and I swear I'll have you fired. That will stop your pension ten years too early. You'll have to get a second job. What are you qualified for? Flipping burgers in a shack in Florida?"

"It would be worth it," hissed Gabe.

"Last warning," growled Kavanaugh. Gabe rethought his retirement. His shame grew with every step he took backward away from the commander.

"That's a good boy." Kavanaugh said in a soothing voice. "Don't worry, I'll get you a good partner to replace her. A male. Or do you want another female?"

"She can't be replaced."

"Oh, how romantic. Where's your balls, Gabe? Christ. Get out of here," said Kavanaugh.

Gabe turned to the door. He contemplated punching Kavanaugh, but then what? An instant of satisfaction and then he would be out on the street with nothing saved. He needed this job more than his pride. He slammed his elbow into the door windowpane and shattered it. Blood soaked his shirt.

"Damnit, Gabe!" yelled Kavanaugh as he jumped up from his seat.

"Shit!" Lonnie covered his face from the flying glass shards. "Glad you came to your senses, Gabe," said Lonnie with a sarcastic tone.

"Go fuck yourself, Lonnie," spat out Gabe.

Gabe walked down the staircase a different man than the one that had run up them. He was going to lose Deanna. How could this happen? Damn this city. Damn this police department. Damn his pension.

Gabe reached Deanna and hung his head low. There was nothing he could have done. Deanna looked at Gabe's arm and touched it gently.

Unfortunately, Deanna had seen how far Gabe's fearlessness stretched and then hit a wall—hard. They both had been beaten down today.

"Let's get the hell out of here," said Deanna.

"Go get some sympathy sex, Gabe," shouted out one of their fellow officers who had already heard of Deanna's firing.

"Fuck all of you," Gabe yelled to the male staff smirking at him and Deanna. They had been jealous of them for years.

Back in Hamtramck, Deanna felt Gabe touch her shoulder lightly as she came back from the memory of her firing.

"Where to? Davenport apartments?" Gabe asked.

"No, we can't risk driving around with Ginny anymore. Go to my uncle's house."

"Sure you want to get them involved?" asked Gabe.

"He can handle it...he's Captain America," Deanna said with a small laugh.

Gabe took off to Uncle Roman's home a few miles away. When they stopped in front of the house Aunt Helen was pushing the lawn mower over her brown grass. She stopped and waved as she saw Gabe and Deanna pull up in front of her home. Deanna looked back at Ginny.

"Ginny, we're going to have you stay here for a while. It's our Aunt Helen and Uncle Roman's home. Aunt Helen is our late grandmother's sister," Deanna didn't know what to say after that.

Gabe opened Ginny's door and helped her out of the car. Deanna went up to Aunt Helen and escorted her into the house. Helen looked curiously at the pretty black girl.

"Who's your friend?" asked Aunt Helen as she took a seat at the kitchen table where Uncle Roman was finishing his evening meal. Deanna stood in the corner of the room. Gabe offered Ginny a seat at the table.

"Where's Stanley?" asked Deanna, stalling her answer to Aunt Helen.

"He works the night shift at the casino," replied Roman.

Uncle Roman and Aunt Helen were silent. They looked at the beautiful woman at their table. Both of them locked into Ginny's green eyes and then looked at each other and then back to Deanna.

"I'm Roman." He wiped off his hand on a napkin and offered it to Ginny who shook it softly.

"Hello," said Ginny.

"This is Helen," said Roman.

Helen offered her hand as well to Ginny who smiled as she shook it.

"And you are?" asked Roman gently.

Deanna stepped forward and put her hand on Ginny's shoulder.

"This is Ginny," said Deanna.

"I'm Wanda's daughter," said Ginny.

"Oh, my," said Helen as she grabbed a handkerchief hidden in her brassiere and brought it to cover her mouth.

Roman pushed himself back in his chair.

"You know about Wanda?" asked Roman.

"Yes, she knows," said Deanna. "Uncle Roman, we need to leave Ginny here while we do some work. We'll pick her up in a few hours. Is that okay?"

"Yes, sure…we can catch up," said Roman as he looked at Helen who nodded supportively.

"Good, walk us to the door Uncle," said Deanna.

"Would you like something to drink?" offered Aunt Helen.

"Yes, please," said Ginny as she looked around the kitchen wondering how many times Wanda sat in the same room, looking at the same flowered wallpaper, talking with Helen and Roman.

"You okay?" Deanna asked Ginny.

"Yes. Thank you," replied Ginny with a smile as she gazed at her newly found aunt and uncle.

On the front porch, Deanna and Gabe talked with Roman.

"What's going on, Deanna?" asked Roman.

"Ginny and Wanda were set to meet for the first time the night Wanda died," explained Deanna.

"Lord have mercy," said Roman. "So she never got to see Wanda?"

"No, she did. For a few seconds. She witnessed the hit and run," said Deanna.

"Christ," said Roman.

"We got some bad cops tailing us. We lost them. But we can't have them find Ginny," said Gabe.

Roman nodded his head, understanding his job to protect Ginny.

"I'm sorry to put you in this situation," said Deanna.

"I wanted to help, that's what family is for," said Roman as he hugged Deanna.

Deanna and Gabe started walking down to the car.

"Who's her father?" Roman yelled out.

Deanna threw her hands in the air. "Don't know…yet."

Gabe and Deanna drove out of Roman's neighborhood.

"Davenport Apartments?" asked Gabe.

"Yeah, to Cass Corridor we go. Fa, la, la, la, la…" Deanna's voiced trail as she worried whether she had done the right thing by depositing Ginny at her uncle's home. She put her mind back to their destination.

Cass Corridor. She hadn't been in that area since last year when she and Gabe were looking for a drug running kid named JoJo. His real name was Joseph DeSoto but was called JoJo due to his stutter. He was only sixteen but on his way up. They never did find him that day.

Deanna rolled down the window and let the stifling heat hit her. Maybe they would see JoJo today. She wasn't sure why she wanted to—somehow she was even nostalgic for criminals. How sad that was to her. She could count on them. They were what they were. Not pretending to be anything different, unlike most of the cops and leaders she had met in the police department.

Gabe flicked on the radio. His shirt was getting wet in his pits, his back, and down his chest. He looked good, real good. Deanna wanted to touch his wet shirt but couldn't find the courage. Why was she feeling this way? In the five years of working with Gabe, she would have never dared touching him even for a second. She wouldn't have let herself. She must be tired. Too many emotions were on her skin's surface. Get them in check, she said to herself. Pull it together. She went back to reviewing the case.

Wanda. Ginny. Limo. Hit twice. The morgue. Two Doppkowskis. Hank Jenkins. Her firing. Uncle Felix. Back to Wanda. Deanna closed her eyes.

Gabe pulled up next to the empty lot next to the dilapidated Davenport Apartments. It was an old building built in 1905 in a classical revival style. Many Detroit buildings were built in beaux-arts classicism. Detroit was compared to Paris at one time in the 1900's. Local historians were listless when analyzing how far it had fallen from those times.

The Davenport building was a three-floor walkup inhabited by young and old, students and retirees, the clean and sober, as well as the drug-affected population. There were tenants that have lived in the apartments for over fifty years and a few young Wayne State University students struggling to pay the cheap rent. The area was known to be dodgy. It had gotten better since the crack-infused drug wars of the 1980's during the Young Boys, Inc. drug ring reign and their war with the Pony Down crew.

The Pony Down gang eventually out—maneuvered Young Boys, Inc. who were once estimated at accruing 100 million dollars of profit from crack sales and employing over 300 people. Drug houses, brothels and liquor stores were mostly what you found in the vicinity. Over the past few years, young artists have been moving into the neighborhood, producing good public relation stories of rejuvenation for the local newscasts but with little results. Soon the artists moved out of the area and left the old neighborhood in a state of disintegration with fresh house paint.

Deanna and Gabe rose out of the car and surveyed the neighborhood.

Gabe gave Deanna a nod of approval to go forward. They both were on high alert. They walked up to the door and looked at the list of names near the door buzzers.

"You think you're going to find someone who remembers Wanda from thirty-five years ago? Good luck on that one," said Gabe.

Deanna was carefully scanning the names on the buzzers.

"Gabe, do you know one way the poor are the same as the rich? They don't move around a lot. They both can't afford it. Middle class jumps around like a bunch of cockroaches trying to get out a slippery toilet. The rich are already out of the toilet and the poor stay put—the climb out is too far for them."

Her fingers touched the apartment nameplates. One typed name in the middle of the list was stained and made years ago on an old typewriter as compared to the rest, which were hand written.

"Look. *E. Lee* in 2C. Second Floor," said Deanna.

"I must have taught you that one," Gabe said as he stared at the names.

"Must have," Deanna said, stroking his ego.

She was patronizing him and he let her. Deanna rang the buzzer twice. After a few moments the speaker crackled to life.

"Yes?" a frail female voice answered.

"Ms. Lee? My name is Deanna Dopp and I have a few questions I would like to ask you."

"I didn't see anything," said Ms. Lee.

Deanna and Gabe both grinned at the most popular line heard by Detroit cops.

"Ma'am, I think you may have known my mother. Her name was Wanda Doppkowski. I wanted to ask you some questions about her."

There was a long pause on Ms. Lee's end.

"You're Wanda's daughter?" Ms. Lee said with a cautious tone.

"Yes, Ma'am."

"Come up, child. I helped Wanda give birth to you."

The news that Ginny was born in the ramshackle apartment building surprised Deanna. She also realized Ms. Lee didn't know that Wanda had given birth to Deanna seven years after Ginny.

The door BUZZED harshly. Gabe grabbed the door and held it open.

"I think she's going to be a little shocked at your color. She was the mid-wife for the birth of a black baby," said Gabe, smirking.

"Shit. I hope she doesn't have a heart attack when she opens the door," said Deanna.

Deanna and Gabe entered the dimly lit vestibule and climbed the narrow staircase. The painting on the walls was peeling off in large layers. It smelled of cat piss, beer and cigarettes. It was quiet. No screaming babies, kids or television sets. Everyone dealing with their lives privately in their own rooms.

Evelyn Lee had lived in the Davenport Apartments for over sixty years. It was a part of her. She had lived there through two marriages with husbands who had both passed on, four children, two of which were dead from drugs, three grandchildren, and a mangy male cat, Mr. Snippy.

Evelyn was eighty-five years old and had lived in her apartment since she was a bride with her first husband, Larry. The apartment was as much a part of her as the gold crucifix she wore around her neck. A deeply religious woman of the Baptist faith, she could no longer walk to church so she settled on watching her favorite pastor on the community television channel every Thursday and Saturday nights.

Deanna and Gabe reached 2C. They peered down the hallway. Still quiet. Gabe put his hand on his gun behind his shirt. Just habit. He didn't think the presumed elderly Ms. Lee was packing heat but she might have a hopped up grandson in her apartment. A majority of senior citizens were raising their grandkids such that he found making these drop-in calls just as dangerous as busting into a dope dealer's house.

Deanna knocked twice on the door.

They heard the shuffling of Evelyn's slippered feet. They didn't hear any other voices in the apartment. That was good. Evelyn straightened her housecoat and looked out her peephole.

"You're white," she exclaimed when she spotted Deanna.

Deanna leaned into the peephole.

"Um, yes, Ma'am. I'm Wanda's *second* daughter. Born seven years after her first one you helped birth. I didn't mean to surprise you," explained Deanna. She was trying to think of what to say so that Evelyn would trust her. "My mother died two days ago. Hit and run. I'm just trying to understand her a little better."

Evelyn leaned her head against the door and clenched her cross when she heard Wanda had died. She then made the sign of the cross across her chest.

"Oh, I'm sorry. She was a sweet lady," said Evelyn.

"I won't stay long. Please," said Deanna.

"Who's that?" asked Evelyn.

137

Shit. Deanna had forgotten to mention Gabe. Nothing could freak out a black woman more than a big white guy like Gabe.

"He looks like a cop," said Evelyn.

Deanna laughed.

"You are a very smart woman, Ms. Lee. Yes, he is, but he's also a friend and helping me figure some things out about Wanda."

"Are *you* a cop?" asked Wanda to Deanna.

"I used to be. Not anymore. Just a civilian." That one was hard for Deanna to say.

Evelyn eyeballed the couple in her peephole then leaned back to think about all of this. Poor Wanda. Good kid. So long ago. Evelyn scratched her chin and the small hairs on it. She could use a chat. She didn't have many people to talk to these days. Her grandchildren just wanted to listen to those damn Apple tune machines. It would be charitable to talk to this girl. She respected Wanda enough to find out more about her daughter.

Evelyn weighed what she could share and what she shouldn't share. She took a deep breath. She remembered that frightful night—yelling, banging, crashing, Wanda's screams, crying. She decided to let the girl and her friend in. The door shuddered as she unbolted the four locks.

Evelyn revealed her face. Her back was slightly curved from untreated scoliosis and she was lean and petite due to her hyperthyroid.

"Come in. Call me Evelyn," she said as she widened the door to let them into her world. Evelyn shuffled to her living room.

Deanna and Gabe both turned to check out every corner in the apartment and counted all of the room doors that could be used for surprise attacks or quick exits, as was the custom for their clientele. Evelyn pointed to a couch across from her worn sofa chair.

"Sit, sit," she encouraged them.

Evelyn was arthritic and moved slow. She sat down and her cat, Mr. Snippy, jumped into her lap. She stroked him as he purred from the attention. Evelyn turned on a light and was able to eye her visitors better.

Yeah, cops, both of them. She wasn't scared. She had seen all that you could see living in Detroit. She wasn't much afraid of anything anymore. She'd seen death upfront, a stabbing of her cousin, drug overdoses, death of infants right after birth in her arms, alcoholism, assassinations, drug wars, strokes, heart attacks, rape, beatings—you name it. In these neighborhoods you saw it all.

"I'm sorry to hear about your mother. She couldn't have been that old. What did you say she died of...hit and run?" asked Evelyn.

"On Mack Avenue," said Deanna.

Evelyn nodded her head. Yeah, she's seen that too. In this town you live by the car and can die by the car.

"Oh, that is awful. Did they catch the person?"

"No. We haven't...yet," said Deanna.

Evelyn nodded again. She heard that loud and clear. Revenge. She had seen a lot of that too. She didn't judge it. Revenge can feel good. Her wisdom told her that it doesn't solve much in the end, but the young ones need it. When you're older you just want peace. Every dog has its day. That was one of Evelyn's favorite sayings. And she believed it, so she never had to arrange any revenge. It had a habit of finding the perpetrator. God made sure of that. He was the biggest bad ass there was, when He was paying attention.

Evelyn eyed Gabe.

"You're handsome," Evelyn said.

Gabe didn't know what to say. "Umm...thank you."

"You're blushing, Gabe," said Deanna which caused Gabe's face to turn even more red. Gabe broke out in a wide grin.

Evelyn liked throwing people off their guard. That was one of the few fun things she was able to do at her age—saying anything she wanted without a filter. She showed off a toothless smile. She covered her mouth up with her hand but her eyes twinkled. They all laughed together. Deanna got quiet first. She was ready.

"Tell me about Wanda. How did you meet?" said Deanna.

Evelyn leaned back in her chair and thought back. She stroked Mr. Snippy.

"That was years ago. Not sure what year. Before the bicentennial. The year Coleman Young was elected. That was a fine year. Maybe not so much for Wanda though," said Evelyn.

Evelyn eyed Deanna over. She didn't mean to hurt her feelings. Deanna sensed Evelyn's sincerity.

"Please go on. Tell me everything you can," said Deanna.

"She came here because the rent was cheap. She told me she couldn't live with her parents anymore and she had just broken up with her boyfriend. Boy, she was pretty. She had...well, you got them, too. Those eyes. Those green eyes. You got your mother's eyes. That was the first thing I noticed about her. I said, a person who was given those eyes by God got to be somebody special. He just don't give those to anybody."

"Yeah, her eyes were beautiful," said Deanna quietly.

"And she could sing. We used to drink wine and she would sing like a bird."

"But she was pregnant," said Deanna. Damn it, she knew it was a stupid statement right when it left her mouth.

"Well, yes, some people have a drink while they're pregnant. Wanda liked to have a glass of wine. Helped her relax. Lot of people do a lot of things when they're pregnant." Evelyn let out a low dirty laugh.

"Yeah, I know," said Deanna, embarrassed at the naiveté that she still had inside.

"I help ladies in the neighborhood have babies," said Evelyn with a wink to Gabe.

"A mid-wife," said Gabe as he winked back. She liked that and returned a blush to Gabe.

"Yes, they call me to delivery their baby...or when they don't want to have a baby."

Both Gabe and Deanna nodded at that last bit of information. Health insurance was non-existent and good medical care was not easily accessible to most of the people in the ghetto. You had to use neighborhood services. It was down to basic survival here and the free neighborhood medical clinics people did find couldn't handle the load.

Most of the residents felt more comfortable using the same known mid-wife for years, generation after generation, like their own tribal medicine man. Homeopathic medicine before it became the rage. Herbs, potions and old wives' tale ingredients to help fertility, deliver babies or conduct abortions. More than half the world had endured this way—why not the people at the Davenport Apartments?

"Things must have been bad with her parents...your grandparents. She pretty much stayed inside every day. She'd never go home even during the holidays. I invited her over to our apartment for all of them. She helped me make pies. She was good at it. Oh, she tried to push some of that Polish food on me, some of it wasn't half bad."

Evelyn adjusted in her chair and Mr. Snippy jumped off her lap.

"I don't know why she didn't have no friends visit. I later found out she was hiding. Hiding out her pregnancy," said Evelyn.

"Of my sister," pointed out Deanna.

Evelyn blinked. Her forehead wrinkled up.

"And your brother," said Evelyn slowly as she leaned toward Deanna.

This information hit Deanna like a shock wave. *Twins?* Deanna could only think of Wanda's eyes. *Was there a little boy baby that had been born with those green eyes, too?*

"Where's the boy?" asked Deanna.

"You didn't know? Wanda...she wanted to keep it a secret. She had to," explained Evelyn.

"What? What happened?" questioned Deanna.

Evelyn hesitated.

"About four months after the twins were born, I heard loud noises from Wanda's apartment across the hall. This wasn't any baby crying, it was Wanda crying *and* yelling. It was a fight. A bad one. Sometimes you hear those types of noises and you keep out of it. But if it's a woman, a single mother, that's when you can stick your nose in it. At least that was what my first husband, Larry, always said. So, Larry went to grab his baseball bat and I got my broom. We busted through the front door. That's when we saw him."

Deanna braced herself and held onto the couch cushion. Hearing her mother fight off a man was hard to hear, even if it happened thirty-five years ago. Gabe put his hand on Deanna's shoulder. She felt his warmth calm her.

"He looked crazy. I'd seen that look. These men get so mad. They get out of their mind. Jealousy, anger, frustration. No stopping them but with a baseball bat. He was already running out the fire escape as we finally busted down the door. Oh, that was bad, such a bad, bad day," said Evelyn as she was wringing her hands.

"Go on, I want to know," said Deanna.

Evelyn dabbed her eyes with her handkerchief.

"Wanda told me afterwards that when she first heard his knock on the door she knew it was her ex-boyfriend and that he had stalked her down. It's hard to get lost in Detroit. He had found out about her having a baby. He shouted through the door that he wanted to talk.

"Her instincts kicked in and she decided to hide those babies. She yelled back that if he went downstairs she would meet him in front of the building. Well, she went and hid the girl in the little broom closet in the kitchen. There weren't no room for her boy there. So she hid him behind her clothes in her bedroom closet. When she opened the door her old boyfriend was hiding around the corner, he covered her mouth and threw her back into her apartment.

"He started hitting her and calling her names. Telling her what a mistake he made taking up with her and that she and the baby wasn't going to ruin him and his chances for a future.

"She was crying and pleading with him. He went searching for his child. Then, all of a sudden, that baby boy started to cry. He was scared in that little closet, all dark, all alone. That's when the boyfriend found him. Wanda fought him but he locked her out of the bedroom. And he...he..." Evelyn started to cry.

"And he strangled that boy...his own son," Evelyn paused to wipe away tears. "By the time we busted in he was out the fire escape window," finished Evelyn.

"And the baby girl?" asked Gabe.

"Wanda ran to the kitchen broom closet after he left. He never knew that she had twins. The baby girl never cried. She stayed quiet. And that's what saved her life. She didn't cry."

"My God," said Deanna.

"No God here that day," replied Evelyn. "I believe Wanda went insane when she found her little boy dead. An innocent. Just an innocent little boy."

"Did you call the police?" asked Deanna.

Evelyn shook her head back and forth slowly. "No."

"Because of who the father was?" asked Deanna.

Evelyn shook her head up and down. "Yes. We wanted to, but she forbade us. Said that he would never be prosecuted and then he would find her and kill the girl. She was panicked about saving the girl."

"Was the man...Hank Jenkins?" asked Deanna.

Evelyn shed a few more tears.

"Yes, yes."

Evelyn continued to cry tears that were thirty-five years old. Deanna kneeled by Evelyn and took her hand and held it. Tears began running down Deanna's face. She tried to stop them.

"What did you do with the boy's body?" asked Gabe.

Evelyn composed herself.

"My husband had a cousin that worked down at the Wayne County morgue. He delivered the body there and his cousin did everything quiet, and arranged a pauper's funeral."

"That's where the second Doppkowski came from in the Medical Examiner's system," said Deanna to Gabe.

"I believed I would go to my grave with this story. I'm glad I told you though, it had to be told" said Evelyn.

"When did she give up the girl for adoption?" asked Deanna.

"Within a week Wanda packed up and swore me to secrecy. She was leaving for Nashville but only for the weekend. She said she had some musician friends that would adopt her baby girl. And then Hank Jenkins would never know about his daughter. But Wanda would have to give her up to save that girl's life. If she'd moved down there he would have eventually tracked her and the girl down. So she went out of town for three days. When she left she was a mother and when she returned she was just Wanda." Evelyn wiped her eyes with her handkerchief.

"She moved out of Cass Corridor and into Hamtramck. That was the last time I saw her. Oh, once in a while she would call, around Christmas. Mainly, when she had been drinking and was real sad. I would just try to listen and encourage her to do her singing. The girl...is she alive?"

"Yes. She witnessed the hit and run," answered Deanna.

"Oh, Lord, Lord have mercy. The poor girl. You think Hank Jenkins had something to do with it?" asked Evelyn.

"We don't know," said Gabe being politically correct.

"I think he did," said Deanna boldly.

Evelyn nodded her head. She heard Deanna's determination.

"Oh, my, my...this *has* to come to an end," said Evelyn. "God forgive me and my husband for not calling the police or at least arranging a hit on Hank Jenkins."

Gabe recoiled back at the casualness of an elderly person like Evelyn talking of contracting a murder. But he considered that she had lived in the corridor most of her life and he had only been there trying to clean it up for twenty years.

"That shock you, boy?" Evelyn asked Gabe.

Gabe didn't give an answer; he just shrugged his shoulder not trying to pass judgment.

"You got to take care of yourself here. And your family and friends," explained Evelyn. "There's a time for mercy and a time for revenge. In my old age I prefer mercy because I know the Lord will take care of all the sinners. But we should try to stop evil whenever we can."

"Yes, Ma'am," Gabe said respectfully. She nodded in appreciation. She could tell by the wear around his eyes that he had probably seen his fair share of pain from this city as well. Either side you are on, the cops or the criminals, you are all just trying to survive.

Deanna got up to leave. Evelyn grabbed her hand.

"I think it helped that I knew Wanda's secret. If she had endured that all alone and had no one to cry to then I think she wouldn't have lived so long," said Evelyn.

"Yes, I think so, too. Thank you for helping her," replied Deanna.

Evelyn smiled a sad but hopeful smile.

"You got her eyes, too, you know," Evelyn reminded Deanna.

"I know," said Deanna.

"You sing?"

"No."

"You going after Hank Jenkins?"

"Yes, Ma'am."

"Good," said Evelyn.

Deanna nodded but didn't say a word and gave Gabe the look that it was time to go.

"Thank you for your time," Gabe said.

"You watch over her, you hear?" directed Evelyn to Gabe.

"Always," replied Gabe.

Evelyn laughed and sparkled in Gabe's handsome presence.

"You two look good together. Are you sweethearts?" Evelyn nosily asked.

Deanna and Gabe weren't expecting this question from the old lady.

"I've asked her out a million times," lied Gabe.

"Why, you say yes, honey. You'll have beautiful children," cackled Evelyn.

"I'll think about it," replied Deanna.

Deanna and Gabe walked out of the apartment. Mr. Snippy jumped back onto Evelyn's lap as she sat in her apartment, alone, thinking back about her time with Wanda and the twins.

CHAPTER 8 – MANOOGIAN NIGHTS

The Manoogian mansion was lit up with party lights and its driveway was filled with expensive SUVs that would never experience an off-road mud pool or mountain pass that the automobile commercials glorified to their urban purchasers. These gas guzzlers were owned by the Detroit suburban elite who were attending the mayor's re-election fundraiser party and were now imbibing in alcohol and conversations with pretty newly graduated female lawyers from the mayor's alma mater—all so earnest in their tight skirts, low cut blouses and fraudulent innocence.

These young women kept the mayor entertained as he vowed off marriage after his relationship with Wanda ended. He settled for brief female encounters that satisfied him physically but only touched the surface of his emotions.

At the party, the women were aware enough to flirt and circulate, not spending too much time with one male attendee, careful not to offset any of the wives of the men who would donate heavily to the mayor's cause and their own, which was to keep the *whitest* black mayor they ever had in office.

The irony of being so relatable to his white fans was not lost on Hank Jenkins. Even though 86% of Detroit was black, 70% of his campaign funding came from suburban white-owned corporations and citizens. They wanted him to stay in office and Hank Jenkins felt conflict deep inside himself. He partly wanted them to hate him, to be opposed to him, as he felt the left over anger from the sixties and seventies.

Hank wanted these whites to hate him like they hated Coleman Young. But when it was Hank's time to develop a running platform and throw his name in the mayor's race twelve years after Coleman Young had left, he realized aligning with whites would make him a far more powerful and richer man. He rationalized that times had changed, that Coleman's anger had pulled Detroit down to the depths of hell. They had received independence but at what cost? The highest murder rate in the country, terrible schools, businesses flying out of the city, with still a heart-wrenching poverty that had its grip on the city.

In his first term, Hank had begun the process of turning the city around. State school tests and high school graduation rates were both slowly rising and the crime rate dropped two percent. The casinos were pouring money into the school aid fund via the city's wagering tax, and even though he hated the casinos, they did help the schools if you kept on top of the casino's net winnings.

Hank was now running for his third four-year term and things were looking good. He had been asked to give the key speech at the U.S. Conference of Mayors held in Miami. He met dignitaries that encouraged him to run for U.S. Senate and even had Barack Obama request his attendance at a dinner in Washington D.C. for later that month. It was the first time he considered living outside of Detroit. He finally felt he could succeed outside the city limits. It made him feel good way down deep, the way he hadn't felt in years.

At times when Hanks mind drifted back to his past and the Davenport Apartments, for brief moments, he couldn't remember if he did or did not kill his own child. But those moments would come to pass and his ego would atone for its sins by condemning Wanda. She had actually helped him by segregating herself from her friends and family after they broke up.

No one was aware she was pregnant and the only way he had discovered it was nine months after he and Wanda had broken up. A friend of Hank's had seen Wanda in Cass Corridor walking to a local liquor store for a bottle of wine. The friend had said that Wanda had gotten fat. Hank quickly processed everything he could remember after his friend reported this information to him.

When Hank was still dating Wanda, she had told Hank she was pregnant, and he had made her get an abortion. A week after the procedure, Hank broke up with her, on the heels of his introductory conversation with Coleman Young. He remembered her crying in his car.

Hank told her that there was no way he could have a worthwhile career if he had to constantly defend their relationship. Wanda didn't say anything. She just cried and then sat with mascara smudging her yellow dress. She fumbled for the handle, opened the door, then turned and slugged Hank in the chin.

Wanda strode away from the car holding her hurt hand. She then felt her stomach. The hell if she was going to abort her baby. To hell with everyone. She turned the corner and headed to the nearest bar.

Hank grabbed his face as blood stained his shirt. He almost called out for her, but the sound of Coleman Young's voice in his head kept his own voice quiet.

Hank re-examined his friend's sighting of Wanda. Could she have tricked him? Lied to him about having the abortion? Why would she cut off all her friends if she weren't hiding something? Drugs? Prostitution? Her Uncle Felix would not have allowed that if he had known about it. Something wasn't right.

Hank staked out the liquor store in Cass Corridor for one month watching every white woman enter and exit. Then he saw her. She had gained a few pounds, her hair was stringy, and she looked tired. He watched her leave the store holding a bottle.

Wanda crossed the street and entered the Davenport apartments. When she went into the building he ran up to it and looked at the names on the buzzer. There were names associated with all the apartments except for 2A. Hank guessed that was Wanda's. When one of the tenants exited the building, he grabbed the door, and ran up a flight of stairs—that is when it all unfolded.

Hank Jenkins finished off his soda water and looked around the beautiful room in his mansion filled with political supporters. He had talked to each benefactor and felt that everyone was having a good time.

The fact that John Floyd was not in attendance didn't seem to upset or arouse suspicion in anyone. Hank felt surprisingly confident without his old colleague by his side. In the morning the Mayor's Office could release a press statement describing how John had moved on to either retirement or another community organization. Hank would let John choose his exit strategy, which was very generous in his opinion.

Max Schwartz was in a corner drinking a Chevas with his wife, Rose, chatting with the president of a large insurance company based in Detroit. Good work, Max. Tell him some good morgue stories and how you cracked a criminal case with your forensic clues—even if it is fictional.

Hank felt a hand pat him on his back and move up his shoulder into a clench. He turned to see that it was one of his oldest friends, Terry Cone.

Hank had treated Terry well by securing him a position as the city planning and development chief. Terry was making good money, had his children all graduate from private schools, and could retire without a worry. Hank kept Terry away from all of his dealings that were outside of Terry's comfort zone, like having young detective Deanna Dopp fired.

Terry was an unknowing accomplice to Deanna's departure. He had gone back to The Blue Monk one night five years ago and ran into Wanda. She was singing that night and was hammered. She had told Terry about how her and Ronnie's daughter, Deanna, was joining the Detroit police department. He congratulated and hugged her when he said goodbye.

Terry still had a crush on Wanda, even after all the years that had passed. She was refreshing in the old days—a spark of wildfire he hadn't seen before in his life. He had felt bad when Hank and Wanda hadn't worked out as a couple, and guessed it was outside pressures that caused them to split.

After his run-in with Wanda, Terry reflected that if she and Hank had met twenty years later, hell even ten years later, they could have made it. A few weeks later after a staff meeting with Hank, Terry told him privately about his encounter with Wanda.

Hank had already known decades ago that Wanda had had a daughter with the bandleader Ronnie Charbonneau. But it was unsettling news to him that Wanda's daughter was joining the Detroit police department. That was too close to home. He had one of his aides track down the young officer and keep tabs on her. One day she will mess up, Hank predicted, and he could quietly make a recommendation that the police department should dispose of Deanna Dopp. Labor union or not, things could still be done. That woman could go walk the beat in the suburbs but not in his city, Hank simmered.

Hank Jenkins had one honest man in his life, his long time friend Terry Cone. This didn't mean that Hank admired him for being honest because he didn't. He viewed Terry as unsophisticated and naïve, but he also recognized that Terry was never a man that could be bribed or influenced by gifts—a very rare trait in a city leader. That is why he appointed Terry into his position but kept him out of any situation or privy to any information that was not suitable for a man of such moral convictions.

Hank was unable to show his friend his true self and that pained him only once every couple of years when Terry would drink too much at the annual Christmas party and reminisce about the old neighborhood. Hank was unable to fully participate and would leave his friend's conversation hanging in the air without input or appreciation. The awkwardness consistently closed down the conversation and Terry felt deep down he never truly knew his friend Hank. There was something that kept both of them at arms length. He by no means pushed Hank on this topic, thinking it was the mayor's political position that caused him to keep his distance from everyone—even old friends.

"Good party, Hank," said Terry with a small slur. Hank saw his friend had drunk one too many whiskeys.

"Thanks, Terry. You may want to slow down a bit," advised Hank.

"Just been working hard, trying to blow off some steam," said Terry.

"This isn't the place for that. Take a day off. You can use the lake house. The boat is all ready for you."

Terry fidgeted. "Oh, thanks, no. We're going to visit Samantha and her fiancé in Atlanta next week. I can relax then. Thank you Hank," Terry swirled the ice in his glass.

"Hey, I heard some bad news."

"What?" asked Hank.

"Wanda...died," said Terry.

Hank didn't know if he should pretend to know this information or not. "I hadn't heard that. How did you find out? In the paper?" asked Hank.

"Oh, I still have some friends at The Blue Monk," said Terry.

"That's too bad," said Hank.

"In case you are wondering she was killed in a hit and run," said Terry as he teetered on his feet.

Hank was quiet. Terry was feeling nostalgic for the old days hanging out with Wanda. Hank was aware Terry had always been fond of her, and his old friend even tried to convince him not to break up with her so many years ago. Or was he probing? Not knowing his friend's intentions was irritating Hank.

"Sad. We had a lot of good times," said Hank who didn't show any emotion as he took another drink from his soda water.

"That's it?"

"That's it," stated Hank.

Terry tried to read Hank's eyes. He couldn't.

"The past is the past, Terry," said Hank.

"Are the police all over this?" asked Terry.

"The police department covers one hundred and forty three square miles and I'm down one hundred and seventy-five officers from three years ago. Is Wanda Doppkowski's hit and run suspect being hounded in every apartment building or bar in Detroit? No. Come on Terry," said Hank as he rolled his eyes. The mayor contemplated why he had just said 'apartment building' in his last sentence. How did he let that slip out, he wondered. Careful, Hank said to himself, be more careful.

"We can call the news, get the word out to all the auto body shops," said Terry.

"I'll see what I can do," said Hank as he walked away slowly knowing he would act on none of his friend's suggestions.

"Good, thanks," said Terry.

Terry watched his old friend walk away. He struggled with having to ask Hank a favor to look into finding the hit and run driver. Why did he have to beg for that?

Terry wondered if Hank feared information linking him to a white woman, especially a white woman with known drug and alcohol problems, was causing him to not pursue capturing the driver of the car. But asking a favor to scrutinize a murder crime was pretty commonplace in Detroit. This city was known as the murder capital of the U.S. for many years after all. This request would not raise suspicions at police headquarters. Everyone in this town had a family member with addiction problems that coincided with an untimely death.

Terry watched Hank work himself away across the room out onto the patio. When exactly was it when he lost Hank? He didn't have to think too hard. The Coleman Young election year. When he had his cousin, John Floyd, find Hank a job on Coleman's staff. By autumn Hank had broken up with Wanda. That's when he lost him completely.

At times, Terry would get glimpses of Hank that reminded him of when they were young and carefree. But he would see Hank close down and that ended all conversations. Terry decided to stay with him almost as a guardian angel. There were actions that Hank didn't include him on and the mayor departmentalized all friends and staff members so that very few knew what the other was doing.

How Hank led such a successful eight years in office was certainly a testament to how much information he could juggle and maintain in his head. He kept directing so many people independently when he could have leaned on Terry more by delegating authority. But that is exactly what Hank didn't want to do because delegation would give someone else information and power that Hank couldn't control. Terry felt sorry for his friend. He had for years. But Hank felt the same sympathy for him.

Hank walked outdoors and wiped the sweat from his brow with a freshly pressed handkerchief. Andy Pierce, Chief Operating Officer of the Detroit Edison Company was talking in depth with a division Vice President from General Motors, Ken Cunningham. They raised their drinks to Hank and smiled. Hank walked up to them.

"How are you boys?"

"Fine, Hank," said Pierce. "We're looking for the results of the Tiger game tonight. Have you heard anything?"

Hank looked around the patio, close by was his junior aide, Shahrok Iranshad, a young Wayne State University intern for the Mayor's Office.

"Shah, can you get the results for the Tiger game?" asked Hank.

The earnest young man whipped out his iPhone and punched a few buttons.

"Eighth inning. Tigers in the lead, three to two over Boston," Shah dutifully reported. The men clenched their hands in victory.

Pierce and Cunningham laughed with the mayor. Hank was a master at small talk. Sports, kids, art, the latest books on the best-seller lists. All the serious business talks and deals were dealt with through aids and attorneys—the go-betweeners.

At times, secretive lunches between business leaders and the mayor were held where they could talk privately about what they each needed. And business leaders always needed something. Even if it was something in the future, they would prepare and make offerings of land, energy and materials to the mayor. In return for meeting their needs, Hank would receive credits for any of his future needs.

For the most part Hank liked the people he dealt with; there was only a small minority considered dangerous to be linked to in the public's eye. But those people never showed up or were invited to these fund raising events.

"Excuse me," Hank said to the men. He walked down the patio stairs to the lawn. He heard footsteps behind him. He turned.

"Hank, sorry. I need a few minutes. Tony Morton, one of the execs at Detroit Entertainment, called me this week," said Pierce who followed him.

"I'm sorry I don't know him," said Hank.

"He was asking for an energy rate cut that was pretty outrageous for his casino."

"I said I'm not familiar…"

"He dropped your name. Said that you were a big supporter of their company," interrupted Pierce.

Hank's temper flared.

"I don't know the man. And I don't appreciate him dropping my name to get a favorable energy rate. In fact, why don't you tell the man to go to hell?"

"We are all happy with the revenues that the casinos are bringing in and I was worried there were discussions that I should know about," said Pierce.

Hank bristled that Pierce was accusing him of a backroom deal.

"There is and never was a conversation that you or Detroit Edison need to be aware of as it concerns any of the casinos in our city. You got that?" Hank said forcefully with a glare that could have melted the ice in Pierce's gin and tonic.

"Got it, Hank. I thought the guy sounded like a crackpot," said Pierce as he backed away so quickly he bumped into a waiter carrying a tray full of water glasses that crashed to the ground. Hank turned and made a mental note to call his Board of Directors contact at Detroit Edison and have Pierce reamed for his accusation.

Hank walked further away from the mansion. It felt cooler on the lawn. He turned and gazed on the party lights and all the pretty people socializing. The summer night was peaceful. The sweltering heat had cooled off to eighty-nine degrees. The sky was clear and the full moon was keeping watch over the city.

He was headed toward the garage. Hank turned to look across the lawn and noticed the garage door was cracked open. A light in the garage lit up a path from the lawn. He figured that Joe Dempsey was working on the limousine.

Hank quietly walked up to the garage. Joe had one of Detroit's cool jazz radio stations playing. Hank stopped and listened to the music. The song 'What's Going On' by Marvin Gaye filled up the surrounding area. It led him back to his early days, better days. Flashes of friends' faces, parties, laughter and passion. How long ago was that? It felt like a different lifetime ago. A different life. A different man. He walked up to the garage door and knocked on it so not to startle Joe. Hank gently opened the door.

The garage held four lease cars paid by the city of Detroit for the service of the mayor. Each of the U.S. automobile maker's flagship car dealerships from Ford, Chrysler and GM gave an outstanding deal to the Mayor's Office that made them practically free. The mayor had his pick of a GM Yukon XL, A Ford Expedition, a Chrysler 300 and Chrysler Crossfire and, of course, his 2006 Cadillac DTS limousine that had hit and killed Wanda Doppkowski. The limousine had a car cover draped over it. Joe was buffing the Chrysler 300 right next to it. He looked up and stopped.

"Evening, Mayor," said Joe.

"Evening Joe," said Hank. He strolled around the garage. Taking it all in. He had never walked inside this building in all of the years that he had occupied his office.

"Good music."

"Yeah, it takes you back," commented Joe.

"I remember seeing Marvin Gaye at the Cavern Room. Did you ever go there?" asked Hank.

"No, I didn't get out much. But I listened to the radio and my cousin had a ton of records that I used to borrow," answered Joe with a smile.

It was a silly question to ask Joe. Joe didn't get out much in his younger days. His driver had his mother and then, of course, his neighborhood that watched out for him. Hank heard that John Floyd had found Joe to be the driver for Coleman Young. Joe drove for Coleman, and then he drove for the mayor that succeeded Coleman, and now Hank.

Hank laughed at the irony that such a plain man, like Joe, had such a large responsibility for the safety of such important men. You would think they would hire an ex-military soldier or retired cop. No, you needed a simple man for this job. A man that didn't socialize too much, if at all. A man that didn't want the spotlight, that took orders to shuffle dignitaries to call girls late in the night, and who would buff out the cars by himself on a Saturday night and think he had the best job in the world. They were gatekeepers. Sound and secure. He wondered how Joe was coping with the order he gave him to drive down Wanda. Perhaps Joe also had the skill to stuff down actions way down deep. So deep that you couldn't remember doing them.

Joe took out a new rag and kept on buffing the car in the presence of the mayor. He had been cleaning non-stop since he drove back to the mansion from The Blue Monk.

Joe remembered pulling into the gates in a numbed state. He drove the mayor up to the front door of the mansion. They idled there for ten minutes before the mayor spoke to Joe who was now breathing shallow.

"Joe, I don't think either one of us has to belabor what happened tonight. You did me a great favor. That woman was a threat to me and all the good things that we can do for the city of Detroit and its future. I want to thank you for your great service. Sometimes we are at war in this city. And we won a small battle just now. You are a soldier. A brave soldier."

And when his speech ended Hank exited the car. The mayor didn't see the tears that were running down Joe's face, the dread, fear and shame bubbling out of his body and soaking his shirt. Joe wiped his eyes the best he could and slowly drove to the garage.

Joe exited and found the car cover for the limousine. He gathered it in his two arms and walked over to the limousine. He dropped the cover on the ground and looked at the damage to the front of the car.

It was dented by Wanda's body.

A small piece of her dress was caught in the grille. He pulled it out. There was blood on it. He pressed the piece of cloth to his cheek. Joe crumpled to the ground and began to wail deep inside.

Why did he listen to the mayor? Why did he obey the command? He had killed her—that woman. No matter what the mayor said, he wasn't at war with anyone. He was just a driver. He was just Joe Dempsey of 255 Erskine Street.

Joe hugged his knees. What was he going to do? He was going to be sent to jail. A woman is dead. The police will find him. The mayor wouldn't be blamed but he would. A hundred fears were bubbling in his brain. It was too much for him and he lay on his side curled up like a baby and cried himself into a semi-sleep state.

He woke three hours later to one of the mansion security dogs barking. The sun was starting to come up. Joe pulled his head up from the cement floor. His eyes looked up to the window on the wall. He breathed deeply. He felt different. He was a soldier. The mayor said so. He would survive this and he knew exactly what to do. What a soldier would do.

Joe stood up and grabbed a bucket and sponge. He walked to the sink, turned on the water faucet and poured liquid soap into the bucket. He walked back over to the limousine and began stroking it with a sponge. He would make this car shine. It was a shame they hit that dog last night. Dogs shouldn't be standing in the street. That was just stupid and dangerous of that dog. Protecting his passengers comes first.

He cleaned off the blood and any dirt. He surveyed the damage and determined how much of the dent he could buff out. If there were larger areas that he couldn't handle he could order a new front or back fender. He would be able to handle the repair and he felt confident.

Damn that dog was big, Joe remembered. He threw the rags in a bag that would go back to his and mother's house and into the laundry. He covered the limousine with the car cover and walked upstairs to the loft over the garage where there was a bed and small television. Joe dropped down on the bed for a nap and for the next two hours tossed and turned as he dreamt of hitting stray dogs in the street over and over.

"How's the limo?" asked Hank watching Joe buff the car.

"Good. Want to see it?" asked Joe boldly. Hank was surprised by Joe's attitude. He sounded confident. Hank didn't want to look at the limousine damage, but he felt he should review the evidence even if it wasn't him behind the wheel.

"Sure," said Hank.

Joe pulled the cover off in one large sweep that had it floating above the car like a cloud hovering over a city before a rainstorm. He snapped it to the ground. Hank watched Joe perform his trick suspiciously and walked over to survey the limousine. He looked at it from five feet away.

Hmmm, there was a dent on the front bumper, but it wasn't that big considering the jolt he remembered from Wanda's body hitting the limo. He walked closer. The shattered windshield had been replaced and the paint job had been re-done. Good. Very good.

Hank examined the back of the limo. Everything looked up to snuff as he inspected the limousine from left to right. Wait. A dent. A large one on the back fender. He looked up at Joe.

"I got a new fender coming in. Ordered it this morning," responded Joe.

"Being sent here?" asked Hank.

"No. To a garage downriver. Under a fake name. It's under control. I'll pay by cash," Joe said.

Joe has covered everything, Hank thought. He's more competent than I give him credit for a lot of times. Would he keep this all a secret, to his grave? Hank would have to know soon. He didn't want it to come down to that. But there were more important things at stake than Joe Dempsey's life. And if this was ever found out then Joe would go to jail, not the mayor. Joe must have figured that out. Certainly, it would politically hurt the mayor, but Hank felt certain he could get the best defense attorneys in the city and wouldn't spend a day in jail. Hell, they couldn't even tie him to the crime scene. He could find an alibi somehow.

The real cost of being caught, in the mayor's mind, would be the missed opportunity on all that he wanted to accomplish within the next four years in office. With the money from the casino that would help the schools, Hank had plans for bringing in new businesses from the suburbs into Detroit and he had housing developments on the river he needed to champion. He wanted to start commissioning three more hotels and a new convention center. Oh, and his dream to get a Trump tower downtown.

"Looks like you've got everything under control," complimented Hank.

Joe started covering the limousine back up.

"This city needs to work on that damn dog problem. They're on every street, running in packs in the 'hood. People hitting them left and right. Lucky we weren't hurt. Could have set off my air bag. I disengaged it in case we hit a dog again," explained Joe.

A dog? Hank watched Joe busy himself on his cars. Where had this man's mind gone? Packs of wild dogs in Detroit? Hank felt a quick passing of shame cross over him. Joe's mind was caught in self-preservation and Hank understood that the mind was limitless in the amount of creative accounts it could fabricate. He had firsthand experience. This may not be a bad thing. In fact, it is the best that could have happened. It may have even saved Joe Dempsey's life.

"Good idea, I'll look into it. Thanks for taking care of all this, Joe," said Hank.

"My pleasure, Mayor. Just part of my job," said Joe as he turned off the radio.

"Oh, do you have an extra key to the garage? I may want take one of the SUVs out for a ride later. Take in the night."

"I can drive you, Mayor."

"No, go home, get some rest."

"If you insist, sir. Here you go." Joe handed him the extra key on the workbench.

"Thank you. Say hello to your mother for me," said Hank as he turned back to his mansion and party attendees.

"I will. She sure is a fan of yours," said Joe as he put away his equipment.

Hank smiled and waved goodbye.

Joe decided it was time to go home and get a good night's sleep. There he could thank the Lord for his good job, a job that fit him so well. And he would pray for his mother and John Floyd for leading him to Hank Jenkins—a powerful man that would watch over him for the rest of his life. He had saved Hank's life from that dog and the mayor would be forever thankful.

Joe turned off the lights in the garage. He grabbed his keys and locked the garage doors. He walked to his old Buick parked down the pathway as a dark figure emerged from the side window of the garage.

It was Terry Cone walking out into the light as he watched Joe walk down the lane. He looked at the garage and then to the mansion where he could hear the music and laughter rising.

Terry took his car keys out of his pocket and walked to his car in the front of the mansion. He got into his car and turned onto Gratiot Avenue. He rolled down the window and the let the nighttime air cool him down. He didn't feel like himself. Everything was off. He had heard Hank and Joe's conversation through the side garage window. To believe that his friend, Hank Jenkins, could have committed a murder was incomprehensible an hour ago—but now it was possible. He had to find the truth.

From the neighborhood that Terry and Hank came from in Detroit, they had many friends that went bad, had committed crimes and murders. Back then they would have never guessed such brutal endings. But he and Hank were in their fifties. Why would Hank put all that at risk? Why kill Wanda?

Terry's car pulled up in front of The Blue Monk. He locked up the car and walked across the street. He stopped in the middle of the lane. Was this where it happened? He looked down to the pavement. He didn't see any bloodstains. He wasn't a cop so he wasn't sure what he should look for on the street. Someone shouted out to him.

"Hey, move it. Get out of the street!" yelled Winston in a panic.

Terry looked up. Across the street, in front of The Blue Monk, stood the doorman. Terry didn't know him. It had been a few years since his last visit. There use to be a time when he was acquainted with the doormen and all the waitresses in the club. He looked both ways and jogged up to Winston.

"Sorry," said Terry.

"Man, this is a busy street. And I don't need no more trouble," said Winston.

"I hear you. I was a friend of Wanda's," said Terry.

Winston looked Terry over. "I haven't seen you around here."

"I'm a friend from way back. When she first started singing. Ronnie Charbonneau pulled her up on to the stage. That was a great night."

"Ronnie?"

"Yeah, that was back in seventy-three."

"Shit, I wasn't even born yet," Winston started laughing. He enjoyed hearing about the old times. He felt it connected him to a history he could be proud of like family.

"Man, I'm going to miss her," confessed Winston.

"We had lost touch. Man, she had a great voice," said Terry.

"Yes, sir. A good set of pipes. Not everyone saw that through the booze. Some gave her a hard time 'cause of her problems."

"Hard not to take shit from someone in this town. Easy to make enemies too."

Winston stayed quiet, watching Terry suspiciously.

"But God, I don't know if Wanda would know anyone in a limo that would want to take her down," Terry said while looking over his shoulder.

"Why'd you say a limo?" asked Winston.

"It wasn't a limo?"

"I don't know. I didn't see it. I was inside."

"Oh," said Terry.

"Are you a cop, a reporter?" said Winston getting into Terry's face.

"Hey, I really am a friend."

"You still haven't answered my question. Why'd you say a limo?" asked Winston.

Terry shrugged his shoulder. "I can't say. I don't want to put you in a bad situation by telling you things you don't need to know."

"Hard to trust people in this town. The good guys and the bad guys all look the same."

"Sometimes they are the same," retorted Terry.

"Yeah," said Winston studying Terry. "Don't seem like the police are looking too hard for the driver."

161

"Nope. They aren't and they won't be."

"Hmmph," Winston grunted. "There's no justice."

"Not unless someone demands it," said Terry.

Winston took in Terry's statement and wiped the sweat from his brow. He had always been quiet and done his job. That was the way he mostly lived since the fourth grade. Keep your head down and it may not be shot off. He couldn't put his finger on Terry but he figured he was old school Detroit. From Terry's clothes, Winston figured he had pulled himself up but that could have been done righteously or by walking on top of his own people.

"Was Wanda singing that night?" asked Terry.

"Yeah, just got done with her last set," answered Winston.

"And she was heading home?"

"I guess."

"Was she alone?"

"Far as I know..." Winston let his answer trail.

"Listen. If you cared so much for Wanda, you need to tell me everything you know."

"I am," said Winston looking around.

"I think there's more," said Terry.

"How do I know you aren't a cop?"

"I guess I have no way to disprove that. I don't blame you. Say too much in this town and you could wind up dead."

"You got that right," agreed Winston with a grunt.

"But Wanda's killer will never get caught unless someone coughs up some information. For Wanda. For her family."

"Her daughter Deanna will track down the person responsible," said Winston.

"Deanna? Wanda's daughter with Ronnie," said Terry.

"Yeah, and she's a cop. Or was a cop before she got fired."

"Fired?" asked Terry.

"One day she's on the force. The next day she's off, and moving out of state. I hear she's back in town. That ain't no secret. People know when people move out or move back in town. This town has eyes and ears."

"Hard to keep a secret, people like to talk," agreed Terry.

"Yeah, I guess. Hey, Julius is the manager is inside. He remembers all the old boys. Why don't you go in," challenged Winston.

"Thanks. I'll pay my respects," said Terry.

Winston opened the door to The Blue Monk and Terry entered. His eyes had to adjust to the pure darkness. He smelled the smoke that had been drifting in the air for forty years. He heard the door close behind him. His eyes could see better now. A slow blues song was playing on the jukebox. The house band was on a break. He scanned the room that had already checked him out. He walked up to the bar.

Travis, the bartender for the past fifteen years, leaned over to Terry. "What can I get you?"

"Jack and Coke," replied Terry.

Terry scanned the bar scene. There were couples and single men and woman all stirring their drinks and looking bored with the lull in music. One man sat alone in a booth—it was Julius. He was dressed all in black and wore a black fedora. His head was so low in his scotch he looked like he was inhaling it through his nose.

Terry paid for his drink and slowly walked over to Julius and wondered if he would remember him as an anxious and agreeable kid in his twenties. Julius was ten years older than him and was now sixty-five. He had been employed by The Blue Monk for over thirty years and had slept on and off with Wanda for twenty.

"Julius," said Terry. He waited for Julius to look up and recognize him. Julius gazed upward and focused his bloodshot eyes.

"Yeah?"

"It's Terry Cone. I used to hang out here in the club with Wanda and the gang years ago. Remember?"

"Terry Cone…you look familiar."

"In seventy-three you had an open mic night. Wanda was in my group of friends. We encouraged her to sing with Ronnie Charbonneau. That was her first time, remember?"

"Oh, I remember that night. The luckiest and unluckiest night of my life. Sure Terry, I remember you. Sit down, man." Julius moved over in the booth.

"Thanks. I wanted to pay you my respects. I heard about Wanda. I'm sorry man," said Terry.

"I can't believe it. Wanda's dead," said Julius as he took a long drag from his cigarette. "I was crazy about her but she could also drive a man crazy. The music kept us together as friends."

Terry nodded his head like he understood the predicament. To tell the truth, Terry never understood the musician lifestyle. He loved the music but not how these people lived by the gig, by the cigarette and by the bottle.

"When was the last time you saw her?" asked Julius.

"Oh, five years ago. I thought about her a lot. Loved her voice. But every time she saw me it made her kind of sad. So I stopped coming by. I always tried to keep tabs on where she had some gigs."

"Well, there's a history she had with your crowd," said Julius.

"I guess there was," replied Terry.

"This place was her home-base. She was safe here. I saw to that but I guess in the end it wasn't," Julius swilled down the rest of his drink.

"I heard it was a hit and run."

"No respect for human life in this town."

"Julius, maybe I can help."

"How?" asked Julius.

"I know people, the police, City Hall."

"Maybe they're the ones that had something to do with this," replied Julius.

"What makes you think that?"

"There seems to be a general ignoring of this situation by the police. Did you hear Deanna got kicked off the force a few months ago?"

"I just heard. You think they're related?"

"Shit. I think this whole thing stinks to high hell."

"What do you know about that night?"

"I was here. Didn't see it happen though. But I walked by the window and saw her body down in the street."

"Hank knows," said Terry.

"I know he knows," said Julius.

"How's that?"

"Who do you think called him that night? You would think he'd help out, all he did was call a squad car down and I haven't heard shit from him. He won't even return my calls. After all those years keeping him in the loop, now he just drops the ball," said Julius as he grabbed his refreshed drink from the waiter.

"Keeping him in the loop?" Terry repeated.

"Hank and I had a mutual agreement. I was supposed to give him updates on Wanda, her boyfriends, overdoses, anything doing with her and in return he kept the cops away from this joint," explained Julius.

This repulsed Terry to his core.

"Did you report that you were fucking Wanda?" asked Terry blankly.

"He knew about it. He didn't give a shit. He just wanted the info. I called him about twice a year. He didn't do anything with the information. I think he was still in love with her, that's all. Just wanted to make sure she was safe."

"Yeah, that was it," said Terry sarcastically. This guy is an idiot on a grand scale, Terry reflected.

"What was the last piece of information you gave him before her death?"

Julius leaned back in the booth and let his stomach out with a belch. "It would have to be Wanda, blasted out of her skull, on the phone squawking about meeting up with...now get this...her daughter."

Julius let out a big belly laugh that shook the table. He failed to tell Terry he was actually eavesdropping on the other phone line as Wanda talked with Ginny.

"Daughter?" said Terry.

"That's right. Long time ago Wanda gave up a kid for adoption. The daughter found her and was coming up to meet her this week. In fact, the night she was killed. I guess that reunion never happened. Shit." Julius was down again.

"You told Hank this?" asked Terry.

"Yeah, he would want to know that one. I asked him if it was their daughter," said Julius with a large laugh. "The son of a bitch got real quiet on the phone, I tell you that."

Terry began piecing the information together...daughter, meeting. Could Wanda and Hank have had a child? This piece of shit, Julius, handed Wanda to Hank on a platter.

"He broke her heart, you know," said Julius.

"I suspect."

"No fucking suspecting. He did. Deanna is going to track down the piece of shit that killed Wanda," said Julius.

"Have you talked with her?" asked Terry.

"She hates my guts. Daughters don't like the men that are fucking their mother."

Terry paused.

"You think she knew him, the driver?" asked Julius.

"Maybe. Don't know. Not sure if it really matters. She's gone. Lots of crimes go unsolved," replied Terry.

"Especially in this town."

"You got Deanna's cell number?" asked Terry.

"What for?" asked Julius coldly. He laid down his drink and stared at Terry, afraid he would tell all his secrets to Deanna.

"I won't say nothing. I just want to give my condolences to her, that's all," lied Terry.

"She moved out of state. Not sure if this number still works. I used to have to call her to pick up Wanda when she was too in the bag to sing," said Julius as he flipped his cell phone cover open. "313-657-3459."

"Thanks," said Terry as he recorded it in his cell phone.

"Did Winston tell you I was in here?" asked Julius.

"No," lied Terry again as he rose from the table. "Where else would you be?" said Terry with his arms stretched out like Jesus.

"I think he saw something that night."

"He said he didn't."

"Yeah, I'm not sure about that."

"I'd believe the kid. I mean he respects you, Julius. He would tell you since you and Wanda were tight. He sees you both as family," said Terry lying through his teeth.

"Stay cool, Terry."

"You too."

Terry headed toward the exit, opened the door and walked up to Winston who was leaning against the wall waiting to check customer's I.D.

"You didn't tell Julius about the limo," said Terry.

Nervously, Winston shook his head.

"No."

"Smart move. That stupid son of a bitch is the reason she's dead," said Terry.

Winston put his head in his hands like he had a headache.

"Son, listen to me. I know you don't know me from shit. But I got to advise you. Get the hell out of here. Leave right now. This bar isn't going to be around much longer and neither is Julius if you get my drift," explained Terry sincerely.

"You serious?" asked Winston.

"You took care of yourself when you didn't tell Julius everything. It was a gut reaction you had. And I'm begging you to listen to your gut right now. Bad things are going to come down upon this place from on high. That is if I can't stop the man who called the hit," said Terry.

"This job is all I have," said Winston.

"No, all you have is your life," said Terry. "Now run, pack up, get lost and find some place safe to crash for a while." Terry took out his business card and gave it to Winston. "Keep in touch. I'll let you know when it's safe."

Terry gave a reassuring pat on Winston's broad shoulder.

"Good luck, kid," said Terry as he walked away.

Winston watched Terry drive away. He grabbed the door of The Blue Monk and something down deep stopped him. He pulled his hand away, looked down the empty streets and abandoned his post. He ran as fast as his legs could carry him to his apartment where he packed up his sparse belongings and sought out a sanctuary deep in a neighborhood across town.

Terry Cone arrived back at the Manoogian Mansion fifteen minutes later. He gave the guard a nod and looked into the main room. The party had thinned down to a handful of people making plans to go to a bar in Greektown. He saw Max teeter on his feet as he put his wife in a car and sent her home while he went off to party with the bar crowd.

Terry scanned the room and didn't see Hank. He walked past the party stragglers on the back porch and headed down the patio stairs toward the garage.

The goal of capturing a picture of the limousine damage caused Terry to run to the garage with nervous energy. He had never taken a picture with his cell phone. Technology was not his strong point but tonight he would put it to use.

Damn. The garage doors were locked.

Terry walked to the side of the garage and saw a window. He tried lifting the window up. It was locked. The window had nine small windowpanes. He looked around for a small rock. He glanced up to the mansion. He didn't hear any more music and laughter but the lights were still on.

He nervously slammed a rock into one pane. Crack!

The window split but didn't break it. He calculated the chances this window was hooked up to an alarm system. Fifty-fifty. The grounds were adequately guarded but he was aware that the administrative and upkeep fees for the mansion were underfunded and renovation was years behind. Similar to how Nancy Reagan found the White House when she came in with her husband Ronald—in total disrepair.

On Terry's second hit the windowpane shattered. He looked around to assess any reactions. He didn't think anyone could have heard it more than thirty feet away. He shoved his hand inside.

"Damn it," he whispered.

He cut his palm deeply on a shard of glass he hadn't seen. He managed to open the lever and pushed up the window. He surveyed his hand. It was a deep cut that would need stitches. He took a handkerchief out of his pocket and wrapped it around his hand. He took one last look at the mansion. It was silent.

Terry lifted one leg and pulled himself through the window. The moonlight cast shadows on the ground, walls and cars in the garage. He wondered if his phone had a flash on it, he wasn't sure.

The garage was hotter than hell, at least ten degrees hotter than it was outside. Terry wiped his forward and tried to adjust his eyes to the darkness. He was able to find a mechanic's light on the workbench. He plugged it in and searched for the limousine. It was right in front of him, covered up as if it was sleeping. He lifted himself up on his heels to look out the small windowpanes in the garage door. No sign of anyone. He estimated he could take the pictures in sixty seconds front and back if he hurried.

He began to pull off the limousine cover carefully with his good hand. It was a struggle. Terry crouched down and aimed the mechanic's light at the front grille. He saw the dented metal and put his head down knowing it was Wanda's body that had made the damage.

"Wanda, I'm so sorry," prayed Terry.

He took out his phone, fumbled with some of the buttons, and held it up to the limousine. He was aiming the phone when it suddenly started ringing. Terry, startled, dropped the phone.

"Shit." He looked at his cell phone. He wasn't familiar with the number.

"Hello?"

"Who is this?" said a female voice.

"No, who is this?" said Terry firmly.

"This is Deanna Dopp."

"Doppkowski?" asked Terry.

"Yeah, Doppkowski," responded Deanna quickly. She and Gabe had been sitting in a diner calling every auto repair shop owner in town for the past two hours. It was nine p.m. now and all of the repair shops were closed.

Deanna shot Gabe a quick glance with her eyes. She had a link to their case on the phone and she straightened up in the booth.

"How did you get my number?" asked Terry.

"You called me and then hung up," explained Deanna in a crackling reception.

"Shit, I must have hit your number by mistake."

"How did you get my number?"

"From Julius Cassidy," said Terry.

"You're friends with that shithead?"

"No, I'm not. I was just stopping in at The Blue Monk."

"What do you want?" asked Deanna.

"I believe I know who killed your mother," said Terry.

Silence on Deanna's end.

"Hello, are you there?" asked Terry.

"Yeah, what do you know?" said Deanna.

"I'm taking a picture of the vehicle that hit your mother."

"Where are you?"

"The Manoogian mansion," stated Terry.

"Christ. Okay, hold on. Don't do anything. My partner and I can get a search warrant by late tomorrow morning," said Deanna.

Terry laughed. "Girl, you ain't going to get any search warrant. You know what you are dealing with here. I'm standing right in front of the limo. I can see the damage."

"Shit. You are in there without a warrant."

"I need to get a picture, before all the evidence is gone."

"Hold on, hold on. What's your name?" asked Deanna.

"Terry Cone."

"And you were friends with Wanda?"

"Yes, from way back when," answered Terry.

"Were you one of her boyfriends?" Deanna asked with distrust.

"No, I was just a friend. Listen, the mayor's driver has plans to fix this limo quick. I see repair tools lined up in the garage. Who knows how long we got. I'll take a few pictures and be out of here in two minutes if I'm not wasting time on the telephone."

"Mr. Cone. Be careful."

"I'll call you when I'm out," said Terry. "I'm sorry about your mother, Deanna."

"Thank you," replied Deanna as she ended the connection.

"He's illegally trespassing, Deanna. This is bullshit," said Gabe.

"I think we are way past search warrants," replied Deanna. Gabe looked at her with worried eyes.

"This is getting bad. Once you go this deep you got to go all the way. Are you sure you want to do this?" he asked.

Deanna chewed on the inside of her lip. She locked eyes with Gabe.

"Yes. How about you? I don't want you to risk your retirement. You got too much to lose," said Deanna.

Gabe batted the situation around for a few seconds. Fuck. He was in love with her. He wouldn't be doing any of this if he weren't. Now it was time to call bullshit and that was what she was doing with him. He looked into her green eyes.

"I'm in. All the way," said Gabe.

Deanna gave him a hopeful but nervous smile. He did love her. She would do everything she could in the future to help him. To hell with his retirement. They would figure something out. No one had ever put their life on the line to help her like he had. She loved this man. She knew they would be together. She felt it deep inside.

Terry went back lining up his phone camera with the front grille. Click, click, click.

He took multiple shots and angles of the front-end damage. Very softly there were steps he heard coming toward the garage. He dropped his cell phone into his left front trouser pocket and turned off the light he was holding.

The garage door unlocked. Terry ran to the side window. The garage doors whipped open. A beam of light blinded Terry as he had one leg out the window. He was caught. He held his hand up to his eyes. He was in a whiteout.

"What are you doing here Terry?" called out Hank in a calm manner. He clicked off his flashlight. It took a few seconds for Terry's eyes to adjust. Hank turned on the lights over the workbench.

"I know, Hank," asked Terry.

"Know what, you damned fool?" said Hank, starting to lose his temper.

Terry climbed down from the window. He pointed to the limousine.

"It was Joe. He thought he saw a dog in the road. He hit her accidentally. I didn't have anything to do with it. I've been trying to protect him. But maybe it's not the right thing to do. What do you think?" said Hank.

Terry shook his head, trying to understand the story he just heard.

"What the hell were you doing at The Blue Monk?" asked Terry.

"First of all, I wasn't in the limo. Joe had dropped me off for the night and was out joyriding. I have no idea what he was doing there. Maybe he frequents bars, picking up women in the limo."

"You mean it was coincidental that your limo hit Wanda?" asked Terry.

"Incredibly, yes. But given the amount of drunks wandering the streets in this town and then combine the great possibility of Wanda drunk and walking in front of The Blue Monk then those statistics get lowered to a reasonable betting number pretty damn quick," sounded off Hank.

Terry shook his head. This was complete bullshit. How could Hank just shovel it out to me, his old friend, Terry fumed.

"Hank come on, it's Terry."

"You're not buying it?"

"No."

"I guess I'm not good at this," confessed Hank.

"Just tell the truth."

"Too tired," said Hank as he quickly walked up to Terry, drew out a gun and pointed it at him. Terry stepped back, startled.

"Now what else do you know?" asked Hank.

"I know you have a daughter," Terry said has he tried to moisten his dry mouth.

"What are you talking about?"

"I know you know."

"I have no children. Who have you been talking to?" asked Hank.

"Wanda was going to meet her that night. Julius told you."

Hank didn't like that his friend had been snooping. "How do you know she's mine?" asked Hank coolly, not trying to hide anything.

"I don't know for sure but neither do you. That's why you showed up that night. To stop any possible reunion. Where is she?"

"I don't know."

"You didn't see her? You don't know where she is?" Terry started to laugh at Hank's mistakes.

"Hell no, I haven't seen her. I still don't believe it. It was a boy," yelled Hank as he grabbed a hammer and slammed it against the wall, making Terry jump.

"A boy? A son?" said Terry.

"A *boy*," said Hank dryly, without emotion. "Wanda gave birth to a boy."

"She gave him up for adoption, too?"

Hank shook his head and gave Terry such a dark look that the worst image came to his mind.

"No...you didn't. My God. What kind of monster are you? Why, Hank? Why?"

"That woman. She was going to ruin me. Ruin my chances. For all of this," Hank raised his arms outward.

"You fool. You arrogant fool. Your own son," said Terry.

Hank snapped his neck to the side.

"Twins. The bitch had twins."

BAM!

A shot rang out as Hank shot Terry in the chest. Terry's eyes bulged out in surprise as he looked down and watched his summer shirt swell in red blood. He grabbed his chest and fell forward on the car cover. Terry looked up to Hank and shook his head.

"No, no, no..." Terry gasped for his last breath of air.

Hank looked down upon Terry's dead body.

"You've complicated this, Terry. Now what am I to do with you?" Hank asked the rhetorical question to the irresponsive body. Hank began to hyperventilate.

"Not now, not now. Stay in control," Hank commanded his body. What was he becoming? Not becoming—he was and always had been...a monster.

"Was she really worth it, Terry? Maybe she was...sorry old friend. But blame her, she brought this upon all of us," Hank said to Terry's body.

Hank determined his next steps. He looked at the limousine. Joe would always be there for him. Hank wouldn't be able to carry the body out of this garage alone. He opened up the limousine's back door and dragged Terry's body inside. His friend was bigger than him and the lifeless body was hard to maneuver.

After a few minutes of struggling, Terry's body was completely inside and Hank sat down in the back seat exhausted. Joe would have to repair the limousine with Terry's body inside. That will give him incentive to complete the job quickly. Then Joe could drive the limousine out at night and dump the body in the Detroit River. A river rumored to be filled with so many bodies that you could hop from Detroit to Windsor, Canada on the floating cadavers.

Hank hauled himself out of the limousine and covered it back up. Terry's bloodstains were on the cover. Damn, another thing that Joe would have to take care of. What would he tell Joe? That Terry had stumbled out here drunk and had started a ruckus when he was checking out the limousine and saw the damage. Hank could blame Joe for not locking up the garage and covering up the limousine appropriately. He would have to do what Hank said, since Joe was, after all, the driver of the limousine that night. No jury would doubt that.

Hank walked back to the mansion. The lights were low. This will be over soon, all this mess and then the re-election. After four years he could decide to move on to national politics. Then he would be free to go anywhere and be anything. It's going to be so peaceful. He just had to be patient. And he was a man filled with patience.

It had been fifty-five minutes since Deanna had talked with Terry Cone on her cell phone. She turned to Gabe.

"Let's go get him," said Deanna.

"To the mansion?" asked Gabe.

"Something's wrong," said Deanna as she and Gabe headed out the diner.

When they were two blocks from the mansion he slowed down and parked his car on a side street.

"We're hoofin' it," announced Gabe.

Gabe and Deanna began a slow jog to the bordering property. They headed toward the back. There was a tall brick wall surrounding the mansion grounds. They looked up front and saw two guards on duty. Gabe took a running leap and grabbed the top of the wall. He hauled himself up and then lent his hand to Deanna. He pulled her up easily. They jumped down onto the mansion property and crouched down. Everything was silent.

"You don't think they have guard dogs, do you?" asked Deanna.

"I guess we'll find out," said Gabe.

Deanna spotted the outline of the garage in the moonlight.

"This way," she said.

They crept up to the garage. Gabe pointed to the lock on the front garage doors. Deanna motioned him to follow her. She led him to the side window that Terry had broken. All was quiet. Deanna poked her head inside, it was so dark in the garage she couldn't see anything.

"I'm going in," said Deanna.

"Right behind you," said Gabe.

"This could be your last chance to save that pension," she said.

"Retirement is overrated," Gabe said dryly.

Gabe helped Deanna inside. She was careful not to be cut by the glass. Gabe followed her in. Deanna retrieved a small pen light out of her purse. She pointed it around the garage. Her toes started to tingle, they always did when things weren't right on a case. She looked directly down and saw smears of blood that revealed draglines to the limousine.

Deanna took out her cell phone and hit the redial button. In a few seconds a ringing was heard coming from the car.

"I guess he wouldn't be taking a nap in the limo?" said Gabe.

"Shit," whispered Deanna.

Deanna quickly grabbed a glove off the workbench and used it to open the back door of the limousine. They found Terry Cone's body crumpled in the back seat. Deanna reached in, searched and grabbed his ringing cell phone in his pocket. She looked at the photos.

"He took the shots," she said. She turned off the phone and put it in her purse. "Somebody caught him in here."

"Let's not have a rerun. Time to go," said Gabe.

"Wait," said Deanna. She had to see the grille for herself.

She walked to the front of the limousine and targeted her penlight on the front of grille. She dropped to her knees and stared. Her hand automatically reached out to touch it but she stopped her hand an inch from the chrome.

"You son of a bitch. You aren't getting away with this," Deanna vowed.

Barking dogs sounded out in the night.

"Fuck, dogs," whaled Gabe. "Come on Deanna, we got to go." He pulled Deanna up from her arm and forced her out the window.

They ran for the wall, the dogs were running and barking toward them but had no idea how close the canines were to them. Gabe reached the wall first, jumped up and grabbed Deanna's hand.

"Jump!" said Gabe.

A black German shepherd lunged in the air just missing Deanna's right foot. Gabe and Deanna went tumbling down on the other side.

"Move your ass Dopp!" Gabe took Deanna's hand and they ran out of sight back to his car.

Gabe revved the engine and headed out of sight. Deanna stared out her window as they passed each city block.

"The Mayor of Detroit killed my mother."

"What a shit hole town," said Gabe.

Deanna was quiet.

"I'm taking you back to my place," said Gabe.

There was no movement on Gabe's street. No sign of Billings and Stevens. It was just after eleven p.m. Gabe guided Deanna to the front door. He opened the door and she walked in and curled up on the couch. Gabe found a blanket and laid it over her. He sauntered over to his refrigerator, searched and opened a bottle of beer. He took in a long slow drink.

"Here's to retirement," he quietly said to himself as he took another swig.

Gabe heard Deanna rise up from the couch and go down the hallway to the back bedroom. His bedroom. He put down his beer and listened to the sound of Deanna lying down in his bed. He held on to the sink.

There hadn't been any woman in his bed for a year. Not since the day he realized he was in love with Deanna. He ran his hand through his hair. These last few days were ugly and things were getting worse. Gabe began to think of the possibility of losing his job but his mind wandered back to Deanna. He wanted to lie down beside her.

Deanna stretched and then curled her body into the sheets. She moved her face over the pillow and smelled deeply. It smelled like Gabe and his aftershave. She fell into the smell and it transported her back into a thousand days of working with him. Knowing what he was thinking and feeling. She never wanted to be with him then. They were partners and they had both respected the line that they had intuitively and consciously drawn and left alone.

Now with her world turned upside down, Deanna was letting herself have feelings that she had denied herself for years. She wanted him to be near physically. She wanted to feel the strength of his arms around her. She needed that strength. She smelled deeply again.

She loved him.

She let the acknowledgement sink in from her heart into every vein and fingertip. She was trying it out. It excited her. She hadn't been in love since...perhaps ever as an adult.

She giggled and buried her smile in the pillow. What a terrible daughter. How hideous. Surrounded by death, disorder and chaos, she was selfishly thinking of herself. A sadness swept over her. Why did this have to happen now and not months ago? Why did it come at the cost of her mother and others?

Deanna would never be able to answer those questions. It was here and now. Her nerves were on edge and her emotional state swung like a pendulum in her body. She'd have to keep this all undercover and cool until they bring down the mayor, she planned. Then, afterwards, she could confess to Gabe her feelings and they could make it work. She couldn't think of being with anyone else that understood her better. Down to her core. It would be hard to find a better man. He was as good as they get. And damn handsome, too.

Gabe pushed himself away from the sink and quietly walked down the hallway. He could hear Deanna softly stir. He stood at the bedroom doorway. In the dark he was able to see the outline of her body on the bed. He took a deep breath, turned away and stepped back down the hallway.

"Gabe," whispered Deanna.

He stopped and turned.

"Lie down," she said.

Gabe didn't know which way he should step.

"Please," she whispered.

Gabe walked into the bedroom and sat on the side of the bed. He nervously found her hand in the dark. Deanna grasped his hand firmly.

"I don't want to see you get hurt, kiddo...I don't know if I could take that," Gabe said softly. Gabe took his hand away from Deanna and wiped away tears from his eyes.

Deanna reached out her hand to his face, wiped a tear and put her finger to her lips. She tasted the tear.

"I belong here," said Deanna.

She leaned forward and set her head against his shoulder. Gabe turned fully toward her and held her face in his hands. Their faces barely touched.

"I never imagined this would be possible," said Gabe. "Are you sure?"

"Yes," answered Deanna.

Deanna leaned into Gabe and kissed him gently. She pulled herself up on her knees and pulled him to her. She kissed his rough shaven face, his forehead and went back to his lips. Gabe looked into her eyes. He couldn't see their full color but he felt they were looking into his soul. He laid her down onto her back and climbed on top of her and kissed her hard.

Deanna's hands clenched Gabe's shoulders, as their passion became a flurry of touching and tasting each other. Clothes fell to the floor as they rolled over. She was beautiful naked. He couldn't stop touching every part of her. They made love quietly over and over until they had smothered the fire burning for five years.

Afterwards, Gabe wrapped the sheet around Deanna and held her.

"I love you," whispered Deanna.

"I know," said Gabe. Deanna ribbed him. "You have always been mine, Deanna. Since Kavanaugh first gave you to me."

Deanna smiled. She fell asleep exhausted and in Gabe's arms.

CHAPTER 9 – A SLIPPERY SLOPE

B AM! A shotgun blast on the porch brought down Uncle Roman to his knees. Jackson Billings glanced over to Deanna witnessing the event.

"It's your fault," Billings said to Deanna with the smoking shotgun in his hands.

Deanna woke with a jolt from her dream. She was sweating and rubbed her face with the bed sheet.

"I got to get Ginny out of there," said Deanna. She reached over in the bed for Gabe but he wasn't there. She looked at the clock on the nightstand. It read 2am. She switched on the nightstand lamp and looked around his room.

His dresser had an old framed picture of his parents and of course, his beloved '68 Detroit Tigers team. The room had a small bookshelf lined with mystery books by Ludlum, Le Carre, and Elmore Leonard, a local favorite of his. The restful state she fell asleep in was over. She tried to recapture it and felt herself between her legs.

Deanna smelled the aroma of bacon in the air and figured Gabe was having his typical late night meal. She pulled on her outfit, strung her hands through her hair and walked down the hall. When she reached the kitchen she saw that Gabe was drinking coffee and eating bacon and eggs.

"Sorry, didn't mean to wake you," said Gabe.

"I see you moonlight as a late night fry cook."

"My next profession," said Gabe as he served Deanna coffee. "Maybe I need to find myself a wife to cook for me." He winked at Deanna who spilled her coffee all over herself and the table.

"Ouch! Ah!" screamed Deanna.

Gabe came running with a towel.

"Damn, Deanna. Just kidding," laughed Gabe.

"Oh, no. I wasn't reacting to that. I'm still asleep," said Deanna. "Gabe, we have to go get Ginny."

"Too much of a burden for your uncle?" asked Gabe.

"Yeah, we need to ship her back to Nashville," said Deanna.

"Safest place for her," agreed Gabe.

They dressed quickly and got into Gabe's car. The night was quiet in the neighborhood streets. Gabe checked for Billings and Stevens. No sign of them.

Deanna kept thinking about Terry Cone's crumpled body in the back of the limousine. She shook the image out of her head and went back to remembering Gabe holding her.

They walked up to her Uncle Roman's home. The porch light was the only one on in the house. Deanna guided Gabe to the back door, not wanting the neighbors to see any commotion. She knocked and heard Uncle Roman descending the stairs. He looked out through the curtains. Deanna could see he had a handgun hidden under his robe. Roman opened up the door.

"What's wrong?" asked Roman.

"We're here to get Ginny," said Deanna.

"Why? What's going on?" asked Roman. Ginny and Aunt Helen held hands as they crept into the kitchen.

"I can't let you take this responsibility. We can protect her. I'm taking her to the airport. She needs to go back home to Nashville," said Deanna.

Ginny stepped up, "Roman, Deanna's right, I appreciate your help."

"That's the least we could do," said Roman. Ginny gave Helen and Roman a hug before she left.

"One day we will have more time, but that isn't now," said Ginny.

Helen started to cry and Roman escorted his wife back up the staircase. Ginny, Gabe and Deanna silently walked to the car.

"So, you'll get on a plane?" asked Gabe.

"Hell no, I just said that so they would feel better," said Ginny.

Gabe shot a surprised look at Deanna as they all slipped into the car.

"You refuse?" asked Deanna.

"Yeah, I refuse. Wherever you go—I go," said Ginny defiantly.

"Bullheaded," whispered Deanna under her breath. "Just like Wanda."

"What did you say?" asked Ginny.

"By not getting on a plane you are putting everything in jeopardy. If the mayor finds out we have you then the investigation stops and we just become your bodyguards. You would blow our cover completely," said Deanna.

"I want to help," said Ginny sternly.

"You want to help, huh? Okay, then we should probably discuss who killed Terry Cone," said Deanna impatiently.

"Someone else was murdered?"

Gabe looked at Deanna to handle the situation.

"Yes. Terry Cone was on Hank Jenkins's staff. Boyhood friends. He knew Wanda," said Deanna.

"What is with this town? People get murdered left and right. Call the goddamn police," pleaded Ginny.

"The mayor's got the police in his back pocket. Want me to call those cops that were tailing us?" asked Deanna.

Ginny looked at Gabe in the rear view mirror for guidance.

"This really is the best way," said Gabe.

"We need conclusive evidence and then we can nail him. At this point he would blame his limo driver for everything and get away with it," said Deanna.

"What other evidence?"

"We believe he was involved in another murder," said Deanna.

Deanna opened her mouth then closed it. Could she tell Ginny that she had had a brother? That Hank Jenkins had killed him? No, that was too much now. How much could Ginny take in a 24-hour timeframe? Deanna confirmed her decision in her head with just a look toward Gabe as he looked deep into her eyes. They had to wait to tell Ginny about the baby boy.

"Whose?" Ginny asked.

"Well, that's the funny part, we don't know. We need to talk to someone downtown."

Ginny looked at both of them suspiciously.

"Are you hiding something from me?" asked Ginny.

Deanna was surprised by Ginny's moxy. And she liked it.

"Yes," said Deanna deciding not to bullshit Ginny.

"Why?" asked Ginny, surprised by Deanna's honesty.

"To protect you."

Deanna stopped. Hank must have known about Wanda meeting Ginny. She couldn't believe it was just coincidence that they were meeting the night Hank showed up with his death mobile limousine.

"What's not to stop me from going straight to the television stations or newspapers right now?" reasserted Ginny.

Deanna stared back at her. Was she bluffing? She looked deep into those green eyes. She could see her reflection in them. Damn.

"Fine, you can come with us," Deanna said coolly.

"What?" said Gabe.

"She isn't bullshitting," said Deanna to a bewildered Gabe.

"I guess you would know," said Gabe.

Gabe marveled at these half-sisters newly reunited. One dark and one light. He noticed they had the same walking gate earlier. Ginny was an inch or two taller than Deanna. But they had the same slender build. Both attractive. He was in love with one of them. His mind went to earlier in the night and how he held Deanna. He hoped that tomorrow night she would stay with him again. He snapped out of his daydream as Deanna spoke to him.

"Let's go back to the Medical Examiner's Office," said Deanna.

"Is that the morgue?" asked Ginny.

"Yeah," said Gabe.

"They're open at this time?"

"Demand is high in this city. We know the night-shift examiner," answered Gabe.

"This is like a bad episode of CSI," said Ginny.

Gabe laughed at the comment but Ginny wasn't laughing and neither was Deanna. Ginny didn't feel like asking any more questions in fear of the answers she may get in return. She slid back and let the sweat of the night heat roll down her forehead.

The car was moving out of the neighborhood and soon they were on the freeway heading downtown. Ginny let the wind from the window cool her off. She closed her eyes and let all the city's sounds, smells and pressures engulf her body.

Deanna looked out the window to the blur of buildings they passed. Warehouses, abandoned churches, and apartment buildings, all with their windows open, some with people leaning outside, unable to sleep, looking for the break in the heat that wasn't coming.

Deanna missed this town. She longed for it even as she drove in Gabe's car. She thought of Wanda and Hank Jenkins. Did he once love her? Did she ever stop loving him? She wanted to understand every detail of their story - that was the detective inside her longing for the motive and, more so, a daughter looking to understand.

They arrived at the morgue.

On the basement floor of the building Jerry listened to his iPod amid dance poses as he performed an autopsy on an eighteen-year old gang member. He pulled out a bullet from the young man's chest and examined it carefully.

"Hmm, you have broken off. Where is the rest of you?" said Jerry. He plunked the bullet down into a metal bowl and dug in deeper into the cadaver.

"Split bullet? Time to go digging," said Gabe as he plunked down the metal bowl hard on the table. Jerry jumped two feet backward.

"Shit, Gabe. Make yourself known when you walk into a room. Christ," Jerry cried out.

Jerry saw Deanna and softened his tone, "Oh, hi, Deanna. Pardon me for swearing." Jerry checked out Ginny. Pretty hot, almost as hot as Deanna.

"No problem. Jerry, this is a friend. She's cool," said Deanna.

"My pleasure," Jerry said with a toothy smile.

184

"You do autopsies?" asked Ginny.

"We're forensic scientists," explained Jerry.

"You put make-up on them, too?" asked Ginny.

Gabe started cracking up.

"He even paints their finger nails," said Gabe.

"No," said Jerry flustered. "The cosmetologists at funeral homes do that. We have to identify the cause of death. Now what can I do for you guys?"

Deanna pointed to one of the computers in the room.

"We want you to look up a record," said Deanna.

Jerry took off his gloves and gown. He took a seat at the computer.

"Nothing new has been added to your mother's file," said Jerry. "I saw Max logged on yesterday to the system."

Deanna shot a look at Gabe.

"God, I hope he didn't get to that other file."

"What file?" Jerry said annoyed.

"Doppkowski. The second one you mentioned," said Deanna.

"Who would that be?" asked Ginny.

Deanna ignored her. Gabe wasn't about to override Deanna's decision of silence.

Ginny grabbed Deanna's shoulder. "Who is the second Doppkowski?" she asked again.

Deanna looked into those eyes that were going to be hurt again. There was no stopping it.

"You had a brother," said Deanna.

Ginny looked confused and then winced in pain.

"Wanda had twins. You and a little boy," explained Deanna.

"A brother? And he's dead? How?"

Deanna hated being the one to tell her.

"Wanda ran away and hid during the pregnancy. Hank Jenkins found out and went after her. She hid you both that night in the apartment. He found the boy and didn't know there were two of you. We have reason to believe he strangled the boy. That's it," said Deanna.

185

"That's it?" cried Ginny. "Why the hell didn't Wanda go to the police? He committed a murder over thirty years ago. He could have been put away!"

Deanna grabbed Ginny's shoulders.

"She did it to save you. He would have tracked you down, in or out of prison. She got you down to Nashville and came back up here and never brought it up again—to protect you," said Deanna.

Ginny fell into Deanna's arms and cried. She put her arms around her sister. Gabe turned away from them and focused his attention back onto a panicked Jerry.

"You okay, Jerry?" asked Gabe.

"Hank Jenkins? The mayor?" said Jerry with a cracking voice.

"He's the goddamned mayor?" asked Ginny as she pulled away from Deanna.

"Yes, the goddamned, fucking mayor. Now Jerry, look up that other Doppkowski file damnit!" yelled Deanna.

"Crap, this is way too hot, Deanna," said Jerry taking off his gloves.

"Just keep cool, Jerry," said Deanna "Sorry I yelled."

"Everyone cool it," Gabe commanded.

Jerry rotated his neck to relax and typed at lightening speed on the computer. He entered his password, opened the program and then bingo. He was in the morgue's deceased file system.

"I'm in," said Jerry.

He started scanning down the list. A...B...C...D. Down he went into the names. He flashed past the Donans, Donners and then went straight to only one Doppkowski file, which was Wanda's.

"It's not here," Jerry said as he spun his chair around to Deanna.

"Check again," Deanna ordered calmly.

Jerry scanned back to the Donners and then went slowly down the list.

"No, it's gone. There is only your mother's file. What the hell?" said Jerry.

"He got to Max. Hank must know we are on to him," Deanna said to Gabe.

Footsteps squeaked down the hallway heading towards them.

"Fast, get out of that program, Jerry," said Gabe.

Jerry hit a few buttons and popped up from the desk.

In staggered Max Schwartz with a purpose and Chevas on his breath. He had decided to drop by the morgue after his barhopping to fire Jerry. The scotch helped his courage. He looked at everyone in the room and recognized them all except the black woman. He tried to focus his eyes on her.

"Why, Deanna and Gabe, how are you? I haven't seen you two in ages. Deanna, I am so sorry to hear about your mother," slurred Max.

Max walked up to Jerry and put his right hand on his shoulder, pushing him back down into the computer chair. Jerry had an awkward smile look on his face. He wasn't good at lying. Deanna took all of this in and in seconds had to figure out her strategy. Her mind was filling with anger, which kept it from formulating a plan.

"Thanks Max. I just needed to see the body again," said Deanna.

"You been drinking, Max?" asked Gabe, smelling the scotch.

"Yes, I have been. A lot, too. You're no stranger to that, are you Gabe?"

"Fuck you," said Gabe.

"No, thank you," replied Max with a smack of his lips. "Deanna, with all due respect, only investigators are allowed down here after the body has been identified." Max turned to Gabe. "Is Gabe on the case?"

Gabe folded his hands across his chest, ready for anything Max was going to throw at him. Deanna realized this could cause more trouble for Gabe back at the precinct.

"No," Deanna said right before Gabe was about to answer yes.

"Who's this?" Max said, pointing to Ginny.

"An old friend," said Deanna.

"Jerry, are you letting anybody in here?" asked Max with his hand still on Jerry's shoulder. Jerry shrunk down even further.

"That is a violation of our department rules," said Max in quiet control of his emotions and his liquor.

"Max, for Christ sake. It's Deanna's mother," said Gabe as he pounded his fist on the examining table. Jerry jumped back in his chair. Max didn't flinch.

"I mean no disrespect. I'm just trying to follow the rules," said Max as he swayed on his feet.

"Like this place ever follows the rules," pointed out Gabe.

"You understand, right, Deanna?" asked Max.

Deanna's head sagged downward. She hesitated in responding to Max and then looked up to him.

"Fuck you, Max," replied Deanna with her head cocked to the side.

Max flinched his head back, shocked by her answer.

"Why, why…" Max stuttered.

Deanna strode toward him.

"You heard me. Fuck you. Fuck you. Fuck you!" she screamed. The demon that Uncle Felix planted in Deanna was out.

Max backed up against the swinging doors, not knowing how to handle such an outward display of anger. Her words rang in his ears.

"Deanna, you are obviously upset and overcome with emotion right now," sputtered Max.

"Fuck you, fuck everything about you. Fuck you, your wife, your kids, your parents and your grandparents. Did you hear me? Fuck you!" Deanna spat as she came after him with a vengeance.

Max fell down and through the swinging doors.

"I'll leave you alone until you calm down, yes, that is a good idea," said Max as he rose and took off speed walking down the hallway.

Deanna wiped her mouth, straightened her hair with her hands and turned back to everyone. Calm, calm down, she repeated to herself. It came out. She wasn't proud of it, but it did feel good.

Gabe was holding his sides laughing. Ginny and Jerry were both wide-eyed and scared senseless. Gabe howled and leaned against the examination table for support.

"Oh, how I have missed you." Gabe wiped tears from his eyes.

"Max is probably halfway done dialing Kavanaugh or the mayor. Now Jerry…" Deanna said.

Jerry jumped back and smashed into a plate of instruments that crashed to the floor.

"Christ, cool it. When did you transfer the old morgue log names into this new database?" Deanna asked.

"I just got done last week," said a freaked-out Jerry. He had never seen Deanna so furious—it made him even more excited and attracted to her.

"Did you keep all the old hard copies of the records?" asked Deanna.

"I threw them in the dumpster this afternoon," answered Jerry as he picked up his dissecting tools off the ground.

"I love dumpster diving during a heat wave. Get up. Lead us to it," Gabe said as he grabbed Jerry from the floor, picking him up with one hand.

They all turned to leave the room when Ginny grabbed Deanna's arm.

"What was that all about?" said Ginny.

"What? Max?"

"Your tirade. And you were worried about me? You just blew our cover," said Ginny.

"I guess I did. I just couldn't take that snake anymore. Anyway, it's hard to have a cover in this town for too long," said Deanna. "But, it is blown, sky high."

"How are we going to protect ourselves? Can't we go to the media?" asked Ginny.

"You need to stop this. You..." Deanna stopped herself and realized she needed to handle Ginny with more gentleness. After all, this was Ginny's first exposure with a murder in Detroit, her own mother's murder. Deanna grabbed Ginny's hand gently.

"We don't have enough evidence. When we do we can go tell everyone. But right now we would get shut down and escorted out of the city. Gabe would lose his job. Shit, he still may. Hang in there. We're almost home," said Deanna.

"How will we know?" asked Ginny.

"When we have solid evidence linking Hank Jenkins to the murder of his son, Wanda and now to Terry Cone," said Deanna.

Ginny breathed deep. She wiped a tear away from her face and nodded her head. "Okay, okay," cried Ginny. "You're one scary sister. You almost made that man crap his pants."

Deanna and Ginny shared a laugh.

"If it's in me, it's in you. Maybe my beast got nurtured more," replied Deanna.

"Perhaps," admitted Ginny.

Deanna and Ginny ran down the hallway after the men.

Outside in the alley dumpster Jerry and Gabe searched through boxes.

"Got it, I got it," yelled Jerry.

Gabe grabbed the box from him and dropped it on the pavement. They jumped out of the dumpster. Jerry got on his knees and started fumbling through the thousands of death certificates that were thankfully still in alphabetical order.

"Bs, Cs, Ds...here they are..." He grabbed an old yellow card. "I got it! See, I'm not crazy. Look Deanna," said Jerry as he handed the card to Deanna.

She read it.

"Date of death—June 17, 1974. Sex—male. Age at death—4 months."

Ginny's legs went weak and she slowly sank to the ground. Gabe went to her aid. Deanna kept reading.

"Cause of death. It's blank. Name—Daniel Doppkowski." Deanna looked down at Ginny.

"Daniel...Daniel," repeated Ginny as Gabe held her hand.

"It has a grave number but doesn't say the name of the cemetery. Do you know where the body could be buried?" asked Deanna.

"No idea. We have pauper gravesites all over this town. The only person that may know is Max," said Jerry.

"Well, we can't ask him," snapped Deanna who immediately regretted her tone. "Jerry, thank you. I owe you. You know you are going to lose your job."

"I know," said Jerry as he nervously played with his tie. "It's the right thing. Max can kiss my ass."

Deanna smiled and reached over and kissed him on the cheek.

"Definitely worth it," Jerry said with a smirk.

"Jerry, take this whole box and go to a friend or relative's—don't go back home. Hold it until I call you. Give me your cell number," said Deanna.

Jerry gave her his cell number.

"Okay, stay low," advised Deanna.

Deanna looked down onto Ginny. She watched Gabe comfort her, so naturally, so much better than she could.

"Guys, we need to go," said Deanna.

"Where?" said Ginny.

"To find the limo driver," said Deanna.

Deanna shoved Daniel Doppkowski's death certificate card in her pocket and strode out of the alley.

Deanna, Gabe and Ginny drove off, leaving Jerry running erratically to his car with the box of death certificates. Jerry dropped the box into his trunk and peeled out of the parking lot, afraid to look over his shoulder.

"I got a friend, Guido, in the motor pool division who can give us the limo driver's name and address," said Gabe as he veered the car into a u-turn in the middle of an intersection.

"Doesn't anyone sleep?" asked Ginny as she slid into the side of the car.

"The police force is 24/7. These guys like working nights. They're the rats of the city. They own it at night," said Gabe.

Ginny sat in the corner of the back seat. She was in a dazed dream and welcomed the silence in the car.

Deanna looked back at Ginny who looked liked she was reeling on a good drug.

Deanna was familiar with the feeling—being with Gabe, the excitement and sickness of their work, driving on these streets, feeling that you are part of this world, this family, loving and hating it all, and feeling alive.

Ginny opened her eyes and smiled faintly at Deanna who smiled back as if to say, take another swig, inhale another toke, snort another line, relax and enjoy it. It was a drug. Deanna closed her eyes and felt the city press down on her chest as Gabe had earlier in the night.

They pulled up into an alley. The car headlights lit up an indiscreet garage door. Gabe honked his car horn twice. The garage door opened and Gabe pulled into a warehouse for police car repairs.

"Give me Terry Cone's cell phone," said Gabe to Deanna. She handed it over.

Gabe stepped out of the car. A scruffy, white, fat cop with grease all over his body, chomping an unlit cigar, met Gabe with a grin and a handshake.

"What's up shit face?" asked Guido.

"What's up fat fuck?" responded Gabe. Both men laughed and hit each other's stomachs.

Deanna watched from the car.

"Why don't we get out?" asked Ginny.

"See that?" said Deanna.

Ginny watched the two men hit each other and swap insults.

"We can't do that. This is their territory. Man's last bastion at the force. The motor pool garage. Gabe will get what we need. We sit out on this," said Deanna.

"What do you want, Gabe? You wouldn't visit this shit hole for no reason," asked Guido.

"I need some information," said Gabe.

"Shoot."

"The mayor's limo driver. What's his name, his story, anything you got?"

Guido was surprised by the request. Not because it was a bold request but because Joe Dempsey was a benign person who he had known since starting in the motor pool department twenty-five years ago after being injured as a flat foot.

"Joe Dempsey is his name. Black guy, lives in Brush Park with his mother. Pretty dull guy. Been a limo driver for three mayors, starting with Coleman Young. Comes in for an oil change on the limo every three thousand miles like clockwork," said Guido.

"That's it?"

"Yeah, nothing. He's dull as shit. Not a lot going on upstairs. Got his job through Coleman's old chief of staff, John Floyd, neighborhood friend," said Guido.

"Can you get me his address?"

"Sure." Guido walked over to an old beat up computer and looked up Joe's contact info. He wrote it down on a piece of paper and handed it to Gabe.

"Slot machines," remembered Guido.

"What?" said Gabe.

"Slot machines. He likes them. We talked about that once when he was here. Has a whole system on how he works them. Hangs out at Motor City Casino."

"Got it."

"Okay, Gabe. What's this about? Sniffing around the mayor? And who the hell are they?" said Guido as he peeked at Deanna and Ginny sitting in Gabe's car.

Guido handed him a beer he hand under his service counter. Gabe took a quick swig.

"The mayor's a piece of shit," said Gabe.

"What do you got?"

"Take a look at this. In your professional opinion, what would cause this kind of damage?"

Gabe took out Terry's cell phone and showed Guido the damaged limo shots.

"Hard to tell, looks pretty deep. Definitely hit something big," said Guido.

"Or someone."

"That's the mayor's limo?" asked Guido.

The men locked eyes.

"That's my ex-partner in the front seat," said Gabe.

"The infamous Deanna Dopp? No wonder you never introduced me to her, I would have stolen her away from you," Guido smirked.

"Yeah, well, her mother was killed a few days ago. Hit and run."

"Whoa, Gabe, careful."

"That's why I need to talk with Joe Dempsey."

"This guy wouldn't hurt a fly," said Guido.

"I'm not sure who was behind the wheel…or who gave the order."

"Who's the other broad?"

"Deanna's sister. Half-sister."

"She's a knock-out, too. Interesting family."

"You don't know the half of it."

"Sure you want to marry into it?" joked Guido.

Gabe laughed and pushed his hair out of his tired eyes.

"Got to go," said Gabe.

"Kavanaugh know you're moonlighting?" asked Guido.

"No, this is pro-bono."

"You're such a fuckin' saint, Gabe," said Guido as he hit the open button on the garage door. He watched as Gabe hopped into his car and backed out of his garage.

"Careful buddy," whispered Guido.

Gabe revved his car's engine as he turned out of the alley.

"That was Guido."

"Yes, he certainly was," said Deanna.

"No introductions?" ribbed Ginny.

"Well, he's a bit crude. I thought I would save you from that," said Gabe.

"Thank you," said Ginny.

"Get what you need?" asked Deanna.

"Joe Dempsey. Apparently, he likes the casinos," Gabe grinned.

Deanna looked at him and his smile. She tried to capture it in a picture in her mind. This was when he was at his happiest. With some critical information. Driving to their destination. In pursuit. She savored the seconds and held on to them in animated suspension.

They pulled up to the Motor City Casino. It was 2:45am and the casino parking lot was packed.

"What's his game?" asked Deanna.

Gabe parked the car with a jolt. "One armed bandits."

"What?" said Ginny.

Deanna got his meaning.

"Slot machines," Gabe said as he jumped out the car and assisted Ginny out of the backseat.

They all walked under the looming Motor City Casino lights that illuminated the street and highlighted the streams of people walking in the doors with cash in their pockets and dreams of winning big on their minds.

As Deanna was about to enter the casino a voice called out.

"Hey cuz!"

Deanna spun around and saw her cousin Stanley smoking against the wall of the casino. He was high.

"Hey Gabe," said Stanley as he shook Gabe's hand.

"Hi Stanley. Good to see you. You back working the kitchen?" asked Gabe who checked out Stanley's dilated eyes discreetly. He was high.

"Yeah, it sucks. But I like the people," said Stanley. "What are you up to?" he asked checking out Ginny.

"Doing some research," said Deanna.

"Who's your friend?" asked Stanley as he flicked his cigarette to the side.

"Hi, I'm Stanley," he said before Gabe or Deanna could answer his question.

"Hi Stanley, I'm Ginny."

Deanna watched to see if Stanley had heard of her through Wanda. But he didn't say anything except, "You have amazing eyes."

"Thank you," said Ginny awkwardly. She wanted to say hello to her cousin but was following Deanna's silence on the subject.

"Can I help you out? I know a lot of people in there," said Stanley.

"We got it under control, but thanks," said Deanna, pissed that her cousin was high again. "We'll see you later."

Ginny and Deanna walked into the casino. Gabe kept back to talk with Stanley.

"Shit, I think she thinks I'm stoned," said Stanley.

"You are," said Gabe.

"What's your point?" asked Stanley.

Gabe laughed at Stanley's drug infused rationality. "You still got my cell number?" asked Gabe.

"Yeah, why?"

"Remember Jackson Billings?"

"Sure, how can I forget that asshole? He's got a green sidekick called Stevens," answered Stanley.

"That's right. If you see them around tonight, give me a buzz," said Gabe as he walked into the casino.

"You got it 'bro," said Stanley, happy that he could help Gabe.

CHAPTER 10 – A BLOWN COVER

Joe Dempsey loved three particular slot machines at his favorite casino. They welcomed him every week to the world of flashing lights, smiles and laughter. The magical sound of the coins that jingled as they fell down into the holding cup made his heart flutter. It made him happy and the attraction fulfilled him in a rather unfulfilling life.

He was taught blackjack by his mother, Bess, as a child but he wasn't good at arithmetic so he would always lose. Ten years ago when one of the Detroit police motor pool mechanics explained to him that the slot machines required no counting whatsoever—Joe was hooked.

He planted himself at the slot machines every Friday and Saturday night after he got off work, usually from 12:30am to 3:30am. Joe had kept his schedule diligently with only a break on Easter and Christmas Day when he was obligated to be with Bess.

Joe even had a special pattern that he had developed that involved sitting at three distinct slot machines for an hour each. He had to use his left hand to reach into the coin bucket, hand-off the coin to the right hand which would insert it into the machine and then pulled with his right hand after waiting for a four second count.

If anything interrupted this sequence, such as a cocktail waitress handing him a drink and him accepting it in the wrong hand, it would be a foiled attempt. He would have to start over if possible or just attribute his loss to the break in his bulletproof system.

Joe did win. Just not often. He allotted himself one hundred dollars every Friday and Saturday night. If he had to work, he would drive over as soon as his event with the mayor was completed. He mostly broke even and kept a meticulous record of his winnings and losses in a spiral notepad in his dresser drawer at his mother's home.

Bess peeked at this notebook the first year he starting going to the casino and had lost interest in a few months after she saw her son was not a big winner or loser. Let him have some fun, she rationalized. He doesn't chase women or men, do drugs or call sex phone lines. Let him have at least this. And she did. She let him have his slot machines, and at times he would take her out to dinner on his winnings. It worked for both of them.

This evening, Joe sat at his third slot machine. It was his favorite one—the fifth slot machine down, in the third row, near the men's bathroom. He had won three hundred more dollars from this slot machine than the rest. The money wasn't enough for him to change his meticulous schedule but he felt happier when he sat in this particular chair and he felt a small spiritual lift that he didn't feel in the other seats.

Left hand coin, right hand coin, slide it in the slot, count to four and pull. The characters blurred in a dizzying circle.

Plop—cherries. Plop—cherries, again.

Just one more cherry he prayed for as he held in his breath.

Plop, joker.

Joe let out his breath, his shoulders slumped and he looked down at his cup with just a few coins left. He looked at his watch. He had forty minutes left at this slot machine before he went home. He pumped himself up and shoved his left hand deep into his coin cup and began his process all over again.

Deanna strode briskly into the main casino room. She had been at stakeouts at this casino before and had memorized the layout of the floor. She nodded to Gabe in the direction of the slot machines.

Ginny took in all the flashing colors, blinking lights and blaring music. She had been to the casinos in Las Vegas before and this had all the similar features but the crowd was a bit rougher, harder, drunker. Cheers from celebrating winners at the black jack, roulette and poker tables screamed in her ears.

"I guess they can build a casino anywhere," said Ginny.

"Their biggest opponent is the mayor. He hates them, but loves the taxes," replied Deanna.

"Give the people what they want," said Gabe. "If they want to piss their money away. So be it."

"Gabe, we've argued about this a thousand times. It brings down the community," said Deanna.

"They would just go to Windsor, so what's the difference?" said Gabe.

"Oh, shut up, Gabe," snapped Deanna.

"There are some things I didn't miss about you," said Gabe as he winked at Ginny who picked up on the teasing Gabe was giving her sister. They were hiding their love from her but she sensed how Deanna felt about Gabe. It was obvious, maybe not to both of them, but to Ginny it had been apparent when she first saw them together.

Deanna and Gabe scanned the crowd to see if they saw any familiar faces, good or bad. Nothing. They looked over at the slot machines and identified three black males fitting Joe's description. One was smoking, the second was finishing a drink with four empty glasses piled up on the machine, the third had an elaborate sequence with the slot machine that they could time their watches to—they had found the driver, Joe Dempsey.

"That's got to be him," said Gabe.

"Let's close in," said Deanna.

"Do you want me to stay here?" asked Ginny.

"No, better to stick by our side," said Deanna.

Gabe led in front of Deanna and Ginny as they slipped through the crowd. They were approaching upon Joe when a dark shadow passed over them and blocked their passage. They looked up and found a 6'5" man with dark hair wearing a suit smiling with his hands folded against his chest.

"Welcome to Motor City Casino, you must be Guido's friends," said the man.

"Shit, Gabe," Deanna whispered.

Guido had sold out Gabe, Deanna judged. That is the first time she had witnessed Gabe make a bad judgment on a fellow cop. She looked at Gabe who was hiding his surprise as best he could.

"Who wants to know?" said Gabe.

"Come with me," the burly man ordered.

"We were about to talk with a friend over there," replied Gabe.

"I know what you were about to do. But now you aren't. Follow me," said the man.

The man led them forty feet away to a quieter corner. Deanna and Gabe kept their eyes on Joe. Ginny couldn't keep her eyes off this large man that scared every part of her down to her tingling toes.

"Tell Guido, fuck you, the next time you see him," said Gabe.

The man put his finger in Gabe's chest and pushed hard on it.

"Calm down. Now what's your business here?" asked the man.

"Who the fuck are you?" asked Deanna.

"Whoa, manners, missy," the man replied.

"We don't have time for this," said Deanna as she stepped up to the man a foot taller than her. The man glared at Deanna.

"You are in my house, and I will determine what you have time for or not. I'm Guido's cousin, Sam. I'm the floor boss here. I run this show. Is that enough?"

Deanna stared right back at Sam. Ginny stepped in-between the giant and Deanna.

"Listen, let's start over. We need to talk to that man," said Ginny pointing at Joe.

Deanna was annoyed at Ginny for butting in on the conversation, but she was right and her temperament was better at the moment.

"Joe Dempsey, the mayor's driver," said Sam.

"You know him?" asked Deanna.

"It's my job to know all of the returning customers," said Sam.

"We need to have a talk with him," said Gabe.

"How much time do you need?" asked Sam.

"Not sure, could be ten minutes, could be an hour," said Deanna.

"Look, you can't drag him out of here in front of everyone." Sam glanced at his watch. "He'll be gambling another forty minutes. Can you wait?" said Sam.

"We don't have time for that," said Gabe.

"The only way we can get him off that seat is if he wins. Then I can escort him to a special room to change out his coins to dollars. Then you can have him."

"Our own interrogation room. Nice," commented Gabe.

"You can do that?" asked Ginny. "Trigger the slot machine?"

Sam looked at Ginny and rolled his eyes.

"Who's your friend from the country?" Sam asked Deanna.

Gabe laughed.

"Well, I was just wondering," Ginny said defending herself.

"Go on. I'll approach him when the coins stop falling. Now stay here," advised Sam.

Sam walked away and talked into his sleeve and pressed an earpiece covertly with his hand.

"We need a winner on slot number eighty-eight." Sam waited for confirmation. "Good. Make it four hundred dollars. Thanks." Sam ended the conversation with the casino control room.

Sam smiled. Anything to bring down the mayor was his pleasure. His bosses will be very happy when they find out that he helped in this if it materializes in bringing down Hank Jenkins. It's worth the risk, Sam calculated. The mayor was too good for this city. And now it sounds like his number was up on a possible murder, he chuckled. Pay that son of a bitch back for not taking any of their bribes to help them change the legislation and ease up on the red tape they had to go through to open this place up and end the continuous audits that got requested from City Hall on their financial records.

They now had all their eyes on Joe Dempsey, but Joe only had eyes for his slot machine. He barely noticed the people, noise and distractions that surrounded him as he grabbed that last special coin.

Right, left, right, count, pull.

Joe watched the three wheels turn.

Plop! Double dollar bills. A good start.

Plop! Double dollar bills. Two! Joe felt the blood rush to his hands. His eyes widened and he held his breath.

Plop! Double dollar bills. Whoo-wee!

Joe's eyes bulged out. He jumped up and knocked his chair away. He stared at the three slot machine windows again. Yes, it was three double dollar bills.

I won! I won!

Joe pushed his hands up into the air in triumph. The first coin hit with a high-pitched ting! Then blat, blat, blat, like a machine gun rattling.

The sixteen hundred coins were raging down the shoot into the cup and began to fall over onto the floor.

"Winner!" Joe shouted to the room. People turned and celebrated.

"Winner! Winner!" others began to shout. Sirens and bells began to sound off. Complete strangers were congratulating Joe and shaking his hand as he desperately tried to capture all the coins on the ground.

"It's my lucky routine, that's what it is," gloated Joe to the crowd.

As Joe was gathering the coins, Sam appeared, looming over him, and showed Joe his casino employee badge.

"Please follow me Mr. Dempsey. I can take you to a private room where we can change out your coins to dollars," stated Sam.

Sam helped Joe gather the remaining coins and grabbed him by the back of his arm and guided him through the buzzing room to a side door. Sam glanced back to Deanna, Gabe and Ginny to follow. Joe embraced two buckets of coins weighing twenty pounds close to his chest and giggled in excitement as Sam escorted him down a dark hallway.

"I knew my system would pay off. It was bound to happen. I just kept telling myself, Joe, keep believing, keep the faith. God gave you the inspiration for the system and let the system guide you," rambled Joe.

"Uh-huh," replied Sam. "Right this way. This is our exchange room." He opened an unmarked door and walked with Joe into the dark room.

"Hey, you said my last name. How's that?" asked Joe playfully.

In the darkness, Sam replied, "It's my job. You come in Friday and Saturday nights after your shift driving for the mayor. Varying times but usually you're in between midnight and one a.m. You have a circuit of three slot machines that you visit, each for one hour." Joe's smile began to fade.

"You have a certain process with your hands, a superstition, that you think helps you manipulate the machine. You have mostly broken even in the ten years you've been a patron of this establishment but we are probably in the lead by four thousand dollars. Not much, considering the free drinks and the entertainment which we provide but you generally ignore," clarified Sam with no expression in his voice or face.

Joe clutched his coins even closer to his chest. He got a tightening feeling in his stomach. He wanted to call out for his mother, call her on his cell phone, but his hands froze in fear.

"How did you know all of that?"

"All gamblers have habits and rituals. Yours was pretty easy to spot," said Sam.

At that moment Sam flicked on a light on a desk. It lit up half the room. It was filled with broken slot machines, furniture and old poker tables. Sam dragged a chair into the middle of the room.

"Sit," commanded Sam. Joe followed orders and sat down.

The door slammed shut and locked. Joe jumped in his seat and turned to the corner where he tried to make out the shadowy outlines of Deanna, Gabe and Ginny.

Deanna stepped forward in the light.

"What's going on here? Who are you?" whispered Joe as he tried to stand up.

Sam put his hand on Joe's shoulder and pushed him down. Coins flew and jangled on the floor. Joe tried to go reach for them but Sam held him back.

"My coins…are you going to exchange them?" asked Joe.

"No, Mr. Dempsey. I'm not. These people want to ask you some questions," replied Sam.

"What, what do you want?" asked Joe. "I didn't cheat. I didn't tilt the machine," claimed Joe.

Deanna unclenched her fists and walked up to Joe. He caught a glance of her green eyes that seemed familiar.

"Hey, you can't keep me here. I work for the mayor. Just one phone call and you all will be in jail," threatened Joe.

Deanna stepped closer.

"Call him. Call the mayor. That would be great. We got some questions for him, too," said Deanna.

"Who the hell are you?" asked Joe.

"I'm Wanda Doppkowski's daughter."

"Who the hell is that? I don't know no Doppkowski."

"It'd be hard to know her now. She's dead. Know how she died? Hit and run," said Deanna.

Joe stopped and focused. He stayed still and looked deep into Deanna's eyes. It was the same eyes. He squinted back to Sam, Gabe, and Ginny in the corner and then focused back on Deanna's eyes.

"What are you talking about? I don't know nothing about that," stated Joe.

"Gabe," said Deanna. She turned to Gabe and held out her hand. He threw Terry Cone's cell phone at her. She flicked it on and called up the pictures of the limousine and shoved it in front of Joe's face.

"What would you say about those dents in the mayor's limo?" she asked.

A bead of sweat began to form on the top of Joe's skull and began to trickle down his scalp.

"How did you get these? You're in big trouble trespassing. And probably without a warrant," rambled Joe.

Deanna raised her hand and hit Joe's two buckets of coins from the bottom. The buckets went flying into the air and hit the ground in a symphony of bouncing coins. Joe reached out trying to catch them. It was useless. He closed his eyes and listened to all the coins settle to the ground and let out a groan from deep within his chest.

Deanna leaned toward him, inches from his face. Close enough to breathe on him. He tried to turn away but she kept pushing her face into his.

"Did you kill my mother like a dog in the street?" she growled.

"I didn't kill your mother. It *was* a dog. It was a stray dog that wandered in the middle of where he shouldn't have been. I couldn't avoid it," explained Joe. Multiple sweat beads were now pouring down his forehead into his eyes causing him to squint.

Deanna waved the cell phone in the air.

"Are you calling my mother a dog?"

Deanna grabbed Joe's neck into a powerful hold. He started to gasp for air.

"This damage wasn't made by a dog," she said as she put the cell phone image an inch from his eyes. "These dents were made by my mother's body."

"Deanna," Gabe's voice warned her to calm down. Deanna let go of Joe's neck and walked off her anger.

Joe's looked up to her in bewilderment. Dog, it was a dog he pushed through his head. He remembered the hit. A yell. A thud. Yellow hair. He looked into Deanna's eyes.

Those eyes. Green eyes. Eyes of a woman. Joe's stomach tightened. The lies that he was telling himself shattered down to one thought. He was a murderer. But I couldn't have done that. I don't kill people. The mayor kills people. He looked into Deanna's eyes and began to plead with her.

"He told me to do it," Joe cried. "He said we were going to meet someone. I thought he was going to listen to some music. Then he saw her. She was crossing the street. He said she was bad, that she was hurting the city and him. He told me to hit her."

"Didn't you ever think of disobeying his order?" asked Deanna.

Joe thought about her answer. He tilted his head and thought harder. He searched every angle to that question and he came up empty. He looked at her with his clenched forehead.

"No."

Deanna walked off the answer like she was a fighter needing to rest in her corner of the ring. Calm, calm. Keep it cool. Walk, walk. This man killed Wanda. Walk it off. He mowed her down. Take a deep breath. Breathe. She felt Gabe's eyes watching her. She felt the strength he was sending her.

Walk it off Dopp. No—walk it off *Doppkowski*. Stay calm.

Deanna stopped in front of Joe and in slow motion she felt herself wheel her hand back and close her fist. Joe watched her turn toward him with a raised arm. He braced himself for the blow he deserved. Deanna's anger channeled to her shoulder, arm and fist. The force of her right arm began to descend.

Apparitions of Wanda, the limo, Joe, Hank and The Blue Monk swirled in Deanna's vision.

Her fist continued on the downward turn. Gabe saw Deanna go to a place that no good cop can go to...but a heartbroken daughter could. He jumped up to stop her. Deanna looked out of the corner of her eye and could see Joe tracking the targeted direction of her fist. She started to close her eyes and her point of impact became closer. *You can't do this*, rang in her head. Good cops don't beat up on their perps, if they do then they crossed the line they vowed they never would.

Ring, Ring Ring!

Gabe's cell phone sounded off. Gabe glanced at the number—it was Stanley calling.

In a fraction of a second Deanna decided to be a good cop and not just Wanda's daughter. She began the backward motion to stop her arm's forward momentum.

Gabe grabbed her arm and ignored answering Stanley's call. Deanna screamed as the contrary forces tore her rotator cuff so that it was hanging by a thread.

"Ah...my arm," Deanna screamed.

She crumbled into Gabe's arms as she cried from the pain. Joe crumpled into his chair and began to hit himself with his left hand when he saw his beating wouldn't come from Deanna.

"Stupid, stupid, stupid." Joe repeatedly hit himself until Sam stopped him by grabbing his bloody fist.

Ginny walked up to Joe and put her hand on his head. She held it there and he calmed himself under her grace. She began to cry and dropped her hand down to her side. Joe grabbed it and kissed it softly.

"I'm sorry. I'm sorry," he cried to Ginny.

"My shoulder. I can't lift my arm." Deanna said quietly, biting her lip.

Gabe felt her back, shoulder and right arm. "Nothing is broke or separated. Deanna, Stanley called my cell phone."

"Shit," said Deanna. "What would he want?"

"I told him to call me if he saw Billings and Stevens in the casino," said Gabe.

"We need to wrap this up," said Deanna. She turned back to Joe. "We have a witness."

"A witness?" Joe asked listlessly.

"My sister. She saw everything." Deanna waved her head toward Ginny.

Joe lowered his head in shame. Ginny cupped Joe's chin in her hand and raised it up.

"I know you aren't a smart man. But you were driving the vehicle and you did it. And you will serve. But we can arrange to make things easier if you tell the truth about the mayor," explained Ginny calm as a nun.

"He could make it bad. For my family. My mother," said Joe.

Deanna, holding her shoulder, cut in front of Ginny.

"You should be more afraid of how bad I will make it for your family. You can go down hard or you can go down *really* hard. You decide," she said staring into his eyes without blinking.

"The mayor was in the back seat, wasn't he?" asked Deanna.

Joe nodded unable to speak.

"Say it, say it," said Deanna beginning to lose her cool.

"Yes, he was. He ordered me to run her down," said Joe as tears came down his face.

Ginny walked back into a dark corner and tried to hold back her tears.

"Are there more bad things the mayor has done?" asked Joe soberly.

"Yes," said Deanna.

"I never thought he would make me a bad man, too," said Joe. "But he did."

Deanna looked over to the corner at Ginny. "Are you okay?"

"Yes. Now what?" asked Ginny.

"Can you hold on to him?" Gabe asked Sam.

Sam looked down to the rolled up mess that Joe had become.

"How long?" asked Sam.

"Twelve hours," responded Gabe.

"No. That's not good. If you guys don't deliver I'm not going to get hung up on kidnapping charges. You've got four hours."

"No way," said Gabe shaking his head.

"Four it is," said Deanna.

"We got a deal. He'll be in room 1724. It seems Mr. Dempsey was comp'd a room after his big win and spent the next two hours doing drugs and passed out," said Sam with a shrug.

"I don't do drugs," replied Joe.

"Not willingly," replied Sam deadpan. Joe grimaced.

"Let's get out of here," said Gabe. He shook Sam's hand. "Thanks and say thanks to Guido."

"Don't mention it," said Sam and then he looked at Deanna. "Get the son of a bitch."

Deanna affirmed his order with a nod, not exactly sure she liked being urged on by a thug from a casino, even if he was helping them.

"Ginny, come on," said Deanna as she grabbed her half-sister's hand and led her out the door.

Gabe called Stanley's number back.

"Stanley's not answering," said Gabe.

Deanna spun Ginny around.

"Ginny, those two cops are back. Stay between Gabe and me, okay?"

"Got it," said Ginny.

Out in the hallway they headed for the sound of the casino beyond the double doors. Deanna and Gabe took out their guns and concealed them down by their legs.

Deanna opened the door to the casino where the lights, buzzing and laughter hit them like a brick wall they had to blast through. Both she and Gabe were scanning the room for Billings and Stevens.

They reached the outside doors. Gabe had Ginny by the arm and Deanna took the point. Gabe's grip hurt Ginny but she was grateful for his protection. She was in over her head but she tried her best not to let on to it by biting her lip until it was bleeding.

Gabe looked toward the side of the building where they last saw Stanley smoking. He spotted the backs of Billings and Stevens huddled over some nearby bushes.

"Deanna, take Ginny to the car," whispered Gabe. He pointed to Billings and Stevens and threw Deanna the car keys. Gabe squatted down and ran quietly up to the two policemen.

"Hold it, don't move," yelled Gabe pointing his gun at Billings and Stevens. They both had their guns in their holsters.

"What are you up to tonight, boys?" asked Gabe.

The men nervously tried to move in front of the bushes.

"Nothing Gabe. Just going to try out those black jack tables. Want to join us?" asked Stevens.

"Get that gun out of my face, Gabe," said Billings.

"What are you hiding behind the bushes?" Gabe peered over and saw Stanley with a twisted neck. He was dead. His cigarette box sat near his broken neck.

"You son of bitches. I should blow you away right now," hissed Gabe.

"We found him this way Gabe. We were about to call it in," said Stevens.

Billings remained quiet, staring at Gabe's gun in his face.

"Just like you called in Wanda's case?" asked Gabe. "Give me your car keys."

Stevens handed them over to Gabe.

"God help you both," said Gabe as he slowly backed away to his car that Deanna had driven toward him.

"Get in," yelled Deanna to Gabe.

"What do we do now Sergeant?" asked Stevens.

"Call Kavanaugh," said Billings as he grabbed one of Stanley's cigarettes and lit it.

Gabe wiped his face and reached between Deanna's legs below her car seat to grab his rum bottle. He took a deep drink.

"Stanley?" asked Deanna.

Gabe shook his head back and forth. Deanna knew what he meant. The wind was knocked out of her. Gabe grabbed the wheel. She shook herself out of it and refocused on the road.

"It's my fault, Deanna," said Gabe tightening his grip on the bottle.

Ginny curled up in the backseat. That nice man she just met was dead she deduced. Her cousin. Gone, just like Wanda.

"We got to keep going, just keep going," said Deanna as she tried to get her head out of the fog.

"Where to now?" asked Ginny quietly.

"We need to pick up our other witness," said Deanna hearing Stanley's music in her head. How was she going to tell Aunt Helen and Uncle Roman their son is dead? She was losing focus. Stop. Concentrate. Her remaining family will be wiped out if she doesn't capture the mayor, she thought. Get back in your head. She gripped the wheel tighter.

"Who would that be?" asked Ginny.

"Evelyn Lee," said Gabe.

CHAPTER 11 – A GRAVE DISCOVERY

Hank Jenkins led Max Schwartz to his library at the mansion. After the run-in with Deanna and Gabe at the morgue, Max thought it wise to go directly back to the Manoogian Mansion to inform the mayor in person and to see what fortuitous items could come his way with his knowledge of the death certificate of Wanda Doppkowski's son.

Max's alcoholic buzz had died down and he now harbored a headache. There also was the added annoyance of his need to fidget with the belt buckle that was pinching his stomach due to a newly added twelve pounds. He tried to get comfortable on the plush black leather sofa, which was impossible.

"What was she looking for?" asked Hank, who handed Max a drink and starting pacing the perimeter of the room. "She's already viewed the body."

"Yes, I know," answered Max as he tried to discreetly adjust his belt notch looser with one hand while balancing his drink in the other. He decided to drink a little more of the hair of the dog. He wiped his mouth with the back of his hand.

"Who's her contact in your department?"

"Jerry Swift, Assistant Medical Examiner," said Max sheepishly.

"I told you to fire him this morning," seethed Hank.

"That is why I went there tonight. I had no one to cover the night shift. I didn't know they would come back."

"You incompetent moron. He must know something,"

"I don't know if he does, but I do," said Max regaining his lost ground.

"Well, tell me damn it," said Hank.

"While I was reviewing Wanda's morgue report, I noticed there was another Doppkowski name in our deceased log."

"Yeah, so? Those Polacks were breeding like crazy when they first got here. Probably one of her cousins, uncles, whatever."

Max shook his head and got up from the couch. He was in the driver's seat now.

"No, no. This wasn't a cousin or uncle. The deceased was a baby. Born in 1974. Four months old…a boy."

Hank stopped twirling the ice in his glass.

"And," said Hank.

"The mother's name listed on the death certificate is Wanda Doppkowski."

Hank put down his drink quietly and squared off against Max whose back was toward him.

"And," Hank said again baiting him along.

"Do you want to know who was named as the father?"

Max turned around and saw that he was in the direct path of a 10-Performance gun by Hilton Yam of Florida, a birthday gift that the Detroit Chief of Police gave the mayor two years ago after a junket trip to Miami.

Max gasped.

He was in deep but he didn't know how deep until he saw the steel.

"Not particularly, Max. But now that you have my full attention. Who?" Hank said coolly.

"No one. It was blank." Max gulped.

Hank acknowledged when he pulled out the gun that there was no going back. Max had always been a squirrelly bastard. Helpful when Hank needed something, but he kept the screws tight on Max for fear of the situation that had resulted right now. Max was trying to turn the tables on the mayor.

Shit. He should have waited until he had heard Max's answer. If that really was the truth and his name wasn't on the death certificate he could have brushed off Max's accusation that he was the father.

"What have you made up in that clever Jewish head of yours Max?" spit out Hank.

"I…I didn't think anything. Just that it was coincidental," backtracked Max.

Hank held the gun steadily pointed at Max. "That's it?" asked Hank.

"Yeah, I wasn't insinuating anything," said Max.

"Really? You weren't thinking of blackmailing me? To keep a secret…secret. What were you going to ask for, Max? Fifty thousand, a hundred thousand? And would that be a one time payment or yearly?" Hank circled the sofa and now was in front of Max.

"To commit a crime and go all the way you need balls, Max. And you don't have them," said Hank with a laugh. "What evidence did you think you had?"

"None, just a hunch," Max managed to get out as his mouth dried up.

"That is why our Medical Examiner's Office is the worst in the nation. Right! No evidence." Hank began to pace the room again. "But even you, not the brightest bulb in the city, found something."

"No, no. I deleted the file. I only have a hardcopy print. Here, here it is," said Max as he hastily dove his hands in his pocket and retrieved the folded piece of paper that contained the baby's death certificate. Hank took the paper and started to read it.

"So it *is* true?" asked Max.

Hank looked at Max hard and didn't answer.

Max wiped his forehead with his drink napkin that tore on his forehead.

"Does anyone else know about this?" asked Hank.

"We just got a new computer system. Jerry was typing in all the old hard copies into the system. He might have seen…"

"Of course he saw it. That was what Detective Dopp was after, you goddamn idiot," interrupted Hank.

Max put his drink down on the bar.

"I should be going," said Max as he tried to leave the room.

Hank clenched his gun and ran over to Max, grabbed him by his shirt and dragged him out to the hallway to a side door.

"Where are we going?" asked Max between gasps of air.

Hank had Max running on the lawn heading toward the garage.

"The death certificate doesn't state a delivery to a funeral home. It states a plot number here," said Hank.

"A pauper's funeral. The family or mother couldn't afford one," said Max.

"It doesn't have a cemetery name. Do you know where this is?" asked Hank as he shoved the paper in Max's face.

"The plot number starts with GC. That stands for Gethsemane Cemetery, on the east side. Gratiot and Outer Drive," Max said quietly. "That's where we send those poor souls."

"Right by the city airport," replied Hank.

Hank threw Max to the ground as they arrived at the garage. He unlocked the door and walked into the garage with Max crawling behind him. Max looked at the limousine and the apparent damage to the front grille and grimaced. His brain began to make the connections between the broken parts of Wanda's body and the dents in the limousine.

A pungent smell hit Max. He recognized the smell from years in the medical examiner's business. Dead body. Going on five to six hours, he thought. The smell was strong due to the stifling heat of the garage and being inside the limousine which doubled the impact of the odor. It was the mayor that hadn't become accustomed to the smell and when it finally hit Hank's nostrils and flew down to his stomach he bent over in a massive dry heave.

Hank composed himself, grabbed two shovels and a pick from the corner of the garage and opened the door to the limo. He threw the tools onto the body of his friend Terry Cone. Hank grabbed a pair of car keys hanging over a bench and threw them at Max.

"You're driving."

"Where to?" asked Max.

"The cemetery, of course. Come on, Max. Keep up with me," said Hank.

"You want to exhume the baby's body?"

"Ding, ding, ding. You win the prize behind door number two. Well done," said Hank as he pointed the gun at Max.

"Now start the limo," Hank growled.

Max nervously put the key into the ignition and started the engine.

"Keep the lights off," ordered Hank.

The limousine slowly pulled out of the garage. It steadily approached the gates. Two security guards standing with their dogs looked confused. Hank jumped out of the car and slapped his hands and rubbed them together like it was chilly in the eighty-five degree weather. The guards approached the mayor.

"Hello, boys. Just taking the limo out for a little spin with an old friend," explained Hank.

The two security guards, James and Kevin, checked out Max in the front seat.

"No Joe tonight?" asked James.

"Nope, he's off," said Hank ad he slapped Kevin on the back.

"Now, don't tell on me, hear?" Hank winked and started laughing. The guards started laughing thinking the mayor had a private party to attend perhaps with some young ladies.

"Yes, sir, have a good night," replied Kevin. "Don't forget to turn on your lights, sir."

"Yes, will do," said Hank as he smiled, walked back to the limo and got in. He waved to the guards as Max drove past them and pulled out onto the street. When the limousine was a block the headlights turned on.

"Where does this Jerry live?" asked Hank.

"I already went to his house earlier. He's not there. And he isn't answering his cell phone," lied Max. He wasn't going to let this lunatic kill one more innocent person.

"Okay, I'll deal with him later. Get us to the cemetery."

The limousine sped away under the city lights.

Deanna slammed the passenger door of the car with her good arm as she, Gabe and Ginny arrived at the Davenport Apartments at 3:45am. Gabe stared down each side of the street. Just the occasional drunk and hooker walking the streets were out and about in the neighborhood. Ginny's foot hit a hidden beer bottle right before the curb that sent her crashing down to the pavement.

"Ahh," she let out a grunt. Her hands slammed down in pain. She jerked her right hand up in lightening speed. A hypodermic needle wavered as it stuck into the palm of her hand. Deanna winced when she saw the needle in the lamppost light.

"Fuck. A needle," said Gabe. He steadied Ginny's hand. Her eyes began to swell.

"Is this real bad?" asked Ginny.

Gabe pulled the needle out quickly and put a handkerchief he had in his pocket around her hand. Gabe didn't answer her question. He looked up to Deanna. She took the needle and examined it.

"If the needle was on the ground a few days then any HIV virus wouldn't still be on it. But we just don't know. We can take you right now to a hospital. There's one just a few blocks away," said Deanna.

"No," said Ginny as she got to her feet. "We got to finish this. I can get checked out later. A few hours isn't going to change anything now." Ginny took her hand away from Gabe.

"Brave girl," said Gabe.

"Possibly stupid," said Deanna.

"You wouldn't do the same?" asked Ginny to Deanna. "This town can't get rid of me that easily."

Deanna looked over her half-sister. At that moment she felt the missed opportunity of not having a sister to grow up with in her life. She saw her own toughness in Ginny and admired it.

She wanted to experience Ginny as ten-year olds running down the alleys, telling each other secrets, laughing together as they walked to the neighborhood store, and watching thunderstorms from their bedroom window together. As sisters, they would have the common bond of their mother but would never talk about it. They would have understood each other and shared the same history. Deanna's imagined memories snapped back to the street as Gabe pushed Evelyn Lee's door buzzer.

Bzzz. Bzzz.

They waited a few seconds for a response.

"Yes?" Evelyn responded fraily. Deanna walked up to the speaker.

"Evelyn, this is Deanna Doppkowski, remember? We're back. Me and my partner. We need to come up and talk with you."

"At this time in the morning?" asked Evelyn.

"It's urgent. Evelyn, we need to know where the grave is…the baby's grave," said Deanna as she laid her head by the speaker.

Silence.

"Come up."

Bzzz.

They grabbed the door and ran up the stairs.

Evelyn's apartment door was unlocked when they reached it. Deanna knocked out of courtesy and opened the door. Evelyn sat in her easy chair sipping a cup of coffee she had just microwaved in the sweltering heat of her apartment.

Deanna came in first and sat down on the sofa. Gabe entered, went to the window and turned off a light so he could keep an eye on the street. Ginny shyly looked around the apartment as if she was reacquainting herself with it.

Evelyn eyed Ginny. She motioned for Ginny to sit, which she did quietly. The old lady looked Ginny over and stopped at her eyes. Evelyn grabbed the crucifix that hung around her neck.

"Oh, sweet Jesus. You've come back," whispered Evelyn.

Ginny broke her eyes away from Evelyn who was overrun with emotion. Deanna began to speak to break the silence.

"Evelyn, this is…"

"Virginia," answered Evelyn.

"Yes…Ginny," replied Deanna. "She came up from Nashville to meet Wanda. She witnessed the hit and run."

"That ain't right. That ain't right at all. I'm so sorry, Virginia," said Evelyn as she shook her head.

"Evelyn, we have a grave number but don't know which cemetery the baby was buried in," said Deanna as she took out the old morgue file.

"You want to find your brother's grave, child?" asked Evelyn to Ginny.

"Yes, Ma'am," answered Ginny. Evelyn smiled, nodded her head and rose from her seat.

"I'll get my sweater," said Evelyn as she shuffled to her closet.

"Evelyn, it's hot outside," said Gabe.

"When you have the circulation of an eighty-year old then you can give me weather advice, handsome," replied Evelyn.

Deanna laughed heartily as Evelyn turned to her.

"Does the mayor know about her?"

"Yes, I believe so," replied Deanna.

"Do you know where *he* is?"

"We believe his mansion," replied Deanna.

"Hot nights. Men can't sleep in this. Especially a man with murder on his mind," said Evelyn.

"We've got only a few hours. Thank you, Evelyn. For helping," said Deanna.

"Time for justice to be done. It's a long time coming," Evelyn said as she slowly shuffled out of her apartment and grabbed Ginny's offered hand to guide her.

"You know how to get to the city airport, boy?" asked Evelyn to Gabe.

"Yes, Ms. Lee," replied Gabe.

"He's buried at the airport?" asked Ginny.

"No, Gethsemane Cemetery. In the shadows of the airport," replied Evelyn.

"Lock the door, handsome," Evelyn called out to Gabe behind her.

"Looks like someone is flirting with you," Deanna said to Gabe.

"I have to fight them off I tell you," he replied.

Gabe grabbed Deanna and kissed her hard.

"Are you okay?" he asked.

"We're almost there," she replied.

"That's what worries me," Gabe replied.

"The boy's body is the last piece to the puzzle we need," she said.

"I hope so," said Gabe.

Deanna walked out into the hallway. Gabe took one last look around the apartment and locked the door as he left.

The Detroit City airport on the east side was named the Coleman Young Airport in 1997. Plans to expand the small airport and displace the graves at Gethsemane Cemetery caused the public to mobilize and shut down those intended plans. People pay more attention to their relatives dead than alive. Detroit cemeteries are packed during the day with people paying respects of solemn prayers to their relatives, but after dusk they leave the premises before they are mugged or carjacked.

The limousine pulled up to the cemetery's wrought iron gate. Hank opened the backseat door and started taking out the tools. He got a whiff of Terry's decaying body and leaned over to throw up. Max got out of the driver's side door and began to back away as he saw Hank distracted. Max walked three steps backward.

"One more step and I will bury you in this cemetery," growled Hank as he cocked the gun toward Max.

"Easy, Mayor," said Max with his hands up.

"Come here and grab these tools," snapped Hank.

Max picked up the shovel and pick from the ground, nervously dropping them as they walked up to the gate. Hank took the tools and threw them up over the cement wall.

"Jump," said Hank as he pointed the gun at Max.

Max backed up and did his best to give himself a running start. He fell short of reaching the top of the wall and was hanging by his fingertips like a rat about to fall overboard.

"You fat piece of shit. Ever think about jogging?" said Hank as he pushed Max's butt from underneath.

Hank then stepped back and was over the wall in two quick steps and a leap. They landed both on the ground on the inside of the cemetery and surveyed the area. It was quiet as it should be. Two lampposts lit up the path fifty feet away. There was a sign ahead. Hank spurred Max on with the gun.

"Which way?" asked Hank.

"Plot GC456J is this way," said Max as he read the death certificate and looked over to a sign on the lawn.

"Fine," replied Hank.

They trudged over gravestones without giving a thought to the inhabitants below. The roar of a jet taking off overhead made them hit the ground. They covered their ears and the jet engines rattled their bodies. The airplane lights veered off to the west.

"Come on," Hank said impatiently.

Over a few small hills and down from an old maple tree they came upon a barren place with plain white cement blocks standing like soldiers. Numbers were engraved on the top of the blocks. Number 456J sat alone on the end of a row. The grass hadn't been mowed in this section for weeks and no flowers adorned this area of paupers' row. Max dropped the tools.

"This is it," said Max as he wiped the sweat off his forehead. His shirt was soaked through and was chaffing his stomach. He rubbed it to relieve the irritated feeling.

Hank looked down on the single marker that lay above his son. He stared at it for a few moments.

Bang! Bang! Bang!

Hank heard the sounds his fist made pounding Wanda's door over thirty-five years ago at the Davenport Apartments. After a brief glimpse, his memory went black. He couldn't remember anything anymore about that ugly evening. Maybe he didn't kill the baby. He looked at his hands. He remembers washing them over and over in his mother's sink that night. He did do it.

If only he hadn't met Wanda that night on the dance floor. Damn her. And damn The Blue Monk. He made a mental note to shut the place down and take care of the manager Julius. It's time for Julius to move on in life. He could suggest that Julius leave the Detroit area. It's getting so violent. Yes, Hank pondered, he could make a few strong suggestions to Julius.

"Dig," said Hank.

He threw a shovel at Max who grimaced, knowing the small body they were about to uncover wasn't going to be a pretty sight. They both began to dig. The grass was tough to get through and the ground was made up of soft clay. Max pulled back exhausted after ten minutes of shoveling.

"What are you going to do with the body?" asked Max, panting.

"You're quite nosy, aren't you Max? Nosey Max, nosey Schwartz. Is that how you got to be in the top three percent of your pathology program? Your inquisitive nature? The nosy Jew from Detroit? Was that your nickname? Is that your claim to fame?"

The anger in Max boiled from his stomach to his brain. Max had heard prejudiced remarks under people's breath before, but there had not been any thrown directly in his face this bluntly since grade school. But he was always on a heightened awareness for it and was prepared as a pit bull to defend himself at any moment on his race and religion. A man could annihilate his character, his business acumen, his pathology skills, parenting and husbandry skills—but he drew the line on his heritage.

Max took his shovel and leveled it in his two hands. Hank raised the gun to defend himself.

"What did you call me?" asked Max.

"You heard me. A *nos-ey* Jew," said Hank slowly articulating every syllable.

"Mayor, if you are going to kill me anyway, then I might as well take my best shot at you right now. Don't ever talk to me that way," seethed Max.

Hank started to laugh. "Christ, Max. You're so sensitive. You know how many times I was called a nigger growing up? Shit, I thought that was my first name until I was ten. Oh, if it makes you feel better, then call me nigger. Go ahead say it,"

"I don't want to."

"Sure you do. It will feel good. N-i-g-g-e-r. Go ahead, you nosey Jew," said Hank, egging Max on.

Max's anger reached its peak as he calculated that his shovel was out of range to be able to hit Hank. The shovel shook in his hands.

"Nigger," Max said quietly. "Nigger, nigger, damn nigger!" yelled Max with spit flying out of his mouth.

Hank stopped laughing.

"Feel better?" asked Hank, who was quietly pleased with himself.

"No," said Max, shaking his head and wiping his face down. "No, damn you. I'm disgusted with myself. I feel sick to my stomach."

"That's too bad. I thought it would make you feel better." Hank paused and then asked, "Max, why in the hell did you end up in a hole like Detroit?" asked Hank.

"I was born here," answered Max.

"It's not a prison sentence. People are allowed to leave."

"I guess...I never wanted to."

"It's because you learned how this city worked and you could work well within it. Me, too. I never wanted to leave. Ever. But lately I feel I would like to push on."

"You didn't answer my question. About the body," said Max.

"The river," Hank answered as he referenced the Detroit River that ran right downtown and separated Detroit from Windsor, Canada.

"And the body in the limo?" asked Max.

"Same place," said Hank.

Max waited a few seconds to ask his third question.

"And me?" asked Max.

Gabe turned off the headlights of his car and cruised the last two blocks in the dark. He slowed down and pulled to the side of Gethsemane Cemetery. Deanna and Evelyn sat in the front seat of the car. Both looked over and spotted the limousine.

"The mayor's limo," said Deanna.

"He came back for his boy," said Evelyn.

Gabe stopped the car. They all sat in silence.

"So who is going to help us? Are there any cops that aren't corrupt that can help us?" asked Ginny.

"There's plenty that aren't. We just have to have all the evidence locked tight. Or no one will touch this, not the DA or the media. They aren't going to hang themselves and their careers on evidence that can be explained away or doesn't directly point to the mayor," said Gabe.

"So what hope do we have?" said Ginny.

"His confession once we subdue him in the act. Get the baby's DNA. Then you can call in the television stations or Canadian Mounties if you want," said Deanna.

"This man has evil in him. The devil but it's way down deep. Hidden from most. That is the worst kind," said Evelyn. "I've seen him do good things for this city. But that doesn't change the past. I prayed many years that he would be caught and brought to justice. Now, I'm done praying."

"So are we just going to try a sneak attack?" asked Ginny.

Deanna laughed. "I guess we are. We go in. Catch him in the act. That's all I got," said Deanna.

"That's enough," said Gabe as he got out of the car as the others followed.

Silently, they closed the car doors and walked up to the gate. Gabe took out a lock pick, leaned over and POP! The gate opened. He pushed it open only a few feet, enough for all to pass through. Deanna was the last one in and her hurt shoulder hit the gate hard. She muffled a scream. The gate slammed shut. It locked. They were now locked in the cemetery.

"We'll worry about that later," said Gabe as he put a hand on Deanna's back to guide her. Deanna took a deep breath.

"Which way, Evelyn?" Deanna asked trying to forget the pain in her shoulder.

Evelyn looked around the dimly lit cemetery. She searched her mind for the memory of visiting the boy's grave with her husband and Wanda over thirty-five years ago. She closed her eyes. She visualized her feet going up two hills, heavy breathing, two trees intertwined like lovers. Evelyn opened her eyes and looked into the distance. She saw the trees that were tangled and now bent over like an old couple.

"This way, over these hills," said Evelyn as she began walking.

Gabe and Deanna took out their guns. Ginny went up to Evelyn and grabbed her arm to assist her. Gabe and Deanna ran ahead of the two, each separating once they reached the top of the hill. Gravestones below the cemetery lights cast long shadows over the lawn.

A jet roared overhead breaking up the calmness. Deanna was first up the hill. She squatted down on one knee. Gabe was fifty feet across from her also looking down the hill.

Evelyn, breathing heavy, and being assisted by Ginny, came up to Deanna. All their eyes focused on two figures digging at a grave. They could hear the clattering of shovels and one of the men grunting every time he pitched a load of dirt.

"Over there, to the left," pointed Evelyn. "That's it. By the stone wall. They're digging up that poor boy's body."

"Both of you stay here. Gabe and I will go down," said Deanna.

Gabe watched Deanna from his post. She pointed to herself and him and then pointed down to the two men. Gabe gave her the thumbs up sign.

"Deanna, give me your phone. Just in case," said Ginny.

Deanna agreed, remembering that Ginny's cell phone was dead back at Gabe's house. She handed over her cell phone.

"Only call the police and media when we subdue him or if it is absolutely necessary. Do you know when that would be?" said Deanna.

"If shots are fired," answered Ginny.

"No, after shots are fired, only if Gabe and I are shot," answered Deanna.

Deanna wasn't going to take a chance with calling the police and having them foul up the plan if there were only shots fired. Even if the mayor was on the run that would be better than the possibility of the police locking down their operation. Sweeping it under a rug would be tougher with a shot witness or a dead body. Or so Deanna thought just a week ago.

"Jesus, you do think you are Starsky and Hutch," said Ginny.

"Which one am I again?" asked Deanna. Ginny looked up to her like she was crazy and saw that it was her sister's twisted cop sense of humor on display to keep all situations under emotional control.

"Starsky. Hutch always drove," said Ginny, trying to beat Deanna at her own game.

Deanna winked at her sister as she and Gabe descended the hill paralleling each other. They crouched down and took advantage of every large headstone to hide behind.

Hank was overlooking Max in the grave and stopped when he thought he heard footsteps. Max dumped a load of dirt out of the hole.

"What? What's wrong?" asked Max, who was frightened to death that Hank was going to hit him over his head with a shovel at the moment they unearthed the child's casket. He tried the best he could to keep an eye on the mayor but as he dug deeper it became harder.

"Shhh…quiet," whispered Hank.

Hank spun around and looked out toward Deanna's direction. Max brought down his shovel. Thump! The shovel hit the wood casket and splintered it. Max tried to release the shovel from the wood casket. It was stuck. He wrestled the shovel off and ran his fingers around the dirt trying to find the edge of the small casket made for infants.

"I can't lift it," said Max.

"Get out of there. I'll do it," whispered Hank as he lifted Max out of the grave. Then he jumped in, bent down and on the count of three he heaved the small box onto the grass. Max let out a heavy sigh as Hank jumped out of the grave.

"Lord have mercy on us," said Max.

Hanks wrestled open the casket cover and tossed it aside. He stepped back to let the moon glow light up the contents of the casket. His eyes looked over the baby blue silk lining that was draped tenderly around the remains. The silk wrap covered the body entirely as if it was wrapped as a present.

Hank reached out and touched the small body and his fingers felt a firm hardness that surprised him. With erroneous reasoning he was expecting a soft return on the body part. But the touch to his finger was hard and stiff and he pulled his hand away. He wanted to see the baby's face. His better judgment told him no. Take the baby, go to the river and dump every body, and that included Max's, into the river.

But the younger Hank, the eager, young lawyer, the one that was Wanda's lover and his mother's eldest son, yearned to see the baby's face. As if it was a newborn and only sleeping. Peaceful and in the hands of God.

That naïve young Hank began to peel back the satin cover. Max saw what Hank was doing and before he could shout out not to do it - Hank had revealed the shrunken head of a black baby that had deteriorated with bacteria decay. Fright flew through Hanks fingers and face. He recoiled at the sight and dropped the dead baby back into its box.

"Hell. What the hell?" reeled Hank.

Max wiped his face of sweat and dirt. "I meant to stop you," he said, "For pauper graves back then, they didn't embalm, the day after they would bury the dead. He has eroded just like anyone would in the ground against the elements."

"I shouldn't have looked," confessed Hank. "It's just a body."

"Your son's body," said Max quietly.

Hank backhanded Max across the face causing them both to tumble on their backs.

Gabe crossed over to the tree closest to Hank and hid behind it. Hank heard Gabe's steps and swirled back onto his feet with his gun out. He scoured the hill with his eyes and then stared at the tree. He began to walk in Gabe's direction. Deanna saw that Hank was headed straight for Gabe.

"Mayor Jenkins," Deanna said as calm as she could but her words came out warbled and uncertain.

Hank spun around facing Deanna and swung the gun in her direction.

"Who's there?" he yelled.

Deanna pointed her gun at Hank. Gabe revealed himself from behind the tree with his gun also pointed at the mayor. They had him pinned down. But with Hank's gun not secured it wasn't controlled yet. Deanna switched her thought to Ginny, *keep your fingers off that cell phone, Ginny. Don't call the police...yet.*

Deanna walked into the light from the lamppost.

"You're her daughter," said Hank remembering Deanna's face from a picture that he had seen from her police file. The one Hank would make an example of, regardless of Commander Kavanaugh's protests.

This was the first time Hank saw Deanna up front and in-person. He looked at her eyes and even in the dimly lit cemetery he could tell they were Wanda's. Deanna's chest tightened. She looked at Hank's fifty-eight year old face and tried to imagine a younger man, a man less evil. A man that her mother loved. She couldn't imagine it and she didn't want to try. She shook her head to shake it out of her mind.

"Detective Deanna Dopp...Doppkowski," she answered.

"You're not a police officer anymore," Hank said covering the fear that crept into his body. He had to keep his cool. He could close all of this down by dawn. It was still possible.

"Yeah, thanks for the early retirement. I got my lawyer working on it," she replied while looking over Max's condition.

"Hello there, Max. Moonlighting? I thought there was a rule about that?"

"Deanna," yelled Max as he ran wildly toward her. "He's crazy. He made me do it," Max screamed.

Hank grabbed Max's collar as he ran by him and hit him once with the gun. Max was out cold. Hank pointed the gun back and forth between Gabe, who had gotten closer, and Deanna.

"Okay, easy Mayor," she said. "This is out of control and you know it. Now drop the gun."

Hank gripped his gun tighter and flashed it back and forth between the Deanna and Gabe.

From the top of the hill, Ginny and Evelyn saw the current situation.

"My God," said Ginny.

"Let's go down there," said Evelyn. "He can't shoot us all down."

Ginny took Evelyn's elbow and headed down the hill slowly against her better judgment. Everything in this town was turned on its head. Ginny didn't know when to act or react, when to stand up or sit down. If asked to take action then she was going to listen and follow orders. She didn't know what else to do if she couldn't be guided by her own senses.

Gabe was within six feet of Hank. Hank pointed the gun straight at him.

"Now, don't be a hero to show off to your girlfriend, Detective Flynn," said Hank.

Gabe stopped. He thought he could always kick out the mayor's feet and grab the gun while he fell. This was his favorite move to un-arm perps. Deanna enabled Gabe to do this stunt dozens of times. She was the only person at risk in this particular move.

The perp would still have two seconds to aim in Deanna's direction while they were falling to the ground. Gabe had taught her to dive left as the perp would fall back to her right. The trajectory of a possible gunshot would have a lesser chance of hitting her in the torso. If at all, she could get shot below the knee. They never had a problem with the move. It made them feel like martial artists in a cheap karate film as time transferred into slow motion when they were in these situations.

"We saw the limo, Hank. We have photos. We saw what you did to Terry," said Deanna trying to divert attention back to her and away from Gabe. But Hank kept his eyes on Gabe.

"All we have to do is make one phone call to the police," added Deanna.

Hank smiled and turned to her. That was the wrong line to feed him. And her attempt to stack the deck against him only made the rage that he had buried deep come bubbling to the surface.

"What you think you have isn't much. I didn't kill your mother. My driver did. He also killed Terry Cone. He's a sociopath. I never knew. He threatened my life if I went to the police. Oh, and they will be on my side. I just pumped sixteen million into their budget. And this little episode, it seems that our city has had a rash of grave robberies and pagan rituals sprouting up. Take your pick," explained Hank as he wiped the back of his neck with a handkerchief.

"Mayor, I'm taking you in. Now put down your weapon and get on the ground," said Deanna.

Hank's options swirled in his head. He couldn't decide which one to shoot first. Deanna or Gabe. He was favoring Gabe.

Crack!

Hank's gun went off. Gabe's chest ripped open, blood ran out of a pure circular hole, his eyes grew wide. He was shot. This isn't how it's supposed to go, Gabe's brain yelled out to his body. The move, they haven't done the move.

Gabe fell to one knee. Deanna screamed and leaned toward him when Hank pistol-whipped her face. Her cheek snapped back in pain as she tried to keep her eye on Gabe and not pass out. Gabe's second knee hit the ground. He was staring at the blood in his hand in disbelief.

Hank yanked the mumbling Max off the ground, grabbed the baby's body wrapped in its blanket and pushed forward up the hill.

"Get up, get up and go!" yelled Hank.

Hank and Max were now running up the hill as Evelyn and Ginny were running down. Max ran straight into Evelyn. They crashed hard. Air pushed out of Evelyn's lung as she was knocked out cold. Max spun around and was caught by Hank.

Ginny screamed as Hank stared straight into her eyes. They froze—locked in a time suspension, searching each other's faces. Internal waves of emotions ran through them.

Hank gazed into her eyes and recognized the green hue. He saw the mix of white and black in her light skin. At first his eyes softened and then he thought of all the trouble she, his daughter, and Wanda had produced for him. His eyes turned cold. Ginny pulled back and leaned down over Evelyn trying to protect her.

Hank dropped Max and yanked Ginny up to her feet.

"Come with me," he growled.

"No, no, I won't," she cried. "Deanna!"

Deanna's eyes focused on a fuzzy lamppost. She concentrated on it and the shape became defined. She turned behind and saw Hank grabbing Ginny's arm. Her gun.

Where is her gun? She felt around her body and came upon the warm steel. She raised it. It felt as if it was fifty pounds. She steadied her hand, closed her left eye and focused on Hank's body.

BAM!

Deanna's gun shot out. The bullet nicked Hank's ear. He ducked down and turned his head. The rage now boiled up inside him. Damn, he didn't take the bitch's gun.

Ginny broke loose and dragged Evelyn behind a gravestone. Hank saw that Deanna was steadying her arm with the gun to take another shot. He grabbed Max and shoved the crying medical examiner between him and Deanna. He was using Max as a human shield.

"Wait, what are you doing? No!" protested Max as a literal bodyguard to the mayor.

"Run, run, you idiot," growled Hank. Deanna held off her shot for fear of hitting Max as he and Hank disappeared over the hill.

"Gabe," whispered Deanna as she turned over and crawled towards him. Gabe fell onto his back.

Gabe's eyes were looking up to the night sky and blinking at lighting speed. He pushed both of his hands down on his chest trying to stop the blood flowing out of his body. Blood trickled out of his mouth. Deanna put her hands on top of his to stop the flow.

"Gabe, no," cried Deanna. Tears rolled down her cheek. She looked into his eyes and saw his bewilderment. The thought of Gabe dying this way, tonight, was never a thought that had crossed her mind or his. Deanna dug deep for strength.

"Ginny. Call 9-1-1," instructed Deanna. "Tell them there's a ten-thirteen—officer down." Ginny's trembling hand fumbled with the keys on the phone as she called the police.

"Gabe, calm your breathing. I want you to look into my eyes," said Deanna.

"Careful. The mayor is a mad dog. He has no fear," said Gabe. A stabbing pain ripped through his body. He groaned and rocked on the ground.

"Gabe, please. I need you," said Deanna.

Gabe laughed roughly. "Deanna, I wish that was true. I love you," he said softly.

"Please no, Gabe. No…it's true," she said crying.

"Tough girl, my tough little city girl..." Gabe smiled and reached up to touch Deanna's face. "I don't think he's worth it. Get out of town. Take Ginny back home," said Gabe.

"No, I won't let him get away with this. God knows where he is now," said Deanna.

"Remember, when they shot that newscast with him on the waterfront? Where he keeps his yacht?" he said softly.

"Tri-Centennial Park Harbor" said Deanna remembering back to a news story her and Gabe watched at a tavern over a year ago.

"That's where he is. He's familiar with that dock. He's going to dump the bodies into the river. If you want him, you need to go, now," wheezed Gabe.

"I'm not leaving you, an ambulance is on its way."

"Too late," Gabe took Deanna's hands away from his chest. "Go, now. Damnit, Deanna, go, or he'll win."

Deanna looked into Gabe's eyes. She wanted to lie down with him and rest. She looked down at her bloody hands then up to Ginny and Evelyn who now stood over Gabe.

"Go, child. He's in the Lord's hands now," said Evelyn. She touched Deanna on the shoulder and guided her up to her feet.

"Gabe..." called out Deanna as she started to back away toward the hill.

He watched her, with heavy eyelids, turn and disappear in the distance. He knew he would never see her again. The woman that he loved. That he could finally admit he loved. As she marched to her destiny he realized his was ending. The pain in his chest was becoming stronger but he welcomed it—it meant he was still alive.

Gabe looked up to Evelyn and Ginny who were now kneeling next to him. Evelyn was reciting the Lord's Prayer and Ginny was treading near shock. Poor girl, a short trip to Detroit and look at all the mayhem she has encountered in three days. He reached out his hand to Ginny. She grabbed it.

"Take care of Deanna for me, okay?" Gabe asked Ginny.

She shook her head to say no. "How could I do that? Look at all I've caused. I'm so sorry," cried Ginny.

"You brought Deanna back. You gave us a shot at something, now we know what we had was real. And now she's doing what she does best. The only thing she knows," said Gabe.

"I'll do anything I can to help her," said Ginny.

"Don't think she doesn't need you. She can be hardheaded but Deanna has craved family her whole life. You're a gift," said Gabe.

Ginny looked upon Gabe as an angel and kissed his hand.

With that confirmation Gabe looked up into the clear night sky and saw stars above him. His pain was gone. He closed his eyes and his spirit was released.

Ginny watched Gabe pass. She spilled backward and rocked herself. She wanted to go home. To Nashville. Where she loved the people, the manners, the streets and music. She missed her house, her fiancé and her parents.

Ginny thought of Deanna and her loss of Gabe. Her little sister will need her to get through this. She wiped away tears. From deep within a strength appeared and began to grow, permeating through her body. She felt alive, more so than she ever had before. It was crystal clear to her. She was here for Deanna. Ginny rose to her feet.

Evelyn had been praying for the Lord to take Gabe away from his pain and He had listened to her. She thanked Him. She put down her hands and touched Gabe's face. Evelyn had seen much death and birth in her eighty years of life. It was all part of a cycle she had learned.

These are dark times and they will be followed by light. But it is all in how you view and forgive it. Some may view the past forty years as bleak but Evelyn had seen hopefulness, in her grandchildren, in her church congregation and that is how she forgave evil.

Evelyn glanced over at Ginny. She had birthed this grown child and brought her into the world. She felt responsible toward her with Wanda gone. She grabbed Ginny's outstretched hand and was brought up to her feet.

"I remember the day you were born. There were thunderstorms, the electricity went out. But there was no stopping you and your brother from coming into the world that night. By candlelight we delivered you both. And when all the crying and the lightening were over, the electricity came back on. But your mother thought you looked so lovely by candlelight, she asked me to turn off the lights and we just stared at you in the glow of a shining candle. Sort of like this moonlight. Your mother would have been proud of you, she always was," said Evelyn.

"And my father? What does he want for me? To be dead? To disappear?"

"Your father was once good. That is why your mother fell in love with him. He let in darkness, it twisted him up inside. He has made mistakes and the Lord will see to it that he pays, in this lifetime or the next."

Ginny scratched her arm, "I hate to think his blood is in mine."

"His blood isn't in you. It's your blood. Yours, Ginny," said Evelyn as she held Ginny's hand so tight it began to hurt.

Ginny pulled her hand away and let Evelyn's words sink deep inside. She had spent so many years imagining where she came from, who her mother and father were, what they were like, that she had ignored what mattered most. Who she was and where she was going. Wanda had lived a harder life than she could have imagined, and her father buried his secrets so far deep that he had become a master of illusion. Ginny decided that they may have made her but they couldn't define her future.

Police and ambulance sirens flooded the cemetery. The sound of running footsteps of men filled the air at the bottom of the hill.

A voice shouted out to Ginny and Evelyn. "Police! Tell us where you are!"

"Here, down the hill, down here!" yelled out Ginny.

The young policeman, followed by three others, ran down the hill and surveyed the scene. One of the young policemen, Harris, talked into his walkie-talkie pinned to his shirt.

"It's clear, come down with the E.M.T.," said Harris.

Two EMT attendants ran down the hill with a stretcher and equipment.

"He's gone," said Evelyn to the EMT attendants as they checked Gabe's vitals.

Officer Harris bent down and saw Gabe's police badge on his belt.

"Flynn," he said as he looked at Evelyn and Ginny.

"Detective Gabe Flynn," stated Ginny.

"I've heard of him. What happened?" asked Harris.

"The shooter ran off, he had dug up a body. We were trying to stop him," Ginny pointed to the baby's grave.

"Jesus," said Harris. "Any idea where he could be?"

"The river. Tri-Centennial Park Harbor," said Evelyn.

"Detective Flynn's partner is there right now pursuing the man who did this," said Ginny.

"Partner? Gabe didn't have a partner. His old one was fired," replied Harris.

"No, she's back," said Evelyn.

Harris grabbed his walkie-talkie. "Get me through to Commander Kavanaugh. Yeah, I don't give a damn. Wake the man up. We have a ten-thirteen. Send four units to Tri-Centennial Park Harbor. Tell Kavanaugh to meet us there," said Harris.

"Now who wants to tell me the whole story?" Harris asked Ginny and Evelyn.

Ginny looked at Evelyn for guidance. Evelyn glared down Harris.

"Take us to the river. We can identify the murderer there," Evelyn said.

"Why do you think I would do that?" asked Harris.

"Officer, how many witnesses step forward in this city? Have you even had one in your career? Well, you've got two right here and we can easily forget what this man looks like unless you take us to the river right this instant," shouted Evelyn.

Officer Harris stumbled back from the force of Evelyn, "Umm, yes, Ma'am. You can ride in my squad car."

"Thank you, Officer," Evelyn took Ginny's hand and started marching up the hill with Harris following them.

"Do you know the murder's name, Ma'am?" asked Harris as they reached the top of the hill.

234

"I may remember it when I see him," said Evelyn. She winked at Ginny and they walked toward the gate of the cemetery. Ginny tightened the grip around Evelyn's hand as they walked out of the cemetery. It was the first time that Ginny felt safe in Detroit. She worried about Deanna and prayed that she would be safe until they arrived. She didn't want to lose her. Not to this town.

CHAPTER 12 – DOWN TO THE RIVER

Located in downtown Detroit was the Tri-Centennial State Park and Harbor. Fifty boat slips were huddled near the fishing piers and benches lining the Detroit river walkway. It was 4:49am and the harbor would have been deserted if it weren't for two homeless men passed out under a shrub bush.

Sounds from the nearby freeway came alive as early morning workers began commuting into Detroit. The lights of the Ambassador Bridge, which connects Detroit to Windsor, lit up the partially dark sky and sent sparkles across the river.

Hank Jenkins' limousine came to a jerking stop in the parking lot two hundred feet from the waterway. Hank pointed his gun at Max.

"Get out and grab the body in the backseat," he ordered Max.

Max reacted slowly as his body was beginning to go into shock from the stress and apparent proximity of his own death. Max opened the door and got out. The smell of the river hit him first. The wind was blowing the factory fumes from downriver up into the city.

His mind swirled in an attempt to find a way out of this situation. If he ran, the mayor would shoot him. If he fought, the mayor would overpower him. He was a man without a plan to save his life. He opened the back door. The second smell that hit him was that of the decaying body of Terry Cone. The window shield separating the front and back of the limo had safeguarded him from this smell on the ride to the river.

Max looked at the crumpled body of Terry. He remembered sharing a drink or two with him when Hank had parties at the mansion. Their personalities never did click but they respected each other's position and importance in running the city so they shared obligatory compliments and small talk. Never in the world did Max think he would one day have to carry Terry's body to dump into the Detroit River.

Max looked at the body and calculated how he was going to haul the one hundred and ninety pound man he estimated Terry to be forward. He pulled Terry's legs together and then grabbed his shoulders as he propped him up. Max leaned into the dead body and put his head under the lifeless right arm and heaved Terry out with a large grunt.

"Shhh, quiet," whispered Hank, who was now carrying the baby's body with both hands, trying to steady his gun in Max's direction.

"This way," Hank directed.

An escape plan hit Max. He dropped the body. The sound of it hitting the ground made Hank jump.

"What the hell? Pick it up," growled Hank.

"He's too heavy. You need to help me," implored Max.

Hank looked at the blanketed body of the baby in his hands and didn't like the sound of Max's plea. He wouldn't be able to securely have the gun on Max.

"No. Drag him if you have to," said Hank.

Max shook his head and put his hands around Terry's torso from his back and began to pull him slowly. The sounds of Terry's shoes dragging on the cement filled the harbor. They continued down the walkway until they reached the jetty. Max stopped.

"Down that way," said Hank.

"Hank, let's talk. I'll help you do this and will never utter a word to anyone. I swear," said Max wiping the sweat from his forehead.

Hank looked around, up and down the pier. "Thanks Max, I know I can trust you."

"Then you'll let me go after this?" asked Max.

"Yeah, sure," said Hank. Max stared at Hank. He didn't believe him.

Deanna skidded Gabe's car into the pier parking lot. She spotted the limousine as she slammed her car door loudly. She was not hiding her arrival or appearance. Deanna was out in the open, stalking Hank Jenkins. She looked down to the pier and saw two figures by the water. One was dragging a body. There they are. She ran toward them.

Deanna kept her eyes focused on Hank. Nothing was going to stop her from killing him. She had never felt this numbness before. She didn't care what happened in the next few minutes. All that consumed her was to stop this man. This monster.

Max looked past Hank's shoulder and saw a figure coming toward them. A flicker of light reflected on the person's face and he saw that it was Deanna. Max looked back to Hank, hoping that he hadn't noticed his averted eyes.

"Now pick up the body," growled Hank.

"Okay, okay," said Max.

Max put his arms around Terry's body and slowly started heaving it down the jetty. The water splashed up on the wood planks making it slippery to walk on. He carefully walked backward keeping one eye on the pathway behind him while also frequently watching the gun that was pointed at him by Hank. He glanced again toward Deanna. She had reached the jetty and was approaching them.

Max's eyes switched back to Hank but it was too late. Hank turned around swiftly and saw Deanna standing within ten feet of them. They both stopped and faced each with raised guns.

"You can't kill your way out of this mess, Mayor," said Deanna.

"I'm prepared to go all the way, Detective. Are you?"

"Yes, I am."

"Really?" said Hank testing her. "Max, throw Terry Cone in the river," he instructed coldly.

Max put down the body and started rolling it toward the edge of the dock. He gave one last grunt and the body splashed into the Detroit River. The sounds of police sirens blared down the street and were getting closer.

"Oh, God help us," cried Max as he watched Terry's body float away. He started to back away from Hank.

"You too, Max," said Hank.

"No, wait. I can help you. No…" pleaded Max.

"Don't do it, mayor. The police are on their way," said Deanna.

Hank's gun fired, Max grabbed his stomach, lost his balance and plunged into the river. Hank raised the baby's body over his head as he prepared to throw it in the river.

Bang!

A shot from Deanna's gun stopped Hank. The bullet hit him in his left thigh. He dropped his gun and crumpled down to the deck with the baby in his arms.

The two police units and Kavanaugh's car spun into the parking lot. The policemen emerged out of their cars and saw the scene on the jetty. Ginny and Evelyn scrambled out of the car.

Evelyn pointed to the water.

"There he is, that's the murderer," said Evelyn.

"Let's go," called out Kavanaugh to the policemen. The officers began to shout out to Deanna and Hank, "Police, stop. Police. Put up your hands!"

"No, damn it. No," Hank screamed. He squirmed in pain. Deanna began to walk directly toward him. Hank frantically searched for his gun. He found it and leveled it at Deanna.

"Stop."

"Mayor, it's over," said Deanna. "You can't get out of this."

Hank looked at the approaching police then back to Deanna.

"No, you're wrong. If you have any witnesses they are the most unreliable sources. Ask any lawyer. You need proof. I didn't kill your mother. My chauffer did. And this gun will be at the bottom of this river soon and can never be traced to me," he said.

Deanna looked down at the baby in Hank's arm.

"Soon this baby will be at the bottom of the river also," said Hank.

He turned over and started to push the baby into the water when Deanna lunged for him. She landed on top of Hank and put one hand on the baby. They wrestled. Deanna's arm screamed in pain.

BAM!

A gun blast sounded off.

Deanna jumped back from Hank with the baby now in her arms. She laid the baby down on the dock and kept her gun pointed at the mayor. She looked back at Hank and saw his gun pull away from his body revealing a wound on the left side of his chest.

Hank grasped for air and began to wheeze. Deanna dove for the gun in his hand and pulled it away from him with little fight. Hank was shocked at the blast that came from his own gun. He covered the hole in his lung with his hand.

The police were running up the jetty. Kavanaugh called out to Deanna, "Drop the gun."

Deanna pointed the gun toward the police. "Hold back. Do you hear me?" she yelled out.

"Stop men. Damn that woman. What's going on Deanna? Who is that with you?" asked Kavanaugh squinting in early morning light.

Deanna looked down at Hank.

"My mother's murderer."

Hank looked up into Deanna's green eyes and saw Wanda for a moment.

"Give me one good reason I shouldn't blow you away?" asked Deanna.

"I loved her," said Hank.

"So did I," said Deanna as she steadied her gun at him.

Hank glanced at the police officers at the end of the dock.

"I never thought the people would understand. A white wife and half-black, half-white baby would have ruined my career, my dreams, and this city's chance for a future," said Hank gasping for air.

"You didn't have enough faith in the people, in Wanda, in yourself."

Hank's breaths were getting shallower. He rested his head on the planks.

"That was my daughter, down at the grave?" asked Hank as he glanced down the dock at Ginny. "At the end of this pier?"

Deanna turned back and saw Ginny and Evelyn holding each other.

"It is," she answered.

"What's her name?"

"Ginny."

Hank looked downriver then back to Deanna.

"My reasons may not be good enough for you, but they were good enough for me…at the time. I'm glad those times are over," said Hank.

With his last bit of strength Mayor Hank Jenkins heaved himself over the dock and into the river. Deanna reached out to grab him but he fell deep into the water.

Hank held his eyes open and looked into the blackness of the river. His last thoughts were of Wanda and the sound of his daughter's name, Ginny, playing over and over in his mind until his heart stopped. His body floated on top of the water and headed downriver.

Deanna dropped to her knees and touched the blue satin blanket that covered the baby. It was over. She dropped her gun to the ground. The police ran down to her and started shouting orders for people to get a police boat to recover the bodies. Ginny and Evelyn ran to Deanna.

Ginny kneeled down to hug Deanna who hesitated slightly and then embraced her sister fully. Deanna let go of Ginny and picked up the baby boy's body and held it close to her chest.

Kavanaugh approached Deanna.

"Deanna, whose body am I going to be dredging from the bottom of our river?"

"The Mayor of Detroit, sir."

"Jesus, what went on in this city tonight?"

"What happens every night Commander? Murder, deceit, people righting a wrong. You'll be able to explain it all to the news teams and the citizens," said Deanna as she walked away with Ginny and Evelyn. "Their mayor was a murderer."

Ambulances, police cars and now the local television news vans pulled into the parking lot. A police boat had fished the mayor's body out of the water. A police officer on one of the police boats spotted Kavanaugh on the pier.

"We got the body, Commander…it's the mayor!"

The crowd shouted out with the surprise news. Kavanaugh rolled his eyes in irritation to the officer on the boat.

"Thank you, Officer. Now shut the hell up," yelled Kavanaugh as he turned Deanna around.

"He killed Gabe?"

Deanna looked at Ginny who nodded an affirmation that Gabe was dead.

"Yes, he killed Gabe," said Deanna as she held back a cry in her throat.

Kavanaugh took off his cap and ruffled his graying hair.

"I'm sorry, Deanna. I'm sorry about everything."

Deanna cradled the baby as she walked behind Ginny and Evelyn.

"You can explain how sorry you are in court, Commander. How you fired me inappropriately, pressured by the mayor and the union. Then I think you really will be sorry."

Kavanaugh took his cap and threw it in the river. Finding the best lawyer in town crossed his mind but then it trailed back to his service and all that he had given to this town. Forty years on the force. Shot twice. He allowed the mayor to pressure him. He let his precinct down. And now Gabe is dead. Kavanaugh put his hands to his head. He had stayed too long in this city. He got greedy. He should have left after thirty years and taken the condo three miles down from the beach.

Deanna, holding the baby, walked with Ginny and Evelyn to the flashing police cars and news crew lights. Deanna handed the baby's body to an EMT attendant. The three women said a prayer and said goodbye to the baby boy. They then walked up to the parking lot.

Deanna felt an intuition to look over her shoulder to the south side of the park. She saw two outlined figures of men standing together in the morning shadows looking straight at her. She focused her eyes and saw that there stood her two uncles, Felix and Roman.

Uncle Roman waved his right hand slowly to her and Uncle Felix nodded his head. She noticed Uncle Felix had on a trench coat, not a typical piece of clothing on such a balmy night; underneath it he held a sawed off shotgun. Deanna nodded back to her uncles, acknowledging their presence and special place in her world as protectors.

"Now what will happen?" asked Ginny.

"Interviews, a trial. Kavanaugh will lose his job, his pension, maybe serve time but probably not. We need to bury Wanda, Stanley...and Gabe." Deanna stopped and crouched over in pain at the thought of Gabe. She covered her eyes to stop her tears.

Ginny kneeled down to hold onto Deanna who took a deep breath and brought her body back up.

"And after that?" asked Ginny softly.

Deanna shook her head and threw her hands in the air. "I don't know, I don't know..."

"Will you head back to Portland?" asked Ginny.

"I don't know where I'll go."

"I do. Nashville. You can come down and stay with me. It's a nice town. Friendly. Good people. Please, Deanna. Come home with me. Your father, Ronnie, is there. Time for you two to talk...to connect," said Ginny.

Deanna's mind swirled. Ronnie. Nashville. She didn't know anything about the city.

"I think that's a real good idea. You two are sisters. Nothing can break the bond of sisters," said Evelyn.

Deanna turned to Evelyn as she felt her brain go into a fog.

Deanna pronounced the sound of the city name from her mouth slowly.

"Nashville...Nashville..."

Deanna kept walking to the parking lot. She turned back toward the river and then to the city skyline. The sun was coming up and reflecting off the skyscrapers. She let out a deep breath.

"Maybe for a while. Until I figure out what I'm going to do," settled Deanna.

"Good. My parents and fiancé, Noah, will make you feel right at home," said Ginny.

"How reassuring," said Deanna with a dry laugh. Her hands began to shake. "God, I'm not sure I can get through this."

Evelyn took Deanna's hands and steadied them.

"You will, you will."

"How do you know?" asked Deanna with tears coming down her face.

"You're from Detroit. Why do you think God put you in this city? He knew you could take it. And you can," responded Evelyn.

"If I leave, I'm never coming back," said Deanna.

"Never say never, child. But if you didn't, I wouldn't blame you," said Evelyn as she let go of Deanna and took a seat in a police car. She began to pray for the souls lost over the past few days and for Deanna to find forgiveness in her heart.

Ginny stared at Deanna and committed a devotion to her half-sister as the police lights swirled in her vision.

Deanna's eyes swept over her city. She felt the rising sun on her face. She wiped the remaining tears away and walked to Gabe's car. She took inventory of any strength remaining inside her body. Deanna leaned her face against the hood of the car and let the heat warm her just as she had rested her head on Gabe's chest earlier in the night and listened to his heart beating. She dreamed of Gabe until she was pulled into a police car and driven back to her uncle's home to rest.

After the funerals and Kavanaugh's conviction, Deanna drove to Nashville in Gabe's car. She felt him with her as she cleared the city limit sign and headed south on Interstate 75. Forgiveness was far off in the distance, and each mile she drove it moved further away, eluding her but inviting her to keep driving.

About the Author

Megan Clare Johnson, a Detroit native, is an author and filmmaker who reaches out to make us think, and experience a wide range of emotions through her unique voice.

Motor City Murder is the first thriller novel installment in Megan's "City Murder" series featuring the hard-hitting female private detective Deanna Dopp who travels city-to-city solving crimes.

Megan is currently producing and directing her original screenplay *Stealing Roses* into a feature length film. She lives in Portland, Oregon with her husband and two Bengal cats.

She invites you to visit her at www.MeganClareJohnson.com for updates on her books and films.

Back cover photo of the author by Greg Wahl-Stephens at www.photographyfirst.com.

LaVergne, TN USA
30 October 2009
162571LV00003B/11/P